About the author

Mo Tritton was born in Oxford and raised in Barnardo's and foster homes. She spent her teenage years on motorcycles and hanging around the Ace Café. She loved the early rock 'n' roll years and still does.

Over the last twenty years or so she has become a vegan and has never felt better.

Mo deeply loves all life forms and would promote the sentiment that all life forms should be loved and respected.

BLAZE OF GLORY

Mo Tritton

BLAZE OF GLORY

Vanguard Press

VANGUARD PAPERBACK

© Copyright 2021
Mo Tritton

The right of Mo Tritton to be identified as author of
this work has been asserted by her in accordance with the
Copyright, Designs and Patents Act 1988.

All Rights Reserved

No reproduction, copy or transmission of this publication
may be made without written permission.
No paragraph of this publication may be reproduced,
copied or transmitted save with the written permission of the publisher, or in
accordance with the provisions
of the Copyright Act 1956 (as amended).

Any person who commits any unauthorised act in relation to
this publication may be liable to criminal
prosecution and civil claims for damages.

A CIP catalogue record for this title is
available from the British Library.

ISBN 978-1-80016-066-8

*Vanguard Press is an imprint of
Pegasus Elliot MacKenzie Publishers Ltd.*
www.pegasuspublishers.com

First Published in 2021

**Vanguard Press
Sheraton House Castle Park
Cambridge England**

Printed & Bound in Great Britain

Dedication

Dedicated to everyone I know and
everyone I don't know

Chapter 1
Uncle Tom

This was not how she intended it to be. She had been affected by family members' deaths many times during her life and had a fascination for the endless ways that people died and were 'put to rest' and the ways that those that remained dealt with their grief, or not, as the case may be.

As far as she could work it out you died when your heart stopped beating so that the blood that was carrying the life-giving oxygen around the body couldn't complete its designated function. She couldn't work out to any satisfactory conclusion if people stopped breathing first and that was what killed them rather than them dying because their heart had stopped beating.

She had actually been present when her uncle had died, her uncle who had spoilt her rotten and was full of energy and laughter. One moment he was joshing with her at the top of a staircase then he was falling backwards making the most dreadful noise as he went down the quick way. He lay quietly at the base of the stairs and not answering when she called his name. She told him sorry, she didn't mean to push him then kissed him and went out in the street to play with a friend from two doors up.

She went over and over it in her mind when all the fuss had died down and her uncle had been cremated. She knew her uncle had been alive when he was at the top of the stairs and was dead by the time he reached the bottom of them so therefore, she concluded, he had died somewhere in the middle, somewhere between the top and the bottom of the stairs. Drat it, she had missed the moment. How could she learn about dying and plan for it if she didn't know what happened when you died?

One day not long after her uncle's death she came bursting into the front room and caught the dregs of a conversation before her parents' conversation dried up. She was intrigued and showed no finesse whatsoever as she asked "What's a post-mortem then?"

Her parents looked at each other and cleared their throats, then her dad excused himself from the room and went upstairs leaving his wife to answer. "Nothing you have to concern yourself with, it's to do with your uncle's death."

She was intrigued, post-mortem, what on earth was it when it was at home? One thing was for sure though, it was part of the death puzzle she was studying; it was one of the many pieces but she had no idea where it fitted.

"Can I come?" she asked outright. "To the post-mortem I mean, I promise to be quiet."

Her mother clasped her to her bosom saying, "No dear, you can't come, it's not for children."

"What happens when a child dies, is it for children then."

Her mother sighed. "You do say strange things sometimes. Your Aunty Jean is coming over to look after you whilst we are gone but we shouldn't be long."

Oh no, she thought, not Aunty Jean, that would explain why her mother had gone into high alert and had gone through the house cleaning it from top to toe, even her room was invaded, a fact she protested strongly about. Not that any notice was taken of her protests. Her Aunty Jean apparently had a peanut allergy and was likely to go into shock if she came in contact with them. Her mother asked her over and over again if she had any peanuts or if she had bought any sweets which contained them to the point where she told her mother she didn't need a baby-sitter, she was old enough to look after herself. So saying she displayed her immaturity by flouncing off to her room and slamming the door.

It had taken her mother a long time to persuade Jean to baby-sit as she had a fear of leaving a known environment but eventually she had given in to her best friend's cajoling and agreed, although she hadn't the faintest idea how to keep an eleven-year-old girl amused and was thankful that it wouldn't be for long. She would have her EpiPen in her bag in case she came into contact with anything that caused a reaction and she reassured her friend, who was now feeling guilty at putting pressure on her, that she would be fine, just fine.

As her parents were leaving, she suddenly hugged them as if she wasn't ever going to see them again, then decided to use one of those endearing childish comments that parents melted over. "I wish Uncle wasn't dead and that he would come and see me, I miss him so much." The comment had the desired effect as her mother gave a sob and hugged her even closer.

She wondered why her mother was crying after all she had never had a kind word to say about her uncle when he was alive. Perhaps she felt guilty for being so horrible to him, perhaps he was her secret lover and they were planning to run away together but now they couldn't or something. She realised making up stories to fit the facts wasn't the way forward; she had to stick to the facts and only the facts otherwise her research would be useless.

She found Aunty Jean utterly boring and found it difficult to be polite. Her Aunty Jean did not have any children of her own (apparently she couldn't) and so had no idea how to engage with an eleven-year-old. Her idea was to put on the television then disappear into the back garden for a smoke and a glass of wine. She wondered how anyone could drink that stuff, and decided that when she grew up she wouldn't. She stared at her Aunty Jean through the kitchen window as she rifled through her handbag that she had left on the kitchen table and came across her EpiPen. It had instructions on it of how to use it before calling 999. She wondered what would happen if she had an allergic reaction and couldn't find her EpiPen, would she die. She fiddled with the EpiPen as she stared out of the window at her Aunty Jean deciding it would be good if she did die because then she wouldn't be able to come and baby-sit her any more. She made coded notes in her notebook and decided the next time she got onto the school computer she would look up allergies and why some people used an EpiPen. She had an unhealthy curiosity

Her parents were only gone a few hours and were strangely quiet when they returned home. Aunty Jean came in from sunbathing (or whatever) in the back garden and was out of the house in minutes walking quickly down the road, a bird set free.

After tea she said she had a headache and went up to her room and got ready for bed. Her daddy came up a few minutes after she had lain down and had kissed her goodnight before going back downstairs. She left it a little while then, when she heard them talking, got out of bed and crept down the stairs and listened at the living room door for a while then returned to bed to mull over what she had heard.

Accidental death. Her uncle had died an accidental death, well died of accidental causes was the term her parents had used. How did they know that? How could they say it was accidental when they weren't even there? What was an accidental cause? Were the stairs classed as an accidental cause, after all her uncle wouldn't have died if he hadn't fallen down the stairs. Did it mean that her uncle hadn't meant to die when he fell down the stairs? She realised that she was tying herself in knots trying to understand adult speech and that things were getting more and more complicated. She must stick to the facts, stick with what she knew to be true. Only she knew that her uncle had been murdered, only she knew that there was nothing accidental about it. Murderer, murderer. She rolled the term around her tongue feeling a delicious sense of excitement. She was a murderer and nobody else knew it, how funny was that.

She wrote her notes in a special code that she had made up to keep things private and mused over her feelings for her uncle. Did she miss him because she loved him, did she miss him because he used to spoil her or was there another reason? Was what she was feeling the same as everyone else was feeling or was it different? So many questions to consider, so many different angles. It was all so fascinating, perhaps, one day, she would become famous for her insight, perhaps not. She didn't really want to become famous, didn't really want people to know of her fascination. After all why write in code so that only she could understand her notes?

She thoroughly enjoyed the funeral and made copious notes so that she could go over them later. It seemed that everybody cried when someone they knew died but she put a question mark against this comment and underlined it to remind herself that as this was the first death she had been witness to she had nothing to compare it to but she did add comments that she had actually cried in the service though mainly because other people near to her were crying and she wanted to go along with them to see what it felt like.

She didn't like it; it was hard work squeezing tears out of her eyes and making her face wet and top of it all people started hugging her and telling her not to cry although they were crying themselves. Incredible, such hypocrites!

She had tried hard to find out how the funeral arrangements were made but she was sent out to play and get on with her life. She didn't want to, she wanted to cloak herself in the arrangements surrounding death but it was withheld from her as if it was a secret. She found it so frustrating. She had wanted to learn all there was to learn about death and all she had was disjointed pieces of information. Oh well, she would just have to wait until the next time someone died. Shame about her uncle though, in a funny kind of way she missed him.

She went around to her grandparents' house as often as she remembered to and watched them as they came to terms with life without the presence of one their sons and every now and then prodded them with a comment about their son that caused them to become tearful, loving the feeling of power it gave her but made sure she did not do it too often. She knew there was a fine line between her being innocently endearing and downright rude so she walked the line. She noticed lots of photographs of her uncle displayed around their living room that she hadn't noticed previously. Was this something that all people did? get out and dust off old photographs, or was it something that only her grandparents did? She had so many questions to answer, so many gaps in her knowledge base to fill and was excited at the prospect of discovering the answers. Her research, which might last her the rest of her life, gave her a purpose and she was truly grateful that the only thing in life she was interested in was death.

She watched her dad cry but did not feel any emotion whatsoever although she managed to appear that she did. She would ball her fists, then rub them vigorously in her eye sockets to make them red and watery and would splash water on her face, not too much, just enough and she learnt to snivel just within earshot to gain attention and also to talk in a quiet stuttery voice that ensured arms of comfort were wrapped around her.

She hated the contact; it made her cringe to be touched by anyone at all but she allowed it to happen so she could learn from the experience. Were people holding her for her to feel comforted, feel better, or were they holding her so that they could feel better or was it a mixture of both?

She was getting frustrated, so many unanswered questions, so many possibilities, she would have to learn patience, learn that time was a factor, things took time. Arrangements took time, people grieving took time but how much time was needed? Was it the same for everybody or was it different for everybody? She didn't know, in fact all she knew was that she would have to see more people die so that she could begin to see a pattern and she hoped that there would be a pattern, that a pattern of some sort would emerge. After all, if every death was different she would be taking on a task far too big for her. Her research would be never ending.

She junked the negative thoughts as soon as they entered her brain as they were not helpful. She needed to see who else was going to die and hopefully die very soon, and mentally examined a list of people she knew. She knew that age didn't come into it at all, anyone could die at any time which was very useful for her to know but also just a little worrying as she realised that it could happen to her, that she could suddenly die without any obvious reason and that if she did she wouldn't be able to finish her research.

She pondered for a long time on these thoughts and noticed that her parents noticed her mood and put it down to her grieving over her uncle and tried to do things to help her lighten up as her dad put it. She was fascinated, in truth she hadn't felt one tiny piece of remorse over her uncle's death, well, that was not completely true, she argued with herself, she had been really pissed off at missing the moment when life became death, but still, her parents' reaction to her perceived grieving made interesting reading in her copious notes.

She was worried about dying but only if she died before she finished her study of death, how bizarre was that she thought and actually enjoyed the moment. She decided that she would run another study alongside her present one. She wanted to go out in a blaze of glory and she would work out how to do just that. She knew that she had to take each day as it came, that she might not have time but she was excited nevertheless. Life is tenuous she thought, having overheard someone else saying so and liking how it sounded although she hadn't got the faintest idea what it meant at the time. She had since looked it up in her well-thumbed dictionary and made more notes selecting the synonym fragile as a definition.

Although she was tired, she was unable to go to sleep so wrote post-mortem in her notebook and underlined it twice, then looked it up in the dictionary realising that she had to work out the order of events after a death happened. Whereabouts a post-mortem came in the order of events after a death she did not know. What she did know was that it was important and that every death (known death) had to have one. It wasn't just an adult phrase rolled out to confuse children. She read through the explanation in her dictionary and wondered if she could get a job as a person who did post-mortems. She didn't know what they were called but she knew they had to be special people, a bit like her, in order to deal with dead people.

After a while she changed her mind. She did not really want to examine dead people at all, not that she minded them being dead, no, not at all. After all, she reasoned the only difference between a dead person and a live person was that they were alive or dead! If only she could have watched the exact moment her uncle had died she would be able to understand the difference a bit more.

Her notebook was fast becoming full and she realised that she had to get more notebooks otherwise she would be writing on toilet paper. This thought made her giggle and she found she couldn't stop. The giggles turned into a coughing fit and her mother appeared in the room and sat her up and gave her a soothing honey and lemon drink to sip slowly. After a while she lay down to sleep watched over by both parents.

She was frustrated, so frustrated, nobody around her was dying, in fact they all looked very healthy. She looked through the daily paper for something to do and immediately cheered up when she read in 'announcements' about people who had died recently. She read through each one savouring them like strawberries and cream then went on to read the death anniversaries: people who were remembering dead people on the date they had died. She found this extraordinary. She could see the point of birthdays and remembering them but death days, really, what on earth was the point? Still, in a way she was glad they did as it gave her something to read to pass the time and, more important she could put it in her notebook as a list of something to consider with regard to dying. She wondered how soon the people who had lost someone arranged to tell all and sundry about it. Why did they feel compelled to do that, was it a ritual or something? Why on earth would anyone else be interested in somebody else's death? Really, people were so confusing.

Although she had only been present at one death she had put a separate book aside and labelled it 'Findings'. Under this heading she had written 'Balance' and underlined it before writing 'Balance, or rather the loss of balance was the cause of death.' She thought this was a very significant point and wondered if it was a factor in everybody's death.

Her parents decided to travel into the city and insisted she went with them although she protested vigorously and sulked all the way. There was too much of everything and she felt really uncomfortable and whispered to herself how much she hated her parents for causing her so much grief. She stood beside them on the crowded train platform staring daggers and pulling faces at a little girl standing nearby. The 'train approaching' sign lit up at the same time as potential passengers were warned to stand behind the yellow line. The crowd shifted back a little as the little girl turned and quickly stuck her tongue out at her. As she was moved back she pushed the little girl forward with her free hand then quickly turned and took hold of her father's hand with both of hers. There were screams, shouts, a sickening thud and screeching brakes although she could not tell in what order these sounds came. "Somebody's fallen under the train," was passed around the crowd like Chinese whispers, then a vacant silence ensued before uproar took over and people fled the platform to get away trampling over each other in their panic. Her parents were part of the rush to escape and dragged her out of the station up into the reasonably fresh air of the city above it where they were glad to find a vacant bench and collapsed on it. Her mother was sobbing uncontrollably and her father had one arm around her to comfort her whilst the other held onto his daughter.

Wow, she thought, that was exciting. So much better than her uncle's death. That wasn't exciting in the least, not like this. She put on her frightened little girl voice. "Daddy, Mummy, what's wrong, why is everybody running away, I'm so scared." Her dad pulled her close and the three of them hugged and were quiet for a time although around them many sirens sounded. Her excitement peaked and she wet herself as she tried to handle her feelings. Her parents noticed but didn't make a fuss thinking that the recent events were the cause of their daughter being so upset and of course they were right though not in the way they thought.

She pulled away from the hug, feeling stifled and turned to watch the people still coming up the steps from the underground, although the stampede had lessened considerably with the volume of people seeking refuge in the sunshine now down to a trickle from this particular entrance.

There were policemen everywhere it seemed, one of whom had a loudspeaker which was issuing out instructions to keep calm as well as appealing for witnesses, whilst others were attempting to cordon off the area with yellow and black sticker tape.

She turned to look at her parents. "Are we witnesses, Mummy, the policeman wants witnesses?"

Her mother shook her head. "No, darling, although we were quite close to where it happened."

I should say we were, she thought, we couldn't have been any closer. Excitement coursed through her that she found difficult to contain as she realised that all this activity was down to her: people shouting, stampeding, escaping, the police, everything that was happening was down to her. She glorified in the moment and fainted.

She came too feeling the worse for wear cradled on her mother's lap. She felt nauseous and was violently sick and cried real tears of distress. She closed her eyes and listened to her parents talk and to the gossip of people passing by. She felt small and vulnerable and was glad of her mother's arms around her.

"Mummy, Mummy, what happened? Why did we run away?" she whispered in a small voice that her mother had to strain to listen to.

"Never you mind, darling" as her forehead was kissed, "don't you worry your pretty little head about anything," and with that they each took a hand either side of her and walked away to find an alternative way home.

By the time the family reached home she was feeling so much better but kept the fact hidden from her parents and let them fuss over her. She closed her eyes the minute she was put into her bed and tucked in whispering, "I love you Mummy and Daddy," before closing her eyes. She had intended to wait for her parents to leave then creep downstairs to hear them talking but to her surprise she went fast asleep so didn't hear any news or conversation.

Once awake she lay still for a while reflecting on the events of the day before and of how she had felt so ill. She got out her notebook and began writing. She stopped briefly to cheerily wish her daddy good morning, said she didn't want breakfast then continued writing once again getting caught up in the excitement of the moment.

Something had happened that was for sure but she only had the reactions of her parents and surrounding people to go by, she had no proof. It was all so frustrating, she didn't know anything for real, at least when her uncle had died she had been able to see him, this time she had seen nothing at all. She wished with all her might that she was taller for if she was she would have seen everything, she was convinced of it, seen every glorious moment as the train killed the little girl who had put her tongue out at her and serve her right for being so rude although she had to admit that she would have pushed her anyway even if she hadn't stuck her tongue out. The opportunity was just too good to pass up.

She stopped writing for a moment and lay quietly looking up at the ceiling thinking. She wouldn't be able to celebrate properly until she had proof, but how to get it was the puzzle. Her phone pinged as if giving her an answer. Of course, she could access the news through her phone. She hurriedly thumbed through it ignoring the text from a friend and there it was, proof. She read through the newspaper footage many times feeling so much better. A child, a little girl, had been killed by a train in the underground. There were a few paragraphs giving comments from the grieving parents but she skipped them to get at the nitty gritty.

She lay back and sighed, thoroughly contented, then had a thought. She hadn't read about her uncle's death in the paper, she hadn't given it a thought at the time. This was a serious oversight on her part, after all how could she wring any pleasure out of the deaths if she was missing out on newspaper reports and television reports even though she doubted that her uncle's death would make national news. She sat up and made more notes and compared the deaths realising that though she hadn't seen the little girl die she had got a lot more pleasure from it than from her uncle's death. She wondered why that was and thought that perhaps it was because there were a lot more people about and they generated the excitement.

She got up at last and got washed and dressed and went downstairs wondering what the time was when she suddenly stood stock still as if in shock then turned and rushed back upstairs again. Time, she had to look at her notes about time. She searched feverishly through her notes, then threw her notebooks down in frustration. Drat it, she had forgotten, on both occasions to write the time of death, the actual (as near as damn it) time of death. She slapped her forehead with the palm of her hand and screamed out loud in frustration. She couldn't believe it; she was leaving out vital information. What was the matter with her? This was crucial, how could she be so stupid? She stomped around her room feeling intense anger with herself but managed to calm down enough to answer her mother who called upstairs to see if she was all right.

She realised that getting angry with herself wasn't helpful and that she should make a note to include it in future research so that she could fill in all of the gaps, could complete her puzzle of death.

Chapter 2
Grandpa

Her parents insisted that she stay off school for at least two days at the end of which she was chomping at the bit, not that she minded staying in her room, she didn't, except when she had to and then she did.

She never thought she would say it but she was pleased to get back to school away from her parents. It felt like they were suffocating her. The thought distracted her for the rest of the day wondering what it was like to be suffocated for real. Was it quick? Was it painful? she didn't know.

In the book she was reading at the moment there was talk of death by natural causes and she wondered if death by suffocating was 'by natural causes' and decided it wasn't, reasoning that a third party (she liked this terminology) had to do it to someone else and therefore murder wasn't a natural cause. So what was a natural cause? she wondered. Did you have to be old to die of a natural cause or could you be young and die of a natural cause? If you were ill in hospital say and you died that wouldn't be classed as a natural cause even if the cause of your illness was something that people naturally got, like the flu or something.

A few times during the day she was pulled up in class for not paying attention and she had to admit she wasn't, she had far too many important things to think about. She found that she hated being in the first year of a secondary school. She had much preferred it when she was in the top year of the junior school she had been in last year. In the school she was in now everyone in the years above her knew the ropes whilst she and her classmates were floundering and would do so for the next few terms. Her day was not completely wasted though, she had typed in EpiPen on one of the school computers and had discovered there was such a thing as anaphylactic shock. She didn't know how to pronounce the word but she liked the feel of it as she said it to herself and although she couldn't understand a lot of the medical terms she could understand enough to realise the severity of the condition if it wasn't treated properly.

She arrived home tired and fed-up because her notebooks had been confiscated at school and she wouldn't get them back until the end of the week. Just because teachers were grown-ups, they thought that they could tell children what to do, it wasn't fair. She started writing her notes in the back of her school books making sure that she wrote in them in her new revised code so that even if they were discovered nobody could read them.

She thought about Aunty Jean and smiled. With a bit of luck she would never have to tolerate her coming around to babysit her ever again. What would happen if she lost the EpiPen? Did she have more than one in case she mislaid or lost one? She made careful notes then returned to thinking about death from natural causes and suffocating and back to where she had thought that a person could only be suffocated by someone else. The more she thought about it the more she realised that she didn't have enough information or experience to come to that conclusion. She was being side-tracked by ideas and she needed to be careful that she didn't lose sight of what she was researching. Just because she thought something was something didn't mean it was. She stared long and hard at what she had written and knew it was important. She mustn't allow herself to get side-tracked by fiction, she must stick to the facts.

She lay back on her bed staring at the ceiling whilst listening to the sounds her mother was making in the kitchen and suddenly took in a big gasp of air and then pressed her hands against her nose and mouth and held her breath. The first ten to twenty seconds were easy but she found she desperately wanted to breathe and began to panic as one part of her tried to breathe whilst another part of her tried to stop it. She gave in, coughing and spluttering and gasping in great gulps of air with her heart pounding madly in her chest and found she was sweating. When she had calmed down sufficiently she wrote a few paragraphs under the heading <u>Suffocation</u>. She noted that if a person was asleep suffocating them would be easy for them and for the person who did it to them but if the person knew someone was trying to suffocate them and was fighting for their life then it could be quite distressing for the person who was being suffocated and difficult for the person who was trying to kill them. She didn't know if a person could die by suffocating themselves accidentally or if a person who had been killed by suffocating was thought to have died naturally. Everything was so complicated. She cheered herself up by reading through the 'Obituary' columns in the local newspaper then went down for tea and even volunteered to wash-up much to her mother's surprise.

Although she looked out for news so that she could understand how a train death was reported she was surprised that it didn't make front page news, at least it didn't in the papers she read at home and at school in the library. Just a few tiny paragraphs in the middle of the paper. This made her cross as she had almost missed some reports due to where they had been placed in the paper. Was this important for her own death? she wondered, realising that she had been so caught up in the demise of other people that she hadn't given her own death a thought. She decided it was and made a note of it. She was surprised that within a few days it seemed that the train death was almost forgotten, unlike murders which made front page news and went on for days or sometimes weeks dragging out each little detail of the person's life before they had died then each little detail of how the family was or wasn't coping after the death.

She thought about who would be upset if she died and wondered how long they would be upset for and also why they would be upset. Her mum and dad would be upset because she was their daughter but how long would they be upset for? Was there a given length of time to be upset? From what she had seen most people seemed to get upset when someone died but supposing that her parents didn't get upset if and when she died, what would that mean? Would it mean that they didn't love her or would it mean that not everyone would get upset at a death of someone they knew?

Questions, questions, so many questions. She asked herself what facts she had found out so far and wrote down that she didn't want to die by falling or being pushed in front of a train, or by falling or being pushed downstairs. Good she thought, she was making progress at last.

On the way home from school on the Friday, having just had her notebooks returned, she suddenly decided to call in to see her grandparents and see how they were coping now that a time had passed since their son's death.

Grandad was sitting in his armchair fast asleep with his glasses perched on top of his head. He was snoring loudly, his head bouncing every time he did so. As she went to kiss the top of his head, she noticed his asthma pump loosely held by one hand in his lap and she prised his hand open and the pump fell to the floor. She looked around as it fell in case her grandmother came in and got angry with her and was relieved to see that she hadn't appeared. She had previously been told that on no circumstances was she to touch it, that Grandpapa had to have it within reach all the time otherwise the alternative would not be worth thinking about. She looked down at the pump then back at Grandpa and went out into the garden to see Grandma and found her chatting to one of her neighbours. She kissed Grandma on the cheek and said she wanted to see they were all right as she missed them, then left to go back home not giving her grandpa a second glance as she passed him to go home.

Asthma, she thought as she skipped home, I wonder what it is, I must read up about it and that is exactly what she did as soon as she got home. 'Asthma is a chronic disease of the respiratory system that causes narrowing of the airways…' She had to look up the word chronic to fully understand what it meant then read through signs and symptoms. Asthma was definitely not a natural cause of death, in fact the more she read the more horrified she became: it was awful. She would definitely add it to the list of how she didn't want to die. Strange, she thought, that she had been thinking a lot about suffocation recently and here was a disease that to her seemed to suffocate you from the inside!

She heard her dad's mobile ringing and wondered if it was Grandma ringing up about Grandpa and realised that she hadn't given him the slightest thought since arriving home. It would be just too awful if he did die but he was old so he wasn't going to last long anyway and he wouldn't mind being part of her research she was sure of it.

She put on her headphones and lay down listening to her favourite music and thinking she would want the band she was listening to, to play live at her funeral, that would be cool. She sat upright and wrote in her notes under 'Church Ceremony' that she wanted live music to be played. Supposing as she got older she didn't like the music she was playing any more, what then? Should she just write 'live band of the day' to play as she lay in her coffin?

She lay on the bed day dreaming about lying in an open coffin looking like Sleeping Beauty with a live band playing as millions of people came to see her who cried and threw flowers all round the coffin and for a moment she couldn't let go of the image as her mother came into the room and shook her to get her attention. She sat up as her mother sat down on the bed beside her, her face distraught. "It's Grandpa, darling, he was taken to hospital earlier but your dad has just phoned to say he's died." As she said these words she burst out crying and put her head down into her open palms whilst her shoulders shook with grief.

She couldn't believe it, the old fool had gone and died and she hadn't been there to see it, to learn from it. She began to get angry and gritted her teeth and forced air back and forth through them. How dare he die when she wasn't there, it wasn't supposed to have been like this, she had wanted to be there at the hospital with him to watch him fight for his life and lose. Her mother threw her arms around her daughter and the pair of them sat there well into the night, one grieving, one seething.

She had lost a valuable opportunity she berated herself. She had wasted time daydreaming and fantasizing when she could have actually been there when her grandpa was taken ill. She could have watched him and been able to write notes on what actually happened and now that opportunity was lost. She could kill herself; she had been so stupid.

Kill herself, hmm, could she, would it hurt? She thought about cutting her wrists but baulked at the thought of the blood and pain. There had to be another way, an overdose, that was it; it didn't hurt and you didn't wake up. Just supposing though that she did wake up, that it didn't work, that would be too dreadful for words.

Wait a minute, just wait a minute. What had killing yourself got to do with a Blaze of Glory, nothing, nothing at all. This was her mind playing cruel tricks on her but she knew what it was capable of now. She wouldn't let it win, she would achieve what she wanted, one day she would die in a Blaze of Glory and there was nothing her mind, or anybody else's, come to that, could do about it.

Chapter 3
Dusty Ledge

She was fed up to the back teeth and no mistake. In fact she almost wished her grandpa was still alive for at least then she would see her daddy more often and they would go out on family trips and have picnics and such. Now she meandered around the house wishing the weekend would hurry up and finish so that she could go back to school. At least there was distraction there. She sighed as she held the washing basket for her mother to put the clothes into that she had taken off the line.

She felt she must be ill or coming down with something as she didn't even want to write up her study. She wondered if she was dying, if this was it. She looked around at the colourful flowers, the trees in full blossom, bees buzzing, butterflies flying and thought I can take this image with me when I die.

Suddenly she wanted to write in her book so as soon as she had finished helping her mother she took the stairs two at a time and opened her book then wrote: 'Do people take an image of the last thing they see with them when they die and go to wherever they go?' She stared hard at what she had written for a moment. Was it relevant to her study and if so whereabouts did it fit in? She decided that it was relevant and that it would fit in just before the moment of death. She got very excited about this decision, it meant that her uncle and the little girl who had died would take an image of her wherever they went after they had died. Her grandfather didn't count at all because he hadn't seen her when she had visited.

Supposing they were cremated and not buried, would they still take the image with them. She pondered this for a while but couldn't make up her mind so left an underlined note to learn more about what happened to the bodies of people who died.

Her mother called her downstairs for dinner twice before the call registered and she slouched downstairs. At the table after they had said grace she asked her mother what happened to bodies when they died and her mother simply cupped a hand over her mouth and ran out of the room closely monitored by her daughter. Wow, she thought, that was some reaction as she carried on eating her dinner, not at all put off by the sounds of her mother throwing up in the downstairs cloakroom.

She carefully washed up her plate and the pots and pans then made a cup of tea for her mother and left it by her plate on the kitchen table then wandered out into the garden for a while. It was Sunday afternoon and she hadn't seen her daddy since Friday evening. How could the death of her grandpa make the time go so slowly? She thought back to when she had seen him last with his head nodding to his loud snores and smiled and told him she loved him even if he was dead and that at least he wouldn't snore any more.

She picked up an apple from the grass under the fruit tree and saw that the underside of it had gone brown; it was going rotten and as she examined it closely she wondered if the same happened to people when they died, they went rotten. She felt tremors of excitement thinking along these lines and wanted to run upstairs to make a note of her thoughts, throwing the apple onto the compost heap as she passed it on the way back in but suddenly changed her mind and decided to check out the shed.

On a dusty ledge in the garden shed she found the remains of some insects. She was heartbroken, she always was when she found any insects that had died by a window thinking they were millimetres away from freedom but they could only escape if someone opened a window for them. She had saved a lot of insects from such a horrible death and even when she had been quite small she would try to pick up worms and hide them from the birds by burying them under piles of leaves. She thought fondly back to those times, when grown-ups had been enchanted by her actions as she 'put the wormy to bed'.

The dead bodies of the insects in the shed had obviously been there a long time; they had almost turned to dust. As she looked at them she thought back to the funeral of her uncle and what the man with the white collar had said that had suddenly made her pay attention during an event she found boring.

"Ashes to ashes, dust to dust…" that was the only bit of the sermon she remembered but now as she looked at the remains of the moths she thought she understood what the man was meaning and she gasped in astonishment with the new understanding. Somehow or other, she didn't yet know how, we all turned back into ashes, back into dust, how amazing was that. The insects, the beautiful insects had helped her to see what happened, well the moths had at least. She was bursting with excitement and needed to share it with someone but not her mother, definitely not her mother, she was weak and stupid.

"Why did Grandpa die" she suddenly asked her mother at the tea table as she spooned raspberry jam onto a crumpet.

"He was ill, darling" her mother finally came out with as she picked up her mug of tea.

"Do all people who are ill die?" she responded.

"No, darling, some recover."

She was quiet for a moment as she ate her crumpet then reached for another. "Then why didn't Grandpa recover?"

"Look, darling, I don't know, I don't know why he didn't recover all right. I really think we should stop talking about it and talk about something else all right. Have you packed your school bag for tomorrow?"

She nodded her head in response to this and for a little while quietness reigned until she asked, "When's the funeral?" Then she jumped in surprise as her mother slammed her open palms down on the table and shouted, "Enough."

She hung her head as if she was sorry then quietly got up from the table and went up to her room, her sanctuary. She leant against the closed door and laughed. Did she or did she not know how to wind her mother up? The silly bitch would come upstairs in a minute or two to say how sorry she was she was sure but her assuredness turned to disappointment as her mother did not come upstairs to speak to her. She was shocked, she thought she knew her mother so well; she was certainly going to have to rethink her strategies.

She made a note to check the obituaries columns in the newspapers tomorrow in the school library as she had already checked Saturday's paper and not found anything interesting apart from someone remembering the anniversary of their beloved dog. She had liked that and had cut it out to stick in her study but had upset her mother who said she hadn't read the paper yet. She had hoped to read about when Grandpa's funeral was going to be as her mother was being stupid at the moment but decided perhaps it was too early. She must remember that time was important in death things.

Now that she knew her grandpa had died, she thought that her parents would have put an announcement of the fact in the local paper and would have to go to a post-mortem meeting and also make decisions as to whether Grandpa was going to be buried or cremated as well as arrange flowers. She looked over her notes pleased with the fact that she knew more about what arrangements were needed when people died but she realised there was a gap, a huge gap, in her research which she didn't know how to fill. It was obvious she was not going to get any sense from her mother, she was far too sensitive. You would have thought that with Grandpa being old and wrinkly she would have expected him to die soon. What on earth was the matter with her or her father come to that? It looked like he was going to spend all of the weekend with his mother when he should be spending it with his family, taking them out and giving them treats and such. Come to think of it he was being totally inconsiderate to his family. She should be his priority not his mother who was old and wrinkly like Grandpa had been. She wrinkled her nose in disgust wondering why old people smelt old. It was horrible the way they hugged you to them so all you could breathe was their oldness. Ugh. She decided that she didn't want to get old after all. Not many people would come to her funeral if she smelt old, now would they?

She had a bath and got herself ready for bed quite excited by the thought that if the funeral was later in the week she could get the day off school.

She said her prayers loudly in case anyone was listening then snuggled up in bed and thought about how her grandpa had died. Nobody had said anything so she didn't know. As she lay there she wondered how she could get more information about how the old fool had died. She remembered he had been in hospital when he died and wondered if she should go there and spin a sob story to see if she could find out more details. After all she had a right to know, she was family after all.

She decided that she would write a page or two of sentimental trash to say at the funeral then it would be out of the way and she could get on with reality so she started to write 'To the bestest grandpa that anybody in the world ever had…'

Chapter 4
Swimming

She had quite enjoyed being at school although she hadn't mixed with anyone and had spent most of her breaks in the library until the teachers turned her out into the playground. She hadn't found any details out about her grandpa's funeral arrangements in the papers so decided to follow through with her idea to go to the hospital.

She thought she had sounded convincing and had got to them having explained to them that her grandpa had died in the hospital and that she wanted to see him as she missed him. She had willingly given her name and address to the kind, soft-talking lady but realised this was a mistake when suddenly her dad appeared and took her home. Her dad kissed her, hugged her tight and called her sweetheart but didn't say anything about Grandpa. She couldn't believe how terrible he looked and for the first time she realised that he was getting old and that one day he would look like Grandpa had. She shuddered in horror, she didn't ever want to look like her grandparents, never ever. Unbelievable, all that effort for nothing, she was still none the wiser. How on earth could she do a proper study if people didn't talk to her. It was not as if she was asking too much of them, was it?

Unbeknown to her, her parents had a letter from the school to go in and see the headteacher. They worried what it might be about but didn't tell their daughter of their intended visit. They talked about it quietly in the kitchen when they were sure their daughter was asleep but had no idea what it could be about, and anyway they had enough to worry about at the moment with the arrangements of Grandpa's funeral and all the other myriad of arrangements required.

The school receptionist showed them into the waiting room and they sat there in awkward silence until they were called into the office. As they entered the headteacher stood up and leaned across the desk to shake hands with them before inviting them to sit, then passed a few pleasantries with them before saying, "You have been called in today so we can discuss some of our concerns regarding your daughter." Her parents did not know how to respond to this remark or even if they should, although there was enough of a pause for them to speak if they wanted to. The headteacher continued, "It has been reported to me on many occasions that your daughter seems to avoid making friends and spends a lot of time on her own and whilst this in itself may not be something to worry about it does raise concern about her social development. This though is not the main reason we called you into the office. Your daughter has spent quite a lot of time in the computer room accessing sites about funerals, post-mortems and burials. As you know it is unusual for an eleven-year-old child to be looking up this kind of information and we wondered if you could enlighten us as to how she has been behaving at home. Have you noticed anything different in her behaviour since she started this school?" The headteacher paused for breath then continued, "A new school is daunting enough for any child and we wish to help her settle in and lessen any anxieties she may have. We know she had time off recently because of a death in the family and we thought you could bring us up to speed."

Her parents looked across at each other then, as his wife dissolved into tears her husband told them of the loss of his father and brother recently and of how close his daughter had been to both of them and of also being in close proximity when a child went under a train.

An hour later they made their way home knowing they had a difficult time ahead of them. They discussed whether they should let their daughter attend the funeral of his father which was scheduled for the following week but did not see how stopping her attending would help her. In fact, they thought the very act of doing so might make things worse as they felt she would feel left out. Perhaps attending the funeral would help bring closure to whatever she was going through and they would watch her closely and help out wherever they saw the need.

The school had suggested that their daughter might be in need of counselling and they had both shaken their heads at the suggestion but now, hours later, they thought that perhaps they had been too hasty and decided that they would agree to their daughter having sessions if they noticed any deterioration in her behaviour.

Whilst on her way home from school she suddenly stepped out into the path of oncoming traffic whilst thinking about something else and was rudely brought back into the moment as a passing adult yanked her back onto the pavement, whilst an oncoming vehicle, swerving to avoid hitting her, smashed into another vehicle. Suddenly a lot of people were shouting at her and she dissolved into tears saying she was sorry, so sorry. She watched the effect her tears had on the adults and marvelled at their power, how they had changed anger into compassion and loved every second of it. They wiped away her tears, blew her nose and sent her on her way home with her promising to watch what she was doing in future. After all there was no real harm done, the only bodies injured were car bodies after all.

As soon as she got home she knew something was up as she was called into the kitchen to speak to her parents. They told her they had gone into her school as concerns had been raised about web sites she was accessing on their computers and that the school was looking for reassurance that everything was as good as it could be at home. She was shocked. How dare the school go behind her back and tell tales, she would have to do something about that. When they told her that she didn't have to go to Grandpa's funeral if she didn't want to she cried and said, "Please please let me go to Grandpa's funeral to say goodbye to him. I promise I will be good, honest. I have written my goodbye to him especially to read out in church so that everyone will know how much we loved him and that he was the best grandpa ever."

Over the next few days at school she made sure that she went into the playground and mixed with some of the girls from her previous school. She found socialising was boring and a waste of her time but she realised that people in power, teachers, parents and the like could use her habit of isolating herself against her. They wouldn't understand but, on the other hand she didn't want them to, didn't want them prying into her life and how she was living it.

Saturday was a very hot day and her parents had the idea of taking her swimming but unfortunately many other people had had the same idea and the pool was packed. She didn't want to go in, all those people crowding her with their funny body odours but her parents were set on the idea and deaf to her suggestions to go elsewhere. How dare they ignore her and make her do things she didn't want to do.

Her parents left her to go and sit up in the gallery so they could watch her as she went downstairs to the changing area and got changed into her swimsuit on her own. Glad not to have her mother fussing around her, she attached the locker key to her clothes with a safety pin which was always attached to her swimsuit for that very purpose.

The pool area was noisy but as she walked past the seating area towards the shallow end she still heard her name called and saw her mother waving wildly at her. She gave a pretty smile and waved back whilst seething inside: parents were so embarrassing sometimes.

The water was freezing and she took a little time to pluck up enough courage to duck under the water but funnily enough, when she had done that, the water didn't seem so cold. There were lots of parents in the shallow end with little children, some of whom were quite happy bobbing around in rubber rings. She walked up the pool until the water was reaching her shoulders and there was space to swim, and held onto the side and looked up towards her parents who weren't looking at her but were watching something at the diving end of the pool. She turned to look in the same direction but had no idea what had got their attention. She checked nobody was coming then struck out and swam a width without stopping and grabbed the opposite rail and turned to look at her parents ready to smile at them and raise her fist in the air but found they still weren't watching her. She waited as a few people swimming lengths went by then struck out again in her favourite front crawl stroke. As soon as she reached the side she wondered if she could manage to swim a width holding her breath and immediately set off again kicking her legs as hard as she could determined not to breathe until she touched the other side but unfortunately she swam in the path of someone who was swimming lengths and they briefly knocked the wind out of each other before continuing their separate ways. She was devastated but realised that it was her fault as much as the other person's; she hadn't checked to see if it was all clear before setting across, so keen was she to complete the width without breathing. She managed to reach the far side of the pool coughing and spluttering from her encounter and decided that she had had enough and holding on to the rail moved down to the crowded shallow end. She reached for her key and took it off of the safety pin as she moved amongst the crowd, her legs bent so the water still covered her shoulders. In front of her a little child was bobbing about quite happily in the water and without thought she jabbed the pin twice in quick succession into the rubber ring as she passed, her actions lost in the crowd. She continued to the steps whilst underwater. She repined her key to her costume and pulled herself up and out then walked around to the gallery to where her parents were sitting and waved at them to get their attention, then signalled she was going to have a shower and get dressed. Her parents waved back at her then she went downstairs and was in the shower when she heard a commotion and saw swimming pool staff running past and messages booming out of the loudspeakers too loud to be deciphered. She took her time and had a long hot shower, then got changed, dried her hair with the dryer then went to meet her parents.

She saw her parents talking to police officers and, for a split second, hesitated then recovered her wits and smiled her sunniest smile as she went up to them saying, "Did you see me, Mummy, I swam three widths, did you see me?" knowing that they hadn't. Her daddy reached for her and held her close and hushed her before continuing talking to the police officers.

Her parents were quiet on the way home and she continually babbled on about swimming three widths but failed to get any reaction from them. On reaching home she was thankful to escape to her room and write in her notebook.

Was drowning like suffocation? she wondered. After all both had a lack of oxygen as the cause of death. She decided she didn't want to drown when she died. She had had a moment's panic when she had collided with that person who was swimming lengths in the pool and had gone under the water spluttering and kicking wildly before she realised she could reach the bottom. She could have drowned right there and then in front of her parents and they wouldn't have noticed, so busy were they watching something or someone else. A familiar anger welled up inside her and she thought bitter thoughts.

She decided to do some work on what she wanted to be done when she died and decided there and then that she would like to die in her thirties when she would still be attractive and full of promise but not old enough to smell old, to become wrinkly and crinkly as she called it. She studied what she had written and thought she had made tremendous progress. All she had to do now was to decide how she would die and so far all she had was information on how she didn't want to die. Still, she was finally getting somewhere and she skipped downstairs for tea.

Chapter 5
Clive

The day of the funeral was a dreary, cold, rainy day and everyone had on thick coats and scarves as they huddled in small groups and stamped their feet on the gravel outside the church whilst waiting for the cortege to arrive.

She had forgotten to bring her gloves and wanted to wait inside the church which although no warmer offered protection from the wind, but her parents had told her no and that was that. She sulked as she put each hand under opposite armpits to keep them warm and wandered over to look at the many flowers and read the inscriptions on the cards. She wondered what happened to the flowers when the funeral was over. After all her grandpa didn't need them, what a waste. As she looked at them she decided that she didn't like cut flowers as from the moment they were cut they were dying and who would want dying flowers brought to a funeral? She decided that dead people didn't have a choice unless they had written instruction to only bring pot plants or things that were living to their funeral. It was alive people who brought dying flowers. She made a note in her mind to write 'no cut flowers' in her notes when she got home.

She was so busy thinking that a touch on her shoulder made her jump. She turned to see her father walking away from her towards the church entrance to where her mother was waiting and beckoning her to hurry up. A black shiny car was parked outside the church and the coffin had already been removed from it and carried into the church. Blast it, she thought, I like that bit, I wanted to see it. They moved quickly down the aisle to sit in the front pew and bowed their heads feeling embarrassed and also feeling that everyone was staring at them for being last in. Her grandma was already sitting there with a warm blanket tucked around her legs and she watched her daddy kiss his mother feeling jealous of his obvious affection for her. Sitting on the other side of her and holding Grandma's hand was cousin Clive and for a moment she felt intensely jealous of her fourteen-year-old cousin. What a creep, she thought, he's only after her money. She didn't know if Grandma had any money or not but she had heard the phrase and liked it so had tucked it away in her memory to be used as and when she felt like it.

The sermon went on and on and she grew restless and wriggled on the wooden pew trying to get comfortable. Her mother gave her one of her looks that warned her to be still, so she clenched her hands in the pockets of her coat and counted up to one hundred then started again until it was time for her to say her piece. She didn't remember her uncle's funeral being so long and boring and wondered why this funeral felt different.

She stood in front of the small congregation and told them she had written about her grandpa, her daddy's daddy. There was a small murmur as she said this, then she opened her notes and read out what she had prepared remembering to put a catch in her voice and to stop and wipe her eyes every now and then. She finished and kept her head bowed as she returned to her place satisfied with the sounds of people sniffing as if her words had made them cry.

Suddenly it was time to close the curtains and everyone except Grandma stood and sang their hearts out as the curtains drew together. She had to admit that she felt a little bit emotional as the curtains finally closed, and was glad that real tears rolled down her cheeks so that she could feel what it was like to feel real emotion. She didn't remember feeling emotional at her uncle's funeral and decided she would have to read her notes when she got home to see if she had cried real or pretend tears.

She followed her parents outside and dutifully stood beside them and shook hands with the few well-wishers waiting outside the entrance. She heard comments, "such a shame" and "we're so sorry" time and time again. Grandma had stood with them for a while then succumbed to her son's insistence and sat in the car to wait until they were ready to leave.

As she sat in the car on the way home holding onto and patting her grandma's hand, she wondered why the coffin was made of wood. Why did trees have to be cut down to make coffins? it didn't make sense. She decided that she wouldn't have a coffin, she would have a beautiful golden cloth draped over her and to make a note of it when she got home. She remembered that she had something else to write down but had to struggle to remember what it was, then remembered that she didn't want cut flowers brought to her funeral when she died. She was pleased that she had new insights to add to her notes.

There were a few parked cars parked on the road outside their house when they returned to it and she was given instructions to greet people politely when they came to the door after she had helped unwrap all the food that she had helped her mother to prepare. Once everybody who was to arrive had arrived she made herself invisible and stood behind groups of people hoping to overhear things that could add to her knowledge of how her grandpa had died. She heard comments similar to those she had heard at the church and had all but given up when she heard, "Oh yes, he must have dropped it," before her presence was seen and the talking stopped. Dropped it, must have dropped it, were they talking about her grandpa dropping his inhaler or were they talking about something else? Why didn't anyone tell her then she would know if her grandpa had died because of her? At the moment for all she knew he had died of natural causes!

Her mother caught hold of her arm and whispered, "Take Clive up to your room out of the way, you children shouldn't be down here listening to all these reminisces." Her heart sank, oh no not cousin Clive, boring old cousin Clive. She never had been able to stand the sight of him, nor he her for that matter and now her mother had told her to take him up to her room.

"Mum," she wailed to no effect as her mother fixed her with one of her looks, then reluctantly turned away to do as she was told all the while muttering fiercely under her breath.

Clive did not want to go with her but didn't want to stay downstairs with the adults either so chose the lesser of the two evils and followed her up to her room, and plonked himself on her bed and looked around. "No posters!"

"NO, obviously," she retorted, her voice sharper than she intended. She toned it down. "My parents won't let me." This wasn't true but it had the desired effect of getting him on side.

"Mine neither," he responded and got up off the bed and strolled around the room looking at her books then picking up one of her notebooks. She opened her mouth to tell him to put it down then relaxed as she thought it's in code, he'll never be able to read it.

"What's this then, Blaze of Glory?" he asked as he started to read her notes.

She snatched it away from him shocked that he could read her private notes "It's none of your business, it's private and anyway how could you read it, it's in code?"

"It's what I do," said Clive proudly. "I'm a code breaker, and a code maker. I am going to work for MI5 or some secret service when I get old enough."

She was impressed despite her intense dislike of him and decided to change the subject, mentally making a note to keep her notebooks out of sight in future. "How do you get on with your dad?"

He was on the defence straight away. "What do you mean get on with my dad?"

"I just wondered that's all," she replied, enjoying his obvious discomfort.

"OK I guess, why do you ask?"

"Does he punish you, you know, beat you?"

"What's it to you if he does?"

"I just wondered that's all. I mean I know he's Mum's brother but he seems..." she hesitated searching for a word.

"Seems what?"

"Seems to be more of a rough diamond if you know what I mean."

"No I don't and anyway doesn't your dad beat you if you've been stroppy?"

She glared at him, her hands on her hips. "I'll have you know my dad has never laid a finger on me, ever, he wouldn't."

Clive said, "You're weird, asking if my dad hits me, you're weird," he finished lamely. Clive suddenly sat down on her bed and wept. She handed him a box of tissues and watched him carefully, curious at how he had suddenly disintegrated in front of her. He hid his face in the crook of his arm for a while then slowly calmed and raised a tear-stained face towards her. "Happy now you've made me cry!"

She looked at his tear-stained face and felt powerful; she had easily reduced him to tears. "No I'm not," she lied. "I didn't know you would get upset otherwise I wouldn't have said anything. I didn't want to upset you, I like him, your dad I mean, I really do like him, though not so much now if he hits you."

"Thank you," he said as if she had given him a present then, "didn't I see you in the swimming pool the other day?"

"I dunno, you might of, why?" she replied aware that she could be stepping on hot stones if she wasn't careful.

"I'm sure it was you; you were swimming widths because you can't swim lengths yet."

She bit the bait. "I could if I wanted to," she said adding, "I just didn't want to."

Clive gave her a knowing look feeling on much firmer ground now. "All right then we can have a race, see whose fastest."

"You're older than me, you're bound to be fastest."

"Scaredy cat, scaredy cat," Clive taunted her, then, "Didn't you know about the baby that drowned in the shallow end!"

For a moment she had lost the thread of the conversation as she reacted to being taunted, then suddenly she was back in the moment. "Baby that drowned, what baby?"

Clive shrugged. "I dunno, some kid in a rubber ring drowned, the police were there and everything, you must have seen something or heard something at least unless of course you are totally stupid." He grinned a superior grin at her then turned to leave the room when she said something that stopped him in his tracks. "If I show you mine will you show me yours." He briefly shook his head and turned to go out of the room when he suddenly changed his mind and stepped back into the room and shut the door behind him and stood with his back against it.

All was quiet for a moment as they stood there looking at each other then she said, "You first."

"Oh no, you first. You show me yours first, then I'll show you mine."

She stood undecided for a minute then put her hand beneath the hem of her dress and pulled it up, then hooked her thumbs over her knickers and pushed them down to her ankles, then stood there looking at his face as he stared at her.

He said, "Why, you're a baby, you haven't got any hair down there yet," then laughed.

She retorted, "I'm not a baby, I'm nearly twelve."

"Yes you are, you're a baby, I bet you haven't even got any tits yet," he sneered at her across the room.

"It's your turn, I've shown you mine now you show me yours," she said as she bent down to pull her knickers up feeling flustered and not knowing why.

Clive laughed, "No way," then said, "Whoa" as she suddenly hurled herself at him and beat at his chest with her fists. She was furious, her anger rising out of the depths and overwhelming her though she did not make a sound. Clive caught hold of her flailing forearms and bent and kissed her full on the mouth. At first she resisted him but gradually began to kiss him back as she grew calmer. At last he pulled away saying, "I love it when you go wild like that." She laughed up at him then bent down again to pull her knickers up when he stopped her, looked behind him at the closed door and listened, holding up a hand for her to be quiet whilst he did so then turned back to her and said, "Leave them there, I want to look at you again, you're so beautiful."

"Why."

"Can't I look at my girlfriend if I want to?"

"Girlfriend!"

"Yes, you will say yes, won't you? You will be my girlfriend?"

She threw herself in his arms and kissed him how she thought grown-ups kissed, then lay back on her bed and let Clive look at her thinking it no big deal and really rather exciting, she had a boyfriend, she had a boyfriend.

Clive reached into his coat pocket and took his mobile out and held it up to take a picture. She immediately sat up. "What you doing, what you taking a picture of me for?"

"I want to remember you on the day you said that you would be my girlfriend. I want to be able to look at you whenever I like and feel close to you." Clive didn't know where the words came from but they sounded sincere enough and obviously worked as she lay back on the bed and let him take some pictures, opening her legs just a little when he asked her to. He then asked her to pull her knees up and let them relax to the sides thinking she would downright refuse him but she meekly did as she was asked and he took photos of her hairless pussy, then put the mobile away and spent some time kissing her and telling her lies about how much he loved her and how he had wanted to get to know her for ages but was frightened that she would turn him down. She lapped up every word but when he asked her to keep their relationship a secret she flared up again. "Why, you ashamed of me?" He told her that grown-ups wouldn't understand that they loved each other and that they should keep it a secret until she was older, then they could get married and have kids and such.

She was immediately transported to the future, picturing herself with children around her as she was cooking his dinner for when he came home. Clive looked into her face as she was daydreaming thinking what a stupid little bitch she was. Marry her, he'd rather marry his granny. However, he made sure none of his thoughts showed in his face; she was his little Lolita and he was going to have some fun with her that was for sure.

After he had left she sat down on her bed and thought about what Clive had said about the baby drowning in the swimming pool. She hadn't seen anything in the papers or on the news. Surely if what he had said was true there would have been some media coverage. She remembered that when she had come out of the changing rooms her parents had been talking to the police so maybe that part of his story was true but they hadn't said anything else and, to be honest she had forgotten all about it and had only briefly flicked through some papers, after all she couldn't use the school computers now without being spied upon. She decided he was winding her up and using part truth part lie so that she would believe his story and decided that he was simply teasing her and that it was something that boyfriends did to their girlfriends. She thought about kissing him, feeling incredible that he should want her, after all she was only twelve (nearly) and wondered how she could please him and make sure that he would never leave her. She thought about how daring they had been with Clive taking pictures of her and kissing her when her parents and guests were actually downstairs without the faintest idea of what they were up to!

For some reason she felt exhausted so she stretched out on her bed and closed her eyes for a moment or two. It had been a long day and she was glad it was coming to an end at last. Funny how some days seemed longer than others. She would just take forty-five as her Dad would say then she would go downstairs and be polite to the guests who were leaving, then help her mother tidy up, deciding she needed to get in her parents' good books as her birthday was coming up soon and she wanted lots of presents.

Her mother went upstairs about thirty minutes or so later and found her asleep on top of her bed, looking angelic. She didn't want to wake her so simply covered her with a duvet and kissed her gently on her forehead. "Night night, darling, sweet dreams."

Chapter 6
Entrapment

She awoke in the early hours of the morning to go to the toilet and changed into her pyjamas before getting back into bed. She tossed and turned but couldn't sleep and at last put the light on and sat up. She thought about the baby in the swimming pool drowning while its parents were close by and felt a thrill of excitement. She mentally told them they were bad parents as they hadn't been able to look after their baby properly. It wasn't her fault at all, they were just bad parents. She felt a little sad that she had not been able to see the baby drown but reckoned that she still would be able to salvage something from the death after all. She took her notebook out and wrote drowning under the list of ways she didn't want to die from, then spent some time working out a new code as she was worried that if Clive ever came into her room again he would be able to read all her notes and then tell someone. All right he was her boyfriend but she didn't know if he was any good at keeping secrets yet. It was best she just made up a new code then she wouldn't have to worry. She couldn't allow anyone to read her notes, she just couldn't.

Thinking of Clive made her squirm with excitement. She had made herself vulnerable in front of him and he had kissed her and asked her to be his girlfriend. How was she supposed to act when she saw him at school? Should she just ignore him as if she didn't know him or should she nod at him and give him a secret smile? After turning options over in her mind she decided she should just ignore him totally then their little secret would be safe. She pictured him kneeling at her feet begging her to marry him, whilst she stood stony faced and staring into the distance pretending she didn't care, then giving in and falling into his loving arms. The image made her feel powerful and she settled back down to sleep feeling so much better. She had a boyfriend; it was her delicious secret and she hugged herself with delight as she pictured him holding her close and telling her how much she meant to him.

When at school it was obvious that Clive had told his mates something despite their agreement not to and she was teased by both girls and boys. In a way she enjoyed getting lots of attention. She used her stony-faced image that she had pictured herself using in her daydream and found that it worked well. When people got no reaction from her they gave up and left her alone. True some of the little shits were persistent but she had clocked them and they would pay.

She joined the after-school drama club as she thought she could learn a lot from it and also spent most of her lunch hour in the school swimming pool. After a few weeks she could swim a length without stopping but she worked herself hard, remorseless to herself in her training. She had always started from the deep end and stayed near the side of the pool figuring that if she got tired at least she could grab onto the side or stand on the bottom of the pool in the shallow end but now she didn't have to do that any more. The only trouble with all the training was that it made her tired and she had to work hard to stay awake during the afternoon lessons with the warm sun slanting onto her through the classroom windows.

Clive continued to call around to see her and was warmly welcomed into the house by her parents who both liked him. He told them that he thought of their daughter as the sister he had never had and laughed inwardly as their faces softened. He also told them that he loved making up codes and stuff and that their daughter did to.

Her birthday was a great disappointment to her. She had asked for a laptop thinking it was the perfect way for her to keep all her notes in one place and free from prying eyes but her parents had refused and instead bought her a cheap phone and had taken her out to the coast for the day. They had suggested that she ask a friend to come with her but she had just shaken her head and told them she wanted them to herself on her special day when, in reality, she couldn't bear for her friend to find out what cheapskates her parents were.

When Clive came around on this particular day both of her parents were out but she let him in anyway knowing that her parents wouldn't mind. Once in her bedroom she went to kiss him but he pushed her away and said, "You've been cheating on me." She was shocked and suddenly scared of losing him.

Her life continued with its ups and downs and suddenly it seemed it was her fourteenth birthday and her parents had actually given her a laptop. True it was not the state of the art one that she wanted but still it was a start. She lost no time in organising her notes on it and realised that she had huge gaps in her study, too many notes on what she didn't want to happen and too few on what she did. She found that because she had changed the code she used to write her notes several times she had difficulty in transcribing some of them and had to spend a lot of time and effort to regain the information. It was Clive's fault she decided, her stuck up sixteen-year-old cousin. If he hadn't broken her earlier code she would never have had to change it in the first place.

She lay back on her bed as she thought of him and of how she rarely even saw him now. She still loved him, she assured herself, but she decided she didn't want to be tied down to just one boy now. He was continuously on at her to go all the way with him and she was getting fed up with it and their ensuing rows. Didn't boys ever think of anything else? She told him she was saving herself for him for when they got married and he had suddenly got angry and told her that if she didn't sleep with him he would no longer be her boyfriend. She very nearly capitulated but pulled back at the last minute. She would give herself to him when they got married and not before. Clive said, "It's over then," and, stony-faced, walked out of the door and for all she knew, out of her life.

She had been inconsolable for a time, breaking into floods of tears at the least little thing. She had changed from the gawky eleven-year-old into an attractive self-assured fourteen-year-old and yet couldn't understand how her eleven-year-old self had hooked Clive whilst her fourteen-year-old self had lost him.

She had still maintained her swimming schedules and this had helped her body development as well as earning a much sought after place in the school swimming team where she was seen as one of the school's greatest assets. She was much admired for her commitment to training and was continuously used as an example by the teachers to other young pretenders.

She had also continued to attend the after school drama class and had performed in many plays gaining confidence and learning new skills. As time went on, she was amazed at all the subtleties she was discovering and tucked them away for future use.

Clive wasn't interested in her now, no doubt about it unless she gave him what he wanted and what he obviously had no difficulty in getting elsewhere with his good looks, toned physique and skill in whatever sport he chose to adopt. Beauty is only skin deep she said to herself time and time again as she thought about him. Was he handsome? She supposed he was but in the long run how he looked would not stop her from extracting revenge. He had used her, abused her and then dumped her but he didn't realise that he would pay dearly one day. She was a spider in waiting, a black widow no less.

She looked at herself in the locker room mirror after she had just completed a particularly gruelling training session and was pleased with what she saw. A figure who had given everything in training, she could barely stand she was so tired. She had that horrible stomach ache again and knew her period was due, not that she would give in to it or lessen her training when it occurred. She hated having periods, messy things, and initially had treated them like an enemy until she realised that it was part of her development from childhood into womanhood and now she just tolerated them. After a long hot shower she stood under the hair dryer loving the way her hair reacted almost with a life of its own as warm air cuddled and dried it. Her mink-coloured hair reached almost to her waist, thick and glossy, stuff to give boys dreams, and they did. She had boys offering to carry her books or school bag nearly every day and she used the sweetest of smiles to ensnare them whilst she refused their offers of help. She was thankful that half term had finally arrived, she could have a lay in at last.

On the way home she called in to see her grandma and found her sorting through a box of faded photographs. She made them both a cup of tea, then sat beside her grandma and looked at the various ones she picked out being particularly interested in the ones that showed her father when he was a boy. There had been three boys, the oldest whom she had never seen had died in the Falklands War before she was born. Tears were running down Grandma's face as she looked at the photographs of her lovely boys as she put it, telling her granddaughter that they were as dear to her now as they ever were even though only one of them was still alive.

She stared at the photograph of the three grinning boys and wondered what it would be like to have siblings and decided that she liked being an only child because it meant that she got all her parents' attention. She asked her grandma if she had had any brothers and sisters and spent the next half hour listening to the merry times her grandma recounted, that she had had two brothers but that she, with her waist-long hair and big brown eyes, had been her father's favourite. She recounted tales of how she used to wind him around her little finger and get her own way when she suddenly lay back in her armchair, mid-sentence, and fell fast asleep. She studied her grandma as she slept for a while, then left her peacefully asleep and continued home looking forward to a long hot shower and an early night.

When she arrived home her mother was in the kitchen baking whilst her father was busy repainting the banisters. She spent a few minutes chatting with them instead of rushing straight upstairs as usual and told them about calling in to see her grandma and of how she had spent the time there looking at old photographs and seeing Dad as a child in a photograph with his brothers before going up to her room.

The shower was heavenly and she spent much longer in it than she meant to before swirling her hair up into a warm towel and going into her room leaving her bedroom door open. It had been a hot dusty day and as she opened the window the draft caused her door to bang causing her to jump. She went back to open it, picking up a slipper to wedge it open when she heard her mother calling, "Clive's here, darling, he's on his way up."

"Oh shit," she said as the door opened in front of her and Clive peered around it.

"Nice to see you too," he said as he viewed her naked body, "very very nice indeed," as he came into the room and shut the door behind him and stood in front of it.

She wasn't the least bit put out by his gaze and stood there in her robe which she had simply slipped on but not tied up therefore displaying all of her many assets. She watched him dispassionately then let her robe slip off of her shoulders and fall to the floor. His eyes followed it to the floor, then travelled slowly up again until he was looking into her face speechless for eternity it seemed.

He suddenly said, in a husky voice, "You remember that time when you said show me yours and I'll show you mine?" She nodded at him with what he saw as a seductive smile on her face then said, "Do you want to see mine?" He was having trouble keeping himself under control as he watched her move slowly over to her mirror, then sit in front of it and begin to tend to her hair. In an instant he was behind her pressing his groin into the back of her neck as he clumsily reached down to roughly fondle her breasts.

She was in charge, she knew exactly what to do, how to make him reach fever pitch. All those years of attending drama classes would not be wasted. She turned on the stool and gripped him around his waist, pressed her face against his chest and said in a husky voice, "At last, I thought you would never ask."

Clive reached behind himself to unclasp her hands, then stepped back from her and undid his trouser button, then the zip, then leant forward and kissed her firmly on her mouth before hooking his thumbs over the waistband of his shorts and pushing them down.

She laughed to herself as his manhood was proudly displayed not a little disappointed with its size but huskily said, "My oh my what a big boy you are." He needed no further encouragement and scooped her up easily and dropped her down onto her bed then knelt beside it and ran his hand over her skin all the while saying how beautiful she was, that she was a temptress and he was her slave. He would give her anything, anything at all. He cupped a hand over her pubic area and shoved two fingers inside her whilst closely watching her face.

Shoving his fingers into her hurt her and she grew angry at his crudity but didn't let him know. She opened her legs for him and told him she wanted the real thing now, now, oh please now. She told him that she had missed him and that she still loved him with all her heart (she had just finished rehearsing a part in Romeo and Juliet and was thankful for the script!). He clumsily climbed on top of her and reached down with one hand to guide himself inside her when she started screaming at the top of her voice and shouting for help. Clive froze for a moment puzzled as to why she was screaming, then opened his mouth to tell her not to worry, everything would be all right, that he would be gentle with her when the bedroom door burst open and her father came into the room. Taking in the scene of Clive lying on top of his screaming daughter he reacted by grabbing hold of the back of Clive's shirt and dragging him, butt naked, off her before punching him in the mouth and knocking him out cold. His wife was a few steps behind him and managed to stop him hitting Clive again before sitting beside her screaming daughter and rocking her gently back and forth to calm her.

She watched as her father left the room then return with a pitcher of cold water which he threw over Clive's head. Clive, coughing and spluttering as he came round was totally unaware of what was going on. She watched her father haul him up onto his feet and drag him out of the room, and his having to shuffle as his trousers were still around his knees, and heard the thumps as he was dragged downstairs followed by a brief silence before the front door slammed.

As he was thrown out of the front door a well-aimed kick to his backside propelled him forward face first onto the front lawn. He lay still for a moment hearing the front door slam but couldn't piece together what had just happened. One moment he had been about to slip the bitch a length and the next he was butt naked in the front garden. He suddenly realised how ludicrous he would look to any passer-by and reached down to pull up his shorts and trousers before pushing himself up, and making his getaway before her dad changed his mind and returned to sort him out.

She carried on crying piteous tears but gradually timed her calming down so that she could gasp out that Clive hadn't been able to rape her only because her daddy had saved her. She had taken to using the term 'dad' lately but she thought that she would be his little girl again if she called him Daddy. They both rallied around her and ran a hot bath for her and brought up her dinner for her on a tray but after the second day of such attention she felt claustrophobic and wanted to scream.

Her parents were insistent on making a report to the police but she refused saying she didn't want to drag up every sordid little detail in front of a stranger, she wanted to put it all behind her and move on after all because of her father intervening Clive hadn't managed to have sex with her. They were persistent, telling her that she was letting Clive get away with it and that if she didn't stop him he might try it on someone else, but she was adamant and in the end they agreed though they made it plain they were not happy with her decision. Her mother phoned her brother and told him what had happened. Her brother was incredulous but said he would get to the bottom of the story. Her mother knew what that meant after all she had grown up with him: Clive was about to get the thrashing of his life and serve him right.

She managed to put up with her parents' attention for another day then said in a brave girly voice that she wasn't going to let him (emphasis on him) spoil her life and make her afraid to go out, she was going out to the local park for a while. Her parents stood holding hands as they watched their daughter walking up the road then turned and went back indoors.

She enjoyed her solitary time in the park, sitting on a bench watching the ducks swimming on the lake. It was so good to be free, to get away from her parents for a while. She thought to the future and wondered what it would be like when both of her parents were dead, when she would be able to do what she liked without them interfering all the time. She sighed deeply and wondered if all parents were like hers, no wonder kids were fed up with them.

On her way home she decided to detour to see Grandma who was busily looking for her glasses which were perched on the top of her head. They both giggled about it then Grandma made her some tea and got out the photographs again. She asked to see a picture of her uncle who had died before she was born then said to her grandma to tell her all about him. Grandma did not need asking twice and told her about her firstborn son, how proud she was of him and of how naughty he was sometimes. During the telling Grandma suddenly sat back in her chair and went to sleep just like she had on a previous occasion.

She looked at her grandma lying fast asleep, her mouth slightly opened and got up and kissed her lightly on the cheek telling her she loved her before she picked up a cushion from the other armchair and placed it over her grandma's face and pressed gently. There was no resistance whatsoever, no clawing hands trying to pull the cushion away, Grandma just slipped quietly away. When she took the cushion away she saw that Grandma looked the same as before she had placed the cushion over her face. She shook the cushion out then brushed it down and replaced it on the chair she had taken it from, kissed her grandma again, took her teacup out into the kitchen and washed it up and put it away then, just as she reached the front door, turned back and said to her grandma, "He might be your son but he's my daddy too and now you're out of the way I will be able to see more of him," then turned away and quietly pulled the front door closed behind her.

Chapter 7
Burial

Her plan of getting more time to spend with her father didn't work out as she had foreseen it. In fact the following week she saw nothing of him at all as he spent his time around his childhood home sorting out possessions. She had called around a couple of times to offer help but the person who opened the door to her, his face riddled with grief, was far removed from the fun-loving dad she had grown up with and thought she knew.

In the end, she gave up, angry that her plan had misfired, that Grandma was still taking her daddy away from her. She was old, of course she was going to die, it was obvious to her but why wasn't it obvious to them, why didn't they accept it?

She took her laptop with her to the local park pleased to be out of the way of her mother who was busy spring-cleaning the house. She had asked for a lock to be put on her door so that her room could be private, saying that since the time that Clive had burst into her room (exaggeration) she needed the security. She thought that this would tip the balance and that her parents would agree but to her surprise they told her no and wouldn't budge, and on top of that wouldn't give a valid reason why they had come to that decision. "It isn't fair," she pouted as she flounced up the stairs, "you're treating me like a baby."

"Well, if you stop acting like one we will stop treating you like one," her mother called up the stairs to her retreating back.

Once inside her room she caught sight of her pouting face in her bedroom mirror and was shocked at how immature it made her look. Her mother was right, she was acting like a baby. She didn't like the feel of being in the wrong whilst her parents were in the right and told herself that it wasn't her fault, they had made her like she was.

On her laptop in the park she continued to look through signs and symptoms of infectious diseases being both fascinated and horrified by their many forms. She found it exciting that many diseases didn't manifest, didn't surface, until they had a deadly grip of the person they inhabited. Some of the diseases had cures but some brought with them the death warrant.

Death warrant, death warrant. She rolled the phrase around her tongue loving the feel of it, it felt powerful, masterful. She closed her laptop and rolled over onto her back enjoying the warmth of the sun on her face and the gentle wind caressing her face. It was good to be alive, good to feel part of nature. She turned back onto her stomach and opened her laptop again thinking people who were dead, people who had been burnt and were turned into a pile of ash could also be a part of nature if their ashes were strewn into the wind. Wow, what an amazing thought.

She knew that being burnt when you were alive was painful but it wasn't when you were dead therefore she should be burnt or cremated as they called it. She was sure she had already written this down in her notes ages ago but was unable to trace it anywhere and was astonished at this oversight. She definitely didn't want to be buried and rot away in the ground although she had to deliberate over the fact that she would, by her demise, offer sustenance to earth creatures. Much as she liked them she decided that she wasn't going to be buried. She closed the subject in her mind, decision made.

It was so good to go back to school away from her mother who was still spring cleaning and having a clear out at the same time. What was wrong with her? She dreaded to think what she might find, what she might lose, whilst she was out. She worked out her frustrations in the school swimming pool being even harder on herself than usual, so much so that she could barely drag herself from the pool. She sat in the shower half listening to the idle chatter of some first-year pupils when her ears pricked up. For a moment she couldn't understand what had caught her attention but as she sank back against the shower wall she heard it again: they were talking about being in someone's will or something.

This was new to her; she hadn't given it a thought but now it was painfully obvious to her. Lots of people when they died, no, no, not when they died, before they died, made wills leaving their stuff to people they chose to receive it. Why was she such a clown that she hadn't thought of it before? And if she hadn't been in the shower to overhear the first-years' gossip she may never have thought of it at all!

She hurried home, her mind busy, and rushed upstairs to her room then stopped in the doorway, shock registering on her face. In place of her much loved but worn-out bed there was a single four poster bed draped with net curtains: it was lovely. She turned to see her mother standing a few feet away watching her and flew into her arms. "I love you, Mummy, I love you so much. Thank you, thank you." She knew she was in danger of overdoing it, of being too effusive, but, in reality, she had been totally taken by surprise and was overwhelmed by it. "Now I really do feel like a princess."

She lay down on the new bed totally captivated by it. This was how it should be when she died, laid to rest so that her adoring public could file past her and show their love for her either by weeping or throwing flowers around the area in which she lay. So real was this image that she lay in state for at least thirty minutes before shaking her head awake and getting out her laptop. She decided that she wanted to be remembered like that princess who was still loved twenty years or so after her tragic death. She spent some time researching her and wondered what it was about her that made so many people love her, was it her looks, her personality or was it because she was a princess, she couldn't make up her mind.

She moved over to her mirror and spent some time looking this way and that trying to decide her best angle, then decided that all angles were her best so that from whatever angle her adoring public saw her from she looked beautiful.

Adoring public, how was she going to manage that one, she tossed ideas around in her mind before deciding that she would become a famous actress and that way would get an army of fans that would follow her every move. She hesitated at this thought, if she had an army of fans to follow her every move wouldn't that be the worst-case scenario? She wouldn't be able to make a move without cameras flashing and fans clamouring for her autograph. Bang goes her freedom of movement, she got shoved off when her parents invaded her privacy, how on earth was she going to cope with millions of fans? Millions of fans, she laughed at herself then thought why not, other people have millions of fans so why can't I have?

She decided that she would talk to her drama teacher and see what he thought about her signing up to an acting school. She would see if she could get him to help her with a CV to pave the way. She had no doubt about her talent; she was sure she would rocket to the top in double time.

She knew her parents were in the kitchen discussing Grandma's funeral arrangements so she went down into the kitchen and asked if she could help with the arrangements. She hadn't seen her father for a few days and was shocked at how old he looked, he even had grey hair at his temples. How come she hadn't noticed it before? She sat down at the table without being asked and took hold of each of her parents' hands as she cried crocodile tears. Her parents told her that most of the arrangements had been made already; the post-mortem that had taken place whilst she was at school had given a 'natural causes' verdict. Now all that was left after the burial was to book a place for the reception to take place. She started, burial, Grandma was going to be buried. Why when Grandpa had been cremated, how would they meet up if they were laid to rest in different ways? Her father told her that Grandma had expressed her wishes in her will and that he would make sure her wishes were honoured.

She jumped up and ran upstairs to her room. Buried, her grandma was going to be buried, how awful was that and how selfish taking up precious space when there was hardly room to move anyway. She must try and persuade her parents to change the burial for a cremation, didn't they know what happened to bodies when they died? She was not sure this approach would succeed in her getting her parents to change their minds but she had to try something.

Try as she might she came up against a brick wall, her parents united in fulfilling the wishes of Grandma. She even began to doubt her acting ability as she had no effect whatsoever. In the end her parents told her enough was enough and that they would hear no more from her. She stopped acting and turned into a little girl again stamping her feet and shouting but was ordered up to her room at once by her father. She had never seen him so angry and realised she had gone too far, had pushed him too far so she hung her head and mumbled that she was sorry, that she had only wanted the best for Grandma and fled upstairs.

School the following day was a welcome relief and she threw herself totally into her lessons to push out unwanted thoughts, the main one being that her grandma would rot in her coffin until only her skeleton was left. Uggh. She spent her dinner break in the pool following a punishing schedule, then checked up the noticeboard to see she was entered in the school swimming gala the following week.

On the day of the funeral a sleek shiny car drew up outside their house and she joined her parents in the car following the hearse to the church. It was a different church to the one where Grandpa had been cremated but she kept quiet, not daring to comment and make her parents angry or upset. Once at the church they walked in single file with their heads bowed to their place at the front of the aisle. Halfway down the aisle she caught sight of Clive and wondered why he was so far back from where the family all sat, then realised he was in disgrace: he had, because of her, become the black sheep of the family. She smiled to herself, serve him right little prick, he'd found out the hard way that she was too hot to handle and for good measure had taken a beating from his father. Her friend who lived a few doors away said she had heard him screaming, not such a big boy after all.

The service droned on and on and she wondered if it was ever going to come to an end before they all died of boredom. She decided that she had preferred her grandpa's funeral, in fact, compared to this morbid affair it was almost enjoyable. After what seemed an age the coffin was lifted off its stand by the pallbearers and carried outside whilst the mourners followed at a decent interval.

Standing around the oblong hole the mourners watched stoically as the coffin was carefully lowered into it. A few words were spoken then she watched her father and her mum's brother pick up handfuls of earth and throw them down onto the coffin. She was fascinated and decided to look it up when she got back home to see if it was an ancient rite or something.

As they made their way back to the waiting cars it started to rain and many of the mourners quickened their paces to their waiting vehicles. She felt really tired, really drained and was going to ask if she could be dropped off home but one look at her father's set face changed her mind.

They arrived first at the reception venue and stood dutifully in line shaking hands and murmuring small consolations to the people that arrived. She was particularly interested to see a distant cousin of hers who was in a wheelchair and thought that she would like to find out a lot more about her.

The food was well prepared and she even managed to sneak a glass of white wine which she screwed her nose up at but drank anyway deciding she would have to get used to it as it was what famous people seemed to drink. She moved around freely but noticed that Clive didn't have the same option and that he stayed in his father's shadow all the time. She shuddered as she gave thanks that his dad wasn't anything like her dad; his dad was stern and not above taking a belt to his son if he thought he deserved it whilst her dad had never hit her, never ever. In fact when she thought about it, it was her mum who had smacked her hand when she was naughty.

As the reception drew to a close and people started to leave, she again stood with her parents at the entrance to shake hands and wish people a safe journey home. Her father and Clive's dad left the line up to help her distant cousin get into her vehicle and stow away her wheelchair when suddenly Clive was standing beside her, towering over her. He leant down as if to kiss her cheek and whispered, "Photos, bitch," into her ear with all the venom he could muster before straightening up with a pleasant smile on his face, nodding his head in the direction of her mother who had seen nothing of his previous action being distracted by watching the men aid their distant cousin.

She watched him suddenly aware of his capabilities of covering things up. If she had reacted immediately she could have caused him more grief and perhaps another beating but now it was too late. As she had written in her notes timing was everything and she had missed her cue. She wondered what he meant 'photos bitch' but couldn't immediately fathom it out so shelved it to think about later.

Her father thanked the staff who worked at the reception centre, then at long last they went home and she thought she was never so glad to see it. She dutifully kissed both her parents goodnight then went up to her room and sat down by her mirror and stared into her reflection. She had made an enemy in Clive, no doubt about it. She must tread very carefully in future to see that she didn't underestimate him, very carefully indeed. Now, what was it he had said to her, oh yes 'photos bitch.' What on earth did it mean? But try as she might she couldn't work out why he had said those words to her, she was frustrated with herself after all they must mean something if he had taken the risk to say them to her.

As she lay in bed she thought back over the long day, she had learned a lot and no mistake, tomorrow after school she must update her notes and get them in order. The most exciting thing about dying naturally, she thought, was that you didn't actually know when it would happen, that is if it was natural. She wondered how many deaths that were classified natural were actually natural and how many deaths there were when someone had tipped the balance just a little.

Her thoughts turned to her distant cousin as she wondered what was actually wrong with her. Why did she have to be in a wheelchair? She was dying to find out but knew she had to wait, had to use what was called common sense. She wondered if her cousin died if it would be classed as a natural death seeing as she had something wrong with her already. It all was getting too complicated for her tired mind. She knew what she meant but couldn't put it into words. It would just have to wait for another day and so saying she turned over and was asleep within minutes.

She attended school the following day even though her parents had given her permission to take the day off. She had had enough of them and their cloying attention, at least at school she had space. She saw Clive in the dinner hall but was careful to stay well away and not give him any excuse to approach her. He was watching her, she knew it, she felt it, it was as if she was being hunted, stalked. She liked the excitement and the fear that the thought brought with it and let it run through her being.

Her drama teacher was delighted that she wanted to go on to have an acting career but told her that in order to progress with it she would need her parents' permission; it wasn't just a simple case of doing something just because she wanted to. She was furious but held herself in check. How dare he say she couldn't do what she wanted without getting the permission of her parents. What did he know? In fact what did they know? How dare they stand in her way. She couldn't see them agreeing to her going on to acting school but she would have to work out how she was going to get her way without appearing to manipulate them. Why was life so complicated? Death was so much easier!

Chapter 8
Outwitted

She hadn't told her parents about wanting to go to acting school although on the way home from school she had thought of many approaches. She couldn't get away from her inner child who kept telling her it wasn't fair, that it was her life and she should be able to do with it what she wanted. She spent a restless night and was in no mood for pleasantries in the morning and was, in fact, very abrupt with her mother who pulled her up sharply.

"Yeah, yeah, whatever," she cried, as she went out of the front door slamming it behind her. She knew it was a childish thing to do but so what if it made her feel better. At school she enjoyed the last lesson of the day, double maths but was irritated when the teacher kept her behind as all the other pupils left. To her surprise the teacher was glowing about her progress and commented that if she carried on the way she was going she could well earn a place in university studying maths.

She left school not really looking where she was going, her mind full of what her maths teacher had said. Of course she wasn't going to go ahead with it, she wanted to go to acting school but still it was nice to hear someone sing her praises. Still distracted by her thoughts she bumped into someone and said sorry before she realised who it was. Clive, all six foot two of him, stood in front of her, barring her way. When she saw it was Clive she went to push past him her face expressing her disgust but he caught hold of her arm and said, "Give us a kiss, bald pussy." He had half a dozen mates with him and they all laughed at his words and the show he was putting on for them. She wasn't intimidated in the least and pulled her arm away from Clive and went to slap his face as hard as she could but he again caught her arm and pulled her towards him.

"You disgust me," she shouted as she tried to pull herself away, when suddenly his mouth was covering hers, his tongue was reaching down her throat making her gag but she couldn't get away no matter how hard she squirmed to get away. She felt the hands of his friends exploring her body in its most intimate places and she could do nothing about it, then suddenly she was free. She closed her eyes and screamed for help and when she opened them neither Clive nor his friends were anywhere to be seen. Two girls walking on the opposite pavement were looking at her curiously and asked what the matter was and if she was all right.

"Those boys, they kept touching me, I couldn't get away."

"Boys, what boys!"

"They were in a gang, they kept touching me, you must have seen them," she wailed.

The girls looked at each other and made the crazy sign to each other and walked away ignoring her pleas for them to help her. She was distressed and couldn't understand why nobody was coming to help her. Those girls across the road had ignored her when she needed help and now there was nobody to turn to. She spun around on the spot looking wildly for anyone to help, then finally made her way home and went into the kitchen to find her mother at the sink. She put her arms around her mother's waist and laid her head against her back and sobbed out her story. Halfway through her mother managed to sit her down and told her to start again, listening carefully and asking a few questions now and again, then went out in the hall to telephone Clive's mother. After what seemed like ages her mother returned to the kitchen and made her a cup of tea, then held her hands and said, "Clive wasn't in school today, he's at home sick. His mother has just gone up to check on him and he is fast asleep in bed."

"But I saw him, it was him. I wasn't mistaken, he put his tongue down my throat and his friends kept touching me."

Her mother continued to hold her hands, her thumbs gently stroking the back of her hands and looked into her daughter's face. "Sweetheart, we have had a lot of trauma in the family recently, what with Grandma and Grandpa dying. I really think you should take a day or two off of school and relax. I'll make an appointment to see the doctor tomorrow."

She pulled her hands away from her mother's grasp, incredulous. "You don't believe me, do you? You think I'm lying, that I'm making it all up."

Her mother tried again. "Darling, just sit down a minute and listen..." but was interrupted by her daughter who was raging at her, swinging at her face with her open hands as she tried to make her mother see sense. She hadn't heard her dad come in but now he had gripped hold of her and had pulled her off his wife, whose cheeks were starkly red where she had been slapped repeatedly. Her father held her tightly whilst she raged against him unable to damn her anger until at last she was spent and obediently sat on the kitchen chair and hung her head as she listened to her mother recount the story she had been told. She looked up and saw her dad embrace his wife and kiss her gently and felt a wave of jealousy and confusion; she was the one who had been hurt, been violated and yet her mother was getting all the attention. She wished with all her heart that she had hit her harder whilst she had had the chance, the bitch was taking her dad away from her. Her mother left the kitchen and went out into the hallway leaving the door open so that she could be heard making an appointment for her daughter with the doctor. Whilst her mother was out of the room she put on an Oscar winning performance for her father who held her in his arms and rocked her gently when she had finished speaking. She went upstairs to bed thinking she would toss and turn all night but was very quickly sound asleep. Her parents remained in the kitchen and discussed how she was and how to help her through it and decided they would talk about it further after the visit to see the doctor. The bottom line was that they did not believe her story and thought that the spate of recent deaths in the family had taken their toll. They wanted to believe her but the evidence was piled against her. Clive was home in bed fast asleep when she said he had waylaid her and there was no disputing that.

She had sat quietly listening to her mother speak to the doctor and was prescribed some medication and rest with a further appointment in a fortnight. She made no protest; she had worn herself out going over and over what had happened. She thought of all the times she had lied before and been believed. Now here she was telling the truth and everyone thought she was lying!

When she returned to school all she heard about was the school swimming gala and how well the teams had done. She couldn't believe it; she hadn't even been missed. She buckled down to her lessons and kept herself to herself for the first few days, until she got back into the rhythm of the school.

She was the only one in the pool at this particular time, churning out length after length of butterfly and freestyle stokes. Halfway down the final length she hit the wall and struggled to reach the side. It had never happened to her before but she knew she had pushed herself too hard. She hung onto the side for what seemed an age, then gradually moved hand over fist down the side to the shallow end thankful when she could finally touch the bottom. She mustered up enough strength to climb out of the water and trudged her way back to the changing area and sat down on the cold floor by the lockers, gripping around her knees whilst her head rested on them. She gradually became aware of a disturbance, odd noises that she couldn't recognise and looked up but could see nothing. She listened carefully for a while and had all but been ready to get up and go to the shower cubicle when she heard the noises again. She eased herself upright and carefully peered into the ladies' dressing area at first not understanding what she was seeing. She pulled back quickly her eyes wide with comprehension then, despite herself, she returned for another look. Clive, his shorts around his ankles was busily servicing someone; the noises she had heard were the grunts made during sexual intercourse. She turned away again but just as quickly turned back to watch finding she was aroused by what she was seeing. She had never actually seen anyone having sex before and she wanted to learn as much as she could. Her eyes had adjusted to the light and now she could see everything along with hearing everything. Clive was taking whoever it was from behind whilst fondling her breasts and kissing the back of her neck and laughing and joking with her. She was astonished, was this how everyone did it now. She cast her mind back to when Clive had attempted to have sex with her. He had lain on top of her when he had tried to put his willy in her. She felt warm between her legs and she began to fondle herself until she was working her fingers in an out of herself in time to Clive's thrusts. She didn't know it yet but she had been seen. Clive had caught a movement in the mirror to the side of him and had quickly identified her although he gave no indication that he had. He upped his game, his buttocks working overtime clenching and relaxing as he drove his penis into the moist welcoming vagina in front of him, never taking his eyes away from where he had seen the movement. The girl groaned beneath him pleading with him not to stop, but she needn't have worried, he had no intention of stopping even if he had wanted to. He was going to discharge his load into her whatever they had agreed.

She felt strange as she experienced new sensations in her groin. She suddenly looked up and was shocked to see Clive was looking at her; he knew she was there. She quickly pulled back into the shadows to be out of sight but was still able to hear the couple reach their respective climaxes before everything went deathly quiet.

She stayed frozen, unable to move, scared at being discovered, then laughed at herself for being so silly. She peered around the corner again but the dressing room was empty. She showered and dressed and went to the area she had seen them having intercourse and found a used condom on the floor where they had been. She recoiled in disgust, then had second thoughts and used a plastic cup to scoop it up into and put it in her locker thinking that one day it might just come in handy. She then went to see the headteacher and recounted what she had just seen. The deputy head was called in and she was made to recount everything that had happened, then tried to answer the questions they seemed to bombard her with. Could she identify the boy?

Yes. How could she identify him when she had only seen him from behind? She had caught his reflection in the mirror in the changing room. Who was the girl? She didn't know. How was she able to identify the boy from behind and not the girl? The questions went on and on. Why were they questioning her when they should be doing their jobs and questioning the guilty party? Suddenly her parents were there and explaining to the headteacher about her being on medication due to losses in the family. They had already informed the school of her fragile state of mind but now they had to decide on a course of action.

She lay resting in the school nurse's room whilst her parents were informed of what she was claiming. The boy in question, Clive, was out playing football at the time he was supposed to have been engaging in sexual activities in the girls' changing room. Both his teacher and fellow pupils had vouched for him. There was concern on the school's part that she was waging a vendetta against Clive and whilst they would continue with their investigations and not make judgements they had an equal duty to both pupils and the school.

Chapter 9
Ward 3

She awoke to find herself in a strange place. The room was cold and the bedding looked like those she had seen when she had visited Grandpa in hospital. She slipped out of bed onto the cold lino floor and went out of the room into a long corridor in which various young people were wandering up and down, many chatting away to themselves. Nobody took the slightest notice of her as she stood and screamed out her frustrations and stamped her feet and demanded to be taken home right this minute.

She lost account of the day and time as she angrily repeated her demands and attacked the staff with so much ferocity that on occasion she had to be restrained.

On this particular day she had groggily awoken and had made it down to the playroom in which a television was displaying children's videos and various staff were interacting with the resident children.

She sat down at an empty table glaring around herself but found nobody was paying her the slightest bit of attention.

"Don't you want to get out of here?" A nearby voice startled her and she looked around to see a young boy on a walking frame.

"Err, what, what did you say?"

The young boy manoeuvred himself onto a chair opposite her and said, "I said don't you want to get out of here?"

"Fuck off," she retorted.

The young boy smiled but didn't move, just sat staring at her.

"What the fuck you looking at?" she snarled at him to scare him off, conversation with a looney was all she needed. The boy shrugged and eased himself up off the chair and moved away, his frame clunking on the floor. She watched him go, then wished she had been nicer after all he was the first young inmate she had spoken to. For the first time she had her meal in the dining hall and to her surprise ate all of it and wanted more. It wasn't surprising that she was hungry as most of her previous meals had been worn by the staff or thrown against her bedroom wall.

She sat and watched a video and dozed off in front of it to be woken by staff at teatime then, after she had taken her plate to the washing area, she walked tiredly back to her room feeling like she had done a real day's work. As she passed the young inmate who had spoken to her earlier in the day she turned and smiled at him, and was rewarded with a cheeky grin which, for some reason, made her feel a whole lot better.

The following day she awoke in time to go down to the hall for breakfast and sat at the table at which the young boy was sitting. "Hello."

"Hello, yourself," he said as he ate his breakfast.

"Why are you in here?" she asked him directly.

"I'm a looney," he answered and burst out laughing.

"No really," she persisted, "why are you in here? You don't sound like a looney."

"Well I am and if you are in here you must be one too," he observed bluntly.

"How dare you, I'm not a looney, how dare you," she shouted at him, then noticed staff looking in her direction so toned her voice down and said, "I'm not so there."

"My, you are prickly, is that why you are in here?" he asked as he got up from the table.

"Don't go, please don't go. Look, I'm sorry I shouted OK?"

The boy moved away from her despite her plea for him to stay and suddenly, for no reason that was obvious to her she burst into floods of tears. A member of staff came over to her and she found herself opening up and saying how much she wanted to see her parents, how much she missed them. She was surprised at herself telling the truth. She really did miss her parents, a strange feeling to her as she thought her parents were there simply to be at her beck and call. This was the first time that she had thought of them since she had arrived and now she had she realised she really did miss them and wondered if they missed her.

A few days later her parents came to visit her and she realised how much of an effort it was for them to come to see her in Ward 3. Not much was said during the visit but a lot of the time she was held tight and hugged whilst her tears were kissed away and her forehead gently stroked. When the time came for them to leave, she broke down and held on to them begging them to take her home and not leave her in this dreadful space. Staff had to intervene and her parents left with the sight of their daughter raging and screaming.

She spent the next couple of days in her room before venturing out again into the playroom. She sat at a table with a half-finished puzzle on it and despite herself she started to complete it.

"How you doing?"

She looked up to see the young boy on his frame looking across the table at her.

She gave him a half grin and he took it as an invitation to sit across from her at the table.

She looked up at him. "How long you been here?"

"Most of my life really," he responded.

"No, what really!"

"Yes, my mum dumps me in here when she can't cope with me," he said looking straight-faced at her, "treats it like a kindergarten."

"How awful." She genuinely felt sorry for him.

"Nah, not really, she can't cope with me and feels guilty all the time."

She didn't know how to reply to this so said nothing and carried on with the puzzle. After a moment's silence the boy said, "You're going the wrong way about it you know."

She stopped doing the puzzle and looked up. "Wrong way about what?"

"Getting out of here."

"So tell me then, how do I get out of here? I mean they can't keep me in here forever, can they, can they?"

"You have to play the game."

"Game! What game?"

The young boy said, "Look, the only way that you will be able to get out of here sooner rather than later is to play the game, go along with them, be nice to the staff and mix, be friendly, take your meds, stop losing the plot."

"If you know so much how come you're still in here then," she retorted, smarting at his comment with regard to losing the plot.

"I like it here. It's like my second home. Actually it's better than my home," he said with a sad look on his face, "and anyway I've become institutionalised."

"What's that, institutionalised? Never heard of it."

"It sort of means that I have become so used to being here over the years that I now depend on coming here."

"I'm so sorry."

"Don't be," he laughed, "as I said I like it here."

She spent the evening pondering over what the young boy had said and decided to follow his suggestions and put it into action the following day, finding it difficult at first but easier as time progressed. She had further visits from her parents with no incidents and was eventually allowed out on a day visit with them. On her return to Ward 3 she looked for her young friend but couldn't find him so thought that he had gone home.

The day before she was due to go home for good she saw him again in the corridor and followed him into the playroom, eager to tell him she was going home for good. He was heavily bandaged on both of his forearms but seemed cheerful enough to her.

"What happened, what have they done to you?" she asked him.

"Oh this," he said holding his bandaged arms aloft "they didn't do anything, I did it myself."

She was shocked. "What do you mean did it yourself?"

"What I said, I did it all by myself," he said as he waved his forearms in the air and grinned cheerfully in her direction.

"Why would you want to do that? I don't understand."

"I don't understand either, it's just that sometimes I feel that I have to do it so I do it. No big deal."

She told him she was going home tomorrow and thanked him for his help but he just shrugged, "I reckon I'm going to die in here, still never mind ay we've all got to die sometime," then proceeded to move off down the corridor without looking back at her.

Chapter 10
Wedding Bells

"Well you can either come with us or we will ask Aunty Jean to come over. Make your mind up."

She didn't like being given ultimations and this was definitely one. She tried another tack. "I'll be on my period."

Her mother did an about turn and strode back into the kitchen calling, "That's it then, I'll phone Aunty Jean."

"No, Mum, no, don't phone her. I'll come to the wedding if it makes you happy."

"This has nothing to do with making me happy, young lady. Now you've said that you are coming to the wedding you'll need to get up early tomorrow as we've got shopping to do."

Shit, she thought to herself. She didn't want to go to the wedding or have Aunty Jean come round. Bloody parents always making their kids do things that they didn't want to. She stamped out her frustration on the stairs causing her mother to call up after her, "That's enough of that, young lady, or I'll tell your father."

Tell her father, so what, he'll never do anything she thought, then thought what would she do if he did smack her. She decided she would run away and then her parents would be sorry that they weren't kinder to her. She looked in the mirror and saw she had her pouting face on and thought that she really needed to stop being childish; she needed to act like a young woman after all she was fourteen.

She thought back to the young boy she had meet on Ward 3 and wondered how he was getting on, wondered if he was still alive. She had really liked him and since her return home three weeks previously, had missed him. She had asked her parents if she could visit him but they told her that they didn't think it would be a good idea for her to go back there so she took to writing to him and poured out her heart in a way that she had never been able to do before, though she never let on to her parents that she was still keeping in contact.

Shopping, why did she hate it so much. True she had finally managed to persuade her mum to buy her a really smart trouser suit but once it was purchased she had gone off the boil and simply followed her mum from shop to shop with a sour look on her face not that she had anything else to do with her time. She had told her mother she looked nice in loads of outfits trying her best to sound sincere so as to hurry her mum up so she could get home but it didn't do any good.

They stopped for a coffee and she caught sight of her miserable expression in the mirror behind the bar and thought how ugly she looked; at this rate she would never get a boyfriend. That thing with Clive had put her off boys altogether although she still had a soft spot for that boy, Tom, in Ward 3. She sighed feeling the world on her shoulders, but was brought abruptly out of her melancholy mood by a woman nearby who was coughing and spluttering as she held her hands to her throat, her eyes wide and desperate. Her mother got up and slapped the woman really hard on her back a few times and helped her compose herself in front of all the prying eyes, giving her tissues to clean herself up. The bar staff had responded slowly but at last came over to check the customer was all right then wiped the table to clean up the spillage that had occurred.

As her mum came back to collect her bag, hopefully not noticing the twenty pound note that she had taken from it, she said, "You saved that woman's life, Mum." Her mother simply looked at her, then shrugged and said for her to hurry up as they still had shopping to do. As she trailed after her mother she enacted the scene that had played out before her, reliving the panic in the woman's face as she struggled to breathe, finding it exciting. She must remember every detail for when she needed to play that part when she became an actress. Shame the woman hadn't died though, she could have actually witnessed that moment between life and death that so alluded her. True she had been there when her grandma had died but she had held a cushion over her face so she couldn't see the actual moment the silly old bag had popped her clogs. She glared at her mother's back, angry at her for taking away from her the one thing she wanted but if her mother felt her daughter's angry glare she didn't respond to it.

Her mother finally chose a colourful dress with a bolero jacket and at long last they could go home. She ran up to her room with her purchase and tried it on turning this way and that to see all angles. Perfect, if she said it herself it was just perfect. She carefully hung it up in her wardrobe, then got out her laptop and made some notes, then lay back on her bed and took the twenty pound note out of her back pocket and held it up to the light turning it over and over as she wondered what she was going to spend it on.

The wedding took place in a small hall in the town hall, then everybody travelled to the reception which was held at a fancy hotel. There were a lot of people present, more than had been at the actual ceremony and she wandered around taking every little detail in, thinking that perhaps when she died, she would have booked a place like this so that her mourners could cry and talk about her in luxurious surroundings. She couldn't wait to get home and start writing.

She hadn't really looked at the man her aunt had married but she suddenly caught sight of him amongst all the guests and stared at him. Although he wasn't as handsome in her eyes as her uncle had been there was something about him that she liked, perhaps it was the way his eyes crinkled as he smiled. She realised she was spending too much time staring so moved on to the young man standing behind him chatting to the bridesmaids, his son James, she had been told when she had asked her mother who he was. Her mother had given her a knowing look and told her to behave herself and she had simply said, "Mother," in a shocked tone and moved away. She caught Clive staring at her on a couple of occasions but totally blanked him and moved off in a different direction.

Later that evening she had been on the dance floor for ages when she caught the son watching her, but pretended she hadn't, though she put all she had into her dance movements to see if she could hook him. Out of the line of reach of her parents she drank glass after glass of chilled white wine and became more and more unsteady. She moved out of the dance hall and looked into some empty rooms in the hallway on her way to the loo when an arm grabbed her around her waist and hooked her into one of the empty rooms. She struggled at first not knowing who it was, then, when she saw who it was, just relaxed in his arms as he kissed her. She kissed him back then in no time at all they were writhing and grunting on the floor in a powerful coupling. He exploded into her as she too climaxed, her vagina gripping and releasing him and heightening his moments of pleasure. They lay panting on the floor then he said, "I've been wanting to do that all evening." She laughed, feeling wonderful and worldly and totally out of it. They coupled again this time not in such a frenzy and she marvelled at the beauty of the act thinking perhaps this was the way she should die, this would be her Blaze of Glory. They rearranged themselves, then separately left the room and continued with the evening as if nothing had happened between them. Her mother noticed how unsteady her daughter's movements had become and made her sit nearby so that she could keep an eye on her, not realising that it was way too late for that protection.

Later that evening she touched herself between her legs wondering if it had all been a dream, wonderful yes but still a dream. She felt different: now she felt she knew what it was like to be a woman. She no longer dreaded the endless summer holidays stretching in front of her, she could find plenty to keep her busy.

As she came quietly down the stairs, she listened to her dad talking about the newlyweds and discussing that it was barely two years since his brother had died and that although he quite liked the man, he still thought it was too early for his brother's wife to remarry. Her mother laughed and called him a stick in the mud, then they changed the subject as she came into the kitchen keeping her face composed so that they would not know that she had overheard their conversation.

Chapter 11
Revenge is Sweet

The summer holidays seemed to go on for ever and she was bored. She wondered what James was doing and if she should call him. After all it had been three days since she had last seen him but decided she should wait a bit longer as she didn't want to appear to be too eager.

She decided she would go to the local library and her mother asked her to collect some fish and chips for tea on the way home as well as pick up some photos from the chemist. Her first reaction was to protest but she managed to hold her tongue and meekly took the money and receipt her mother held out.

She spent far longer in the library than she intended having spent the time going through the newspapers looking up how they reported deaths and reading the 'In remembrance' columns. She found quite a nice write-up about her grandma in one of the papers and discovered she had worked in a munitions factory during the war.

The queue in the fish and chip shop was long and she was beginning to get fed up with waiting when she caught sight of James across the road walking hand in hand with a girl that she knew used to be in Clive's class. She was tempted to go over the road and face them but she kept her head down and resisted the impulse. He was hers; she had slept with him and now he was hers. How dare he walk out with another girl, just wait till she saw him next she would give him what for and might even refuse to have sex with him, now that would teach him. She watched the couple walking and talking until they were out of sight and wished she had gone over and confronted them when she had the opportunity, Now, if she ran after them, she would look like a silly besotted little girl. She bought the fish and chips, then went home but her mind was in a turmoil and she didn't manage to eat her portion despite it being one of her favourite meals and, to top it all, she had forgotten to go into the chemist to pick up the stupid photos, nor could she find the receipt her mother had given her to get them.

It was difficult to know how she arrived at the conclusion that it was all Clive's fault. After all she hadn't spoken to him since the incident in the street. The fact that the girl she had seen James with had been in Clive's class confirmed to her that he was plotting against her and had persuaded the girl to go out with James just to get back at her. The more she ran it through her mind the more credible it became, until she was convinced she was right.

That night she lay awake for hours tossing and turning as she thought about how to get revenge but in the early hours of the morning she suddenly sat up in shock. Photos, photos as she suddenly remembered what Clive had been hinting at. She had all but forgotten it had been so long ago but now she remembered everything in vivid detail as if it had been only yesterday, of Clive taking photos of her as she lay on the bed with her legs spread. Surely he couldn't still have the photos, it was so long ago that he took them but she knew that he still did have them, that he was reminding her that he still had them when he had whispered 'photos bitch' in her ear. As if the sudden influx of memory wasn't enough, she topped it off with the cherry on the cake, with what Clive had said to her when he and his mates had molested her when she was coming home late from school. He had called her 'bald pussy' and although at the time she hadn't given it much attention he was, even then, hinting at the photos he had taken. Bald Pussy was his nickname for her back then and she had thought of it as a term of endearment but not, as she later found out, a description of her fanny. Why boys called that bit down there a pussy she would never know! She had thought that all the boys had liked her and wanted to go out with her but now she could see that Clive had shown them the photos of her and that they weren't admiring her, they were laughing at her! He was going to pay for her embarrassment big time.

In the morning she helped her mother with a few chores around the house before catching the train into town and wandering through second-hand shops and the local lively market. By one of the stalls a lone girl was playing a sad song on a violin and, as she stood and watched, her tears rolled down her cheeks. On her way home she called into the library and booked on one of the computers available and did a search on under age sex. There was a lot of information and she spent a long time absorbing it but, by the time she had finished she had the bare bones of revenge laid out in her mind.

On reaching home she started to put her plan into action and only managed to eat a few mouthfuls of her dinner (luckily she had stuffed up whilst she had been out), and hung her head as she moped around the house and nibbled her nails. Her parents took notice but simply put her behaviour down to being a teenager.

During this time she had been unable to help herself and had gone around to James's house. She had steeled herself up to let rip at him but when he opened the door, she couldn't do it. She just stood there like a little dumb girl. When he saw who it was James opened the door wider and invited her in, and despite wanting to flee she meekly followed him indoors. She wanted to tell him that she loved him, that she wanted his baby, that she knew she was a bit young for him but if he waited for her, she would be everything that he could ever want. James offered her a cup of tea and she meekly accepted, then sat twiddling her thumbs whilst she waited for it. It was all Clive's fault, he had got her into this mess she thought furiously as she gazed longingly into James's handsome face.

She finally got up to leave and suddenly James was very close, too close for her to think clearly. "What did you come round for" he asked then leant and whispered in her ear, "More of the same?" She flushed, guilty at her reason for going round to be discovered so easily, but was a willing participant as James bent her face down over the kitchen table, pulled down her underwear and entered her from behind almost in one swift movement as if he had done it many times before. All she could think of was that this was how she had seen Clive doing it though James didn't fondle her breasts or whisper in her ear like she had seen Clive do. She tried hard to be in the moment and concentrate on what James was doing but the picture of Clive in the girls' locker room got in her way and she hated him all over again. James had a big smile on his face though, although she couldn't see it and perhaps it was lucky for her that she didn't as it wasn't a particularly nice smile. He gazed down at her back and thought that she had great timing in coming around as he had been about to give himself a hand job and this was a better option, not much better but beggars can't be choosers, he thought. He pulled back from her when he had finished and looked dispassionately at the bare buttocks on display as he tucked his tired penis back into his shorts.

She had confirmation now that he loved her and turned and hugged him telling him she was his forever. He unclasped her hands from around his waist and told her that she should get dressed as his mother was due home any minute and he didn't want her to be embarrassed. She hurriedly dressed, then fiercely kissed him and left blowing him kisses. James hurriedly shut the door and thought, now where was I before I was so rudely interrupted... oh yes, and went down the garden to the shed in which he kept his train sets.

On her way home she wondered why she hadn't fronted him about the girl she had seen him with but decided that now it didn't matter. The girl was of no consequence, James had shown her that he loved her. She almost felt sorry for the other girl, almost but not quite.

On her way home she suddenly remembered the used condom she had picked up from the girls' changing room at school after Clive had bonked that girl and wondered how best she could use it. She went over the plan in her mind again and again until she reached what she considered to be a fool proof solution. Clive was going to get his big time, a beating from his dad would be the least of his problems.

She continued to be morose at home then, when her mother had told her to pull herself together and stop being so miserable, she had burst into floods of tears that momentarily took her parents by surprise, before they were all over her trying to comfort her.

"Whatever's wrong?" her mother asked.

She kept her head down and prepared herself for the performance of her life. "I, I can't tell you, you'll hate me and you'll send me away," she sobbed.

"Darling, look, come over here and sit down," said her dad as he patted a space beside him on the sofa. She shook her head and grizzled some more but eventually allowed herself to be persuaded to sit beside her dad who said, "Look, sweetheart, if you don't tell us we can't help you, we need to know, come on, darling."

"Clive took some photos," she managed, "rude ones of down there," as she pointed down between her legs. "He said I should let him take them to prove to him how much I loved him. He said all the boys had photos of their girlfriends; it wasn't wrong if it proved how much they loved their boyfriends."

There was a shocked silence then her dad cleared his throat. "Clive, you mean cousin Clive?"

"Yes, Daddy." She raised a tearstained face up towards him. "He said he would wait for me to get older and then he would marry me and we would have loads of children. I love him." And with that she dissolved into gulping sobs. "Don't hate me, Daddy, don't send me away."

"Did you," embarrassed cough, "did you ever have sex with him?" her mother asked her in shocked tones.

"No, Mummy, we split up because I wouldn't do it and he said that he didn't want to know me until I agreed to go all the way with him." About here she threw in some half-truths so that her parents would have no doubt that she was telling the truth. "That time that Daddy threw him out was the first time he tried to. I had just got out of the bath and had no clothes on when he barged into my room. I was frightened when he just picked me up and put me on the bed, then climbed on top of me. I told him to leave me alone but he wouldn't listen. I screamed and Daddy came in and hit him." She wiped her nose on her dressing gown and said, "You hate me now, don't you?"

Her father held her close against him and signalled his wife to get a cup of tea as he gently rocked his daughter, totally shocked at what she had been saying. His wife came into the room with a tray of drinks and said, "I'm going to phone Ricky (her brother) right now."

She suddenly sat up in alarm. "No, Mummy, no Mummy, please don't, he'll simply delete the photos off his phone and you will think I am lying again and send me to Ward 3 like you did before. Everything I said then was true but you didn't believe me." She looked at the shocked faces of her parents, then drove the nail home. "He left a used condom on the floor and I picked it up and put it in my locker and then, with all the questioning that took place I forgot I had it. It's proof I was telling the truth."

She had calmed down quite considerably now and was able to repeat everything she had said, only now and then sniffing or wiping away an imaginary tear.

Her father patted her hand, then told her to go upstairs and lay down whilst he talked things over with her mother. As she went sadly upstairs, a totally crestfallen and defeated figure she recreated in her mind how she had cried her way through her story and then thought how she would relay it to the police, a new audience, she couldn't wait! Her parents were bound to want to go to the police after all she and Clive were both under age and she knew that what she had to tell them would be taken pretty seriously. She thought how much she liked the uniforms the police wore and thought that perhaps one day she would join the police.

The following day she sloped bleary-eyed downstairs to have her breakfast and to find out what action her parents had decided to take and bumped into Aunty Jean and thought, what the hell is that old bat doing here, but managed to keep her face straight and give a quiet tearful welcome thinking fast on her feet although she was confused. Aunty Jean only came around when her parents wanted a baby-sitter but she wouldn't need one if she was going with her parents to the police station. What was going on! She stared into Aunty Jean's face when she was looking elsewhere, wondering how much she had been told and it was obvious to her that she had been told something, but what? Aunty Jean gave her a quick cuddle, then got breakfast ready for her and she let her do it. After all she was the injured party and needed to be handled with kid gloves so that she didn't breakdown, didn't she? She used the downstairs loo, then opened the downstairs closet and carefully wiped her sesame seed snack over the collar and lapels of Aunty Jean's coat then popped the biscuit in her mouth and went to finish her breakfast.

As she was finishing her parents came into the kitchen and looked out of the window into the garden where Aunty Jean was sitting smoking a cigarette, before giving their daughter a peck on the cheek and leaving the house. It was all completely different to what she had envisaged and she was thrown out of kilter with her mind working overtime to find out what was happening. There obviously had been a change of plan but she, the one whom all the fuss was about, wasn't informed. It wasn't fair, it just wasn't fair, how could she plan her sob story if her parents kept changing the script without her knowledge. At that particular moment she felt pure hatred towards her parents. How dare they treat her like a child, how dare they keep her in the dark. Perhaps they didn't believe her. Perhaps they were trying to catch her out, yes, that must be it. They thought that she was lying and that Clive was telling the truth and that they were, at this very moment, arranging for her to go back to Ward 3.

Aunty Jean didn't like baby-sitting and every time she agreed to do it, she wondered why she hadn't just refused. She only needed to face up to them once and then they would never ask her again, she reasoned, as she sat outside in the garden smoking her fifth cigarette of the day, five already and it was only mid-morning. She ran over again in her mind how she had been coerced again and sighed knowing that however much she rallied against herself she would always be easily persuaded to do what she didn't want to do. She was just that sort of person. Still, she thought, the jumped-up little brat would soon be able to be old enough to be left on her own then she wouldn't have to put up with her any more. The time couldn't come soon enough for her, she couldn't wait. The morning sun beat down on her face and pretty soon she dozed off, her half-smoked cigarette falling from her relaxed hand onto the concrete pathway and burning itself out.

She watched her aunt dozing in the garden from the kitchen, then examined the contents of the handbag her aunt had left on the kitchen table, took a £10 note from her purse and, after second thoughts, also took some small change and the left hand of her gloves and cut the fingers off before shoving the pieces deep in the bin. She didn't know why she did it, she had just acted on the spur of the moment and now it was done. Further rummaging in the side pockets caused her fingers to connect with an EpiPen and, without forethought she dropped it on the floor and stamped on it a few times, then kicked what pieces she could see under the freezer, then finished her breakfast, washed up and went upstairs to shower.

She had been getting a bit fed up with having to keep repeating her story but perhaps that was just how grown-ups were, she thought, children had to repeat themselves over and over again to them before they were believed, or not. Her parents had been distraught, she believed, and only too willing to believe every lie she told. She had also innocently recounted how she had been molested on her way home from school that time knowing that the point would strike home, and that her mummy and daddy hadn't believed her nor had the school, they had believed Clive instead of her, but that was all right as she still loved Clive and wanted to marry him. She told her parents that Clive had threatened to download the photos he had taken of her onto a porn website (whatever that was) and she would be shamed forever.

Meanwhile her parents called around to Clive's home and, after a few attempts, told his parents every sordid detail, leaving nothing out. When they had finished speaking there was a shocked silence before everyone took a deep breath and then started throwing questions at each other. Clive had, luckily for him as it turned out, spent the night at a friend's house and knew nothing of the hornet's nest he would be returning to.

After a few hours the parents decided that they would keep the police out of it and deal with the problem themselves, keep it in the family so to speak. They decided that this was the best course of action as they did not want two young lives ruined. Clive's mother wept uncontrollably and clung on to her sister-in-law for comfort, begging forgiveness for the way he had acted and thanking them for the plan they had concocted between them. It would break her heart to move, she confessed but move they would and far far away to where nobody knew them and hopefully where they could start a new life. Clive's dad said he would have no trouble finding work, he was a jack of all trades and not in the least bit worried about doing hard graft. They shook hands politely at the front door knowing this would be the last time they would see each other for a long time, if ever, then went their separate ways.

At long last her parents returned home and her mother gave Aunty Jean a big thank you hug, then kissed her on each cheek before Aunty Jean left the house.

She couldn't believe it, after all that had happened she just couldn't believe what her parents were trying to explain to her. Aunty Jean had long since left and the family had the house to themselves and her parents were presented with a side to their daughter they had never previously known existed. She was not sulky or having a tantrum, she was cold and calculating and, for a moment, actually scared her parents as the venom poured out of her. Who the hell did they think they were, running her life for her and making decisions about her without including her? She had very nearly (not) been raped and humiliated and now she was being told that everything was going to be swept under the carpet as if it had never happened. That Clive was going to get away scot free and that only she would have to bear the burden and suffer the rest of her life. She stormed up to her room and slammed the door and screamed out her frustration and kicked and punched the closed door. James wouldn't let him get away with it, she thought, James would be her knight in shining armour who would sweep her up in his arms then charge to her defence. She hurriedly showered then quickly left the house, for once not bothering to lurk outside in the hallway to overhear what was being said by her parents. James would know what to do she was sure of it.

Confronted by his dad the minute he entered the house, Clive freely handed over his mobile phone having completely forgotten to wipe the photographs he no longer accessed from it but not in the least bit worried. True he had frequently accessed them years ago when he had first taken them, but when his penis no longer stood to attention when he looked at them, he simply went on to pastures new and they lay dormant on his phone. True he had briefly rediscovered them just before a funeral reception and was able to whisper a threat in her ear but in reality he meant to wipe them and he really should have done that. After all it would have saved him so much pain. Clive had been taken completely by surprise by the suddenness of what was happening and couldn't think straight beyond thinking that the bitch had stitched him up again. He didn't know why he had whispered 'photos bitch' into her ear at the reception as he had no intention of doing anything with them, he had just wanted to hurt her. After all she had caused him to get a good hiding and he owed her one big time. His father knew enough about mobile phones to access the 'bald pussy' file in which the photos were stored, then passed them on to his wife to see whilst he propelled his son into the back room and before too long had passed, his belt was connecting with his son's bare buttocks and now his son had two good reasons to owe her big time.

Chapter 12
Aunty Jean

Jean was so happy to get out of the house, she almost skipped down the road to the bus stop. She couldn't wait to get home and shut herself away from the noise and confusion of daily life where the only one who made demands on her was herself, and she liked it that way. She lived a quiet simple life and was, for most of the time, happy except when she was asked to do things, like baby-sitting, that she felt uncomfortable with.

There were a few people waiting at the bus stop so she stood aside from them and watched the passing traffic until her bus came, then she let anyone who wanted to get on the bus go in front of her before she swiped her bus pass and found an empty seat and settled down for the ride, thinking she quite liked riding on buses when there were not too many people on them.

It was perhaps fifteen minutes or so later when she started to feel uncomfortable but didn't immediately figure out why as there was no obvious reason for her to be so. Nobody was sitting next to her and nobody was staring at her so what was wrong? Why did she feel so panicky? She became sick and dizzy and started wheezing as she struggled to breathe. She recognised that she was having an allergic attack of some sort and searched her bag looking for her EpiPen, becoming increasingly anxious as she couldn't seem to find it. It's in here, I know I put it in here she kept saying to herself as she continued the futile search of her bag.

Other people around her on the bus noticed her distress and a concerned lady leaned over her asking, "You all right, dear?" but Jean could only manage "EpiPen" over and over again. The world was spinning and she tried to reach for the hand rail to steady herself. She couldn't breathe, oh somebody, somebody help me, she thought, as she passed out onto the floor of the bus.

Somebody helped by informing the driver and he pulled over at the first opportunity whilst one of the passengers rang for an ambulance and another checked through her bag for the EpiPen that had been asked for. She was not able to find it but did find a purse which she pocketed.

Aunty Jean had been put in the recovery position by someone else who had done first aid a long time ago and who had struggled to remember the sequence to go through though Aunty Jean was passed caring, slipping as she was in and out of consciousness.

She watched her mother take the call that Aunty Jean had had an bad allergic reaction to something and had died on the bus and was curious at her reactions, first of all putting a hand to her mouth and mouthing 'no' before sinking down onto one of the kitchen chairs and crying.

People were funny, she thought. She had heard her mother loads of times slagging Aunty Jean off for smoking or for never going out but now she was weeping for her and thought how two-faced she was. For her part she had no reason to feel sad in the least. At last she was free of the silly bitch. She wouldn't have to put up with the silly cow any more although she would have to attend her funeral. She could pull herself up to do that, make her parents believe she was as shocked as they were, then she could get on with her life without stupid people getting in the way.

As she sat in the cool church on a hot summer's day she looked around the sparse congregation on the pews, not many friends then but she wasn't surprised. After all she didn't like her and expected that not many other people did also. This would be nothing like her funeral she thought, with crowds of people having to wait outside as the church was packed with her adoring fans. Pity in a way that she would be dead so that she wouldn't see them, although part of her laughed as she imagined the golden cloth that would be covering her, slipping gracefully off as she suddenly sat up and yawned. She giggled then quickly turned it into a cough and covered her face with her cupped hands as if she was distressed, whilst her father put a comforting arm around her shoulder.

She was pleased it was to be a cremation and wondered if her parents had asked to receive her ashes so that they could scatter them for, as far as she knew, Aunty Jean had no relatives whatsoever. She wasn't even a real aunty; she had just called her that when she was a toddler and somehow the name had stuck. In reality Aunty Jean was an old school friend of her mother's, nothing more. How awful, she thought, not to have anyone at all who cared for her. She almost felt sorry for the woman.

The congregation stood to sing one final hymn as the curtains slowly closed around the coffin, then everyone piled outside into the warm sunshine, blinking in the sudden brightness of the day.

Her mother had prepared some food and had invited people back to the house but nobody accepted and they found themselves alone with plates of covered food that nobody fancied eating. She made an effort and sat on the settee and dutifully chewed her way through a plate of sandwiches, wondering when would be the best time to ask if Aunty Jean had made a will.

Chapter 13
Two-timer

She just missed a bus as she rounded the corner and clenched her fists and stamped her feet with frustration. She checked the bus timetable although she knew she had twenty minutes to wait for the next one and briefly thought about walking, before dismissing the idea and leaning against the bus stop. She was so engrossed in the scene playing out in her mind that she almost missed the next bus and had to fumble about for her pass. She had a ten-minute journey so she settled down again to try and pick up where she had left off in her daydream, but this time it eluded her and she hunched down in her seat and stared moodily out of the window. She didn't feel right today and guessed her periods were not too far off and wondered if James would have sex with her if she was on her period. She decided that she didn't really like the idea but that she would go along with it if that was what her boyfriend wanted to do.

Finally it was time to get off of the bus and walk the few short blocks to James's house and her mood lightened as she imagined his welcome and covering her in passionate kisses. She giggled with anticipation looking forward to tell him all the gossip about Clive and knocked on the door. She knocked on the door again and then, a few minutes later again though this time a bit louder. Finally, she got hold of the knocker and really slammed it down against the door and was rewarded with, "All right, all right, I'm coming."

The door opened and she saw the rather tousled form of James framed in it and looking none too pleased. "Yes," he said rather pointedly, "what do you want?"

"James, darling, it's me, your girlfriend, sorry to bang so loud," as she reached forwards with her arms to hug him, completely missing the cues of his irritation at her disturbing him.

He stepped back from her to avoid her arms and she caught sight of movement behind him and saw the girl she had seen him with previously although this time she was scantily clad. It suddenly dawned on her what she had interrupted and her face flushed with anger and her outstretched open hands became fists which she pummelled on James's chest calling him a two-timing bastard before turning and running blindly away, tears streaming down her face. James watched her go with a smirk on his face, then turned towards the scantily clad girl behind him "Now where was I, oh yes, come here, sweetheart," he said, as he cupped one of her breasts whilst his other hand explored between her legs.

"That poor little girl, she's got a crush on you. You could have been kinder to her."

"Of course she's got a crush on me, all the girls have don't you know."

As she opened her legs to allow penetration, she said, "A bit young for you though, didn't know you were the baby-sitter."

"I'll show you baby-sitter" he replied, as he thrust himself into her continuing from where they had been so rudely interrupted.

She didn't know how long she ran for or even where she was as she stopped suddenly, then dropped to the ground and drummed her heels onto the ground as she back fisted her fists into the ground. The wasteland she found herself on was full of rubbish but somehow beautiful.

"You all right, girl?"

She looked up shielding her eyes from the sun to get a better look at the figure speaking to her and saw the outline of a young man standing over her.

"Fuck off," she snapped nastily then immediately wished she hadn't as the figure turned and started moving away.

"Sorry," she called then louder, "I'm sorry."

The figure stopped and came back towards her and sat down nearby saying, "Boyfriend trouble!"

"Two-timing bastard," she shouted. "I hate him, I really hate him."

"That's boys for you, can't trust them an inch," he replied, as he smiled at her and, despite herself, she smiled back. "That's better, you look really pretty when you smile."

She sat up and really looked at him. "I don't feel pretty, I think my period's due."

"Wow, that's too much information."

"Oh, sorry, I didn't mean to blurt that out. I mean I'm sorry to share that with you."

"That's all right, I've got sisters, two of them to be exact, one older and one younger."

She smiled at him and said, "Look I'd best be going."

"Me too. Hey I think I know you, you're that swimming girl from school, Monarch's School, aren't you?"

"Yes, if you must know, why, what class you in?"

They both stood up and dusted themselves down, then walked on chatting quite comfortably.

On reaching home she made herself a drink, then spent a few pleasant hours updating her research before thinking about James and bursting into tears. He had used her, all this time he had used her like a throw away tissue. Yes, it was Clive's fault that he had got to know the girl in the first place but he didn't need to keep seeing her, did he? Nobody forced him to. She wailed loudly, pleased that the house was empty and that she could cry as loudly as she wanted to, and she wanted to so she did.

Later, when she had calmed she thought about the girl she had seen and realised that she wasn't in Clive's class at all as she had previously thought, she was in the year above hers. If the girl was out of the way James would be bound to want her back but this time she wouldn't give in so easily. She had in her mind the image of herself standing serene and aloof while James grovelled at her feet although this time she wouldn't give in, she would make him suffer. It was one of her favourite scenarios and she replayed it tirelessly.

She wondered why her parents had never said anything about Grandma's will. She was sure she had one, after all if she hadn't, all of her possessions would have gone to the state and they hadn't. She'd even seen her mother wearing some of Grandma's old jewellery, not that she wanted it of course, but it might be worth something in the pawnbrokers. She wandered into her parents' bedroom and idly searched through their possessions, occasionally trying on some of the clothes she found and looking at her reflection in their wardrobe mirror. She pocketed some of the jewellery she found thinking that it was hers anyway or it would be when her mother died so she might as well have it now, and then lay in the middle of her parents' double bed, luxuriating in the size of it. She spread out her arms and legs and gazed up at the ceiling thinking how wonderful if she and James could make love on it. She sat up suddenly her mood changing and went back into her room, deciding that she would make out her will now whilst she thought about it even though she had nothing to leave anybody.

The school holidays seemed to go on for ever and now that she hadn't got a boyfriend to spend time with she spent her time swimming and researching and, very occasionally helping her mother make cakes.

Whilst on the web she looked at various wheelchairs, especially the brakes and even went to the mobility shop in town so she could get hands on, easily conning the sales people into letting her examine various products.

Keeping herself thus occupied and, of course, attending Aunty Jean's funeral, the time flew by and in no time at all it was time to go back to school, and the first person she bumped into was the boy she had met on the waste ground near the reservoir. She smiled at him in a friendly way and fluttered her eyelashes just a little thinking that he might be useful to get onside and, for his part, he was quite happy with her advances but not in the least bit fooled by her. He had her pegged as a manipulator and, to give him credit, he wasn't far wrong.

She decided that whilst she was at school she would pretend she was a private eye and follow James's girlfriend to find out where she lived but she soon got fed up with the notion as she found it was easier said than done.

To her delight she got a place in the county swimming team and even had a few columns written about her in the local paper. Her parents had a photograph taken with her and for days afterwards she bathed in the glory and knew that above everything else she wanted fame. She bought loads of newspapers and took cuttings and stuck them in her 'Book Towards Fame' as she called it.

Her parents were adamant they would not support her going to acting school. They had been informed by her maths teacher that she had a brilliant future in mathematics and would easily get a place in university, coupling that with her swimming prowess she would have her pick of universities.

She told her drama teacher that her parents had finally agreed that if she made sufficient progress and was accepted at interview then she would be able to go to acting college. The drama teacher was delighted but said that she had to really knuckle down and work hard and that yes, whilst she had a natural talent there was no way she would get in without further hard work.

She went to bed that night with her ego bolstered, the drama teacher had said she had a natural talent, natural talent, oh yes. She knew it, all this time she knew it and now the drama teacher had confirmed it: she was going to be A STAR!

Chapter 14
Needlework

When she woke the next morning, she decided that today she would have a lay in, she deserved it, but her mother put paid to her plans when she came in and told her to hurry up and get ready for school or she would be late. "I've got a study day," she responded thinking off the top of her head.

"In that case you can come with me to a coffee morning, come on, get up and stop being so lazy."

"Oh, Mum," she moaned, but got up anyway as she knew by the tone of her mother's voice that she would keep on at her until she did get up.

"Who's having a coffee morning then?" she asked and was so surprised by the answer she had to sit down for a minute and think, then, just before she went downstairs, she picked up a packet of fine sewing needles and put them in her cardigan pocket planning to put one or two in James's bed to really give him the needle. She didn't notice the irony of the thought and was not smiling as she thought it.

Later, standing by the bus stop she asked her mother why they hadn't got a car. Everyone else did after all but she got the standard reply that they couldn't afford to buy one.

"How come everyone else can afford it?" she continued to whinge tucking her hair back into her hood for the umpteenth time as the wind howled around them.

Luckily the bus came and she went and sat upstairs away from her mother and frowned out of the window until she caught sight of her reflection and realised that frowning was unbecoming. She composed her expression and stared out of the window at the passing scenery, wondering how she could persuade her parents that they needed to get a car.

The coffee morning was in full swing by the time they arrived at the house and they were soon settled in the back room holding cups of coffee and chatting nineteen to the dozen. She listened in for a while then excused herself and went upstairs on the pretext of going to the toilet then, checking behind herself to see if anyone was about, she went into James's room surprised to find that the door wasn't locked. She slipped quietly into the room as if expecting it to be occupied and stood with her back against the closed door surveying the room, then she suddenly spat on the rug and rubbed it in with her shoe, then looked around the room and began opening the dresser drawers and came across the condoms. She stopped for a minute surprised that there were so many; he obviously aimed to be a busy boy. She didn't know he had them as he hadn't used one when they had had sex in the kitchen that time, he just went straight into her, wham bang thank you, mam. She felt herself getting angry at being used and breathed deeply to calm herself as her mind raced. Why hadn't he used a condom? Why hadn't he taken precautions against her getting pregnant unless of course he wanted to get her pregnant so that he would have to marry her? She held on to the image for a while, hope filling her heart then suddenly shook her head. He didn't want her; he had just used her as a convenience. She had walked in the door at the wrong time for her, young and vulnerable as she was, and the right time for him. In a way, she thought it was her fault, she had offered herself up on a plate and he had taken advantage of the offer. He was still going to pay though, right through the nose! An inspiration came into her mind and she smiled unpleasantly and took out her packet of fine needles from her cardigan pocket and carefully and precisely punctured every packet two or three times, only stopping every now and then to listen in case anyone came up the stairs. She had originally wanted to put the needles in his bed but this was a much better idea. She carefully closed the dresser drawer and did a quick recce before being satisfied that the room looked as she had found it, then carefully opened the door to see if it was all clear and went into the toilet and flushed it before going back downstairs to join the group of chatting women. She even asked one of the women knitting to show her how to knit although she wasn't in the least bit interested, she just thought it would help to pass the time. She glanced over at her mother and found she was watching and smiling at her attempts to mix in with the group.

As she sat there in the background, she overheard quite a lot about James (apparently he worked in the city as a surveyor) and his girlfriend Myleen.

An engagement was on the cards any time soon and she smiled and told his mother how wonderful that was and how proud she must be, whilst thinking Myleen, what sort of a name is that? She dutifully passed around pictures of the happy couple that were being shared, whilst listening to everyone saying how happy they looked together although she kept quiet and said nothing. She wondered if his parents had any idea of the things their son got up to and was almost tempted to spill the beans, almost. But luckily, she held back after all she didn't want her own part in the story becoming common knowledge and she was far too involved to think straight.

She was quiet on the way home although her brain was shouting Myleen over and over again. It was wearing her out. She helped her mother do some shopping and carry it home then had to tidy her room and help with general chores around the house, so that she began to wish that she had gone to school for a bit of peace and quiet.

At last she had some me time and flung herself on her bed with an exasperated sound and, clasping her hands across her chest, stared unblinkingly at the ceiling.

The thought suddenly came to her where she had seen that name before. It was on the school sports notice board and she was pretty sure that Myleen was a member of the hockey team, the name had stuck out because it was so unusual. She was not sure of the position Myleen played but she would look that up when she went to school tomorrow. At last she had something to go on but she had to be careful, Myleen had seen her the last time she had gone around to see James and could make her a laughing stock. She had to admit it though, Myleen was pretty, if you liked that sort of thing, and James obviously did. Myleen was a year older than her so that would make her sixteenish and possibly be reaching seventeen if she became pregnant and had a baby. Even her parents would be able to do the maths on that one!

She suddenly sat up in bed with a big grin on her face. Of course, of course, why on earth was she panicking, all she had to do was sit back and wait and let nature do its work. In three months or so she would be able to tell if Myleen was pregnant or not and she could just sit back and watch the shit hit the fan. All she had to do in the meantime was to hope that James used his stash of condoms and find out where Myleen lived. She thought back to her last attempt to find out and decided that this time it would work. This time she was going to put more effort into it. Everything could, of course, go horribly wrong if Myleen decided to get an abortion but she would cross that bridge when she came to it.

She briefly thought about Aunty Jean and realised that she didn't miss her in the least. Must be sad in a way to have no one remember you although sadness seemed to be a big part of dying if she thought about the way her parents and the people in the congregation acted. Miserable sods the lot of them, she thought, weeping into soggy tissues and blowing runny noses, their sorrow made them all look so ugly! She got out her computer and wrote down that she didn't want any sadness at her funeral in the least, everybody was to be happy. Soggy tissues and runny noses weren't allowed.

Chapter 15
New Arrival

She buckled down at school and really worked hard so as to get the time to pass quickly. She had a swimming gala to attend on Saturday so spent her spare time training as hard as she could. She bumped into Myleen as she got out of the pool and started to say sorry until she saw who it was. Myleen grinned at her then turned and said something to the friends she was with and three pairs of curious eyes looked at her before turning away. She felt herself flush with embarrassment and walked away as if nothing had happened, all the time aware of the giggling, whispering group of girls.

Once in the locker room she covered her face with her hands and repeated over and over how much she hated Myleen until she calmed down saying all she had to do was wait. Myleen might be laughing now but before long she would find out that she had crossed the wrong person and she would be sorry, very sorry indeed.

The weeks flew by and half term came and went when she finally had the conformation she was seeking. She happened to be in the toilet at the time when she heard the outside door bang then, "She's about nine weeks pregnant! I told her to get rid of it but she won't" and "Whose is it anyway?" She flushed the toilet and came out to wash her hands deliberately not reacting to the sudden quietness around her. As she was leaving the whispering started up again but she knew all she needed to know and all she had to now hope for was that the bitch didn't abort and fuck her plans up.

The news went viral around the school and Myleen found herself the centre of attention wherever she went and kept bursting into tears. Her parents were called into the school and a few weeks later Myleen ceased to attend although her pregnancy still remained high on the gossip agenda.

Finding out where Myleen lived had been easy. She had been sent to the secretary's office to fetch the class register and had found it empty so. Keeping one eye on the door she had looked through the filing cabinet and had easily accessed the address. All she had to do now was wait but she was finding waiting very difficult and felt life wasn't fair. Life was passing her by and she was being held back; she was fifteen and her parents still treated her like a kid, stopping her from doing things she wanted to do. She still hadn't managed to persuade her parents to get a car and felt awful at being poor. She should have been born into a rich family and no mistake.

Christmas came and went without any major surprises then in the Easter holidays she had reluctantly gone up to town with her mother, moaning as usual, when she stopped in mid-sentence as she came face to face with Myleen, but not the pretty self-assured Myleen of old. This Myleen was heavily pregnant and looked worn out, haggard even. She made a point of shouting out, "Hello Myleen," she said, so that people surrounding them would look their way as Myleen lowered her head and tried to scuttle away unnoticed. She called again, louder this time, "Myleen, wow, you're looking big, how long have you got to go?" Myleen mumbled something she didn't quite hear. "Sorry, didn't catch that, oh mid-May, best of luck then." A woman, quite possibly her mother, took hold of Myleen's arm, stared back at them for a moment, then steered Myleen away through the crowd and out of sight.

As soon as she got home she lay back on her bed and thought over what she had seen and decided there and then that no way was she ever going to get pregnant if that was how it made you look. She got out her laptop and made notes to the fact putting them in bold and double underlining them, then lay back and went over every detail she had seen.

As she lay there she suddenly thought about James becoming a daddy very soon and how that would make him feel and hoped with all her might that he would feel like he had a millstone around his neck and serve him right if he did. He had two-timed her and now he was paying the price but it was not enough, not nearly enough.

She picked up her phone and dialled the surveying firm where James worked.

"D. C. Andrews, can I help you?"

"Yes please, I'd like to speak to James Millet please."

"Sorry he's on the other line at the moment. Can I take a message?"

"Well, it is rather urgent, you see I'm his girlfriend and my waters have just broken," she made a few groaning noises, "and I am being taken by my parents to the labour ward at St. George's Hospital." She groaned again for good measure and clicked the off button on her mobile, then put it on the bed beside her and went into a bout of hysterical laughter which seemed to go on for ages. Her sides ached and she sat up holding her stomach trying to catch her breath and looked over at her reflection in her dressing table mirror and grinned like a Cheshire cat as she thought of James's reaction when given the news. She almost purred.

The drama class performed Romeo and Juliet for the whole school and parents and got a standing ovation which she thought was all down to her. She had been brilliant and had outshone everyone else as far as she could fathom. As the cast took their bows at the end she again knew that this was what she was made for She was a star and without her they were nothing.

When they arrived home after the performance she made as if to go upstairs when her parents asked her to sit down as they had something to say to her. She thought they were going to tell her how proud they were of her and how well she had performed but instead she was told that they had been talking to the drama class teacher who had informed them that he was delighted that they had agreed for their daughter to go to acting school but had soon put him right on that point. They told her that if she wanted to go into acting school she could do so after she had gained qualifications at university, for then they knew that she would have a career to fall back on.

"You did what?" she exploded jumping to her feet and momentarily gritting her teeth. She made a growling sound in her throat. "Why won't you listen to me? Didn't you see me tonight? Didn't you see how natural I am? I was born to be an actress." She stamped her feet and whirled around on the spot throwing her arms wide. "Why aren't you supporting me?" then slumped down in a chair.

"You were good but you were not the only one in the play, it takes more than one person to make a good performance you know."

"How am I going to face the drama teacher now, you've made me look stupid. I hate you, I hate you," she cried, as she jumped to her feet again and thrust her face towards her parents.

She stopped suddenly as her father got to his feet and thundered, "Go to your room before I do something I'll later regret," as one arm pointed upstairs.

She had overstepped the mark but her anger wouldn't subside and she wouldn't back down. She turned and suddenly curled her fingers into her mother's hair and shouted, "It's your fault, you bitch," whilst dragging out clumps of hair. She felt her father trying to pull her away and let go off her mother and turned to punch him as hard as she could but the next moment she found herself splayed over her father's lap, her pants pulled down and in receipt of the first spanking she had ever had in her whole life. She wriggled and screamed abuse at her parents. How dare they humiliate her this way but eventually started crying real tears.

Her father stopped, pulled up her pants and said, "Now go to your room," and she fled upstairs and threw herself face down on the bed continuing to cry real tears. She couldn't believe it, has father had actually hit her!

Her father stood at the base of the stairs watching her go up and sighed deeply, then went into the front room to comfort his wife who was weeping on the settee. He took her in his arms and held her head against his chest and kissed the top of her head with great tenderness. His wife's voice was muffled against his chest and he had to release his hold on her so that he could hear what she was saying. "If you had done that years ago instead of letting her get away with things we might well not be in the situation we are in now!"

"I haven't let her get away with anything," was his immediate response followed with the lame excuse, "You know how I feel about punishment and now I have actually gone against something I believe in. I just hope that she comes to her senses. I don't want to go through that ever again."

"Do you think we should take her for counselling, after all she has displayed worrying behaviours what with all the misfortune this family have had."

They both were quiet for a moment thinking back to the time when their daughter was admitted to Ward 3 and feeling incredibly guilty in agreeing to send her there although at the time it had seemed to do her good.

After a while her dad said, "When are you going to tell her?"

"Well not now obviously, I can't now."

"Well you've got to tell her soon. I mean she'll be even more upset if we leave it till she finds out for herself."

"What do you mean by that?"

"Well, you know, when you start getting bigger, she's bound to notice, she's not stupid."

"I'll leave it a couple of days till this dies down then see if I can find a quiet time to tell her."

"Do you think she'll be pleased?"

"To tell the truth I don't know, she's very temperamental these days."

"Being a teenager I suppose, although I don't remember having mood swings like she does."

"Well, whether she likes it or not she's going to have to learn to get on with it. That young madam has had her own way for far too long, let's see how she'll like being second for a change."

Her dad went into the kitchen to get the first-aid tin and, putting the kettle on for a nice strong cup of tea, went to attend to his wife's wounds and try to soothe their frayed nerves.

Meanwhile the subject of their anguish lay upstairs crying on her bed. As she calmed she slipped a hand beneath her pants and laid it on the flesh of her throbbing bottom which felt hot on both cheeks. She imagined it to be bright red with her father's handprints on it. She suddenly withdrew her hand and began to vigorously masturbate not caring how much pain she caused herself in the process. She experienced an orgasm that made her body tremble, then fell into a deep sleep.

Over the next few days she was very subdued and obedient. She knew that her father would be mortified that he had succumbed to punishing her and she planned on how she could use his guilt to her advantage in the future. She would get her own back one way or the other but her revenge would have to be put on hold for a while, she had bigger fish to fry.

She continued scouring the 'In memorium' columns in the papers as well as the birth announcement section and eventually came across *Mr & Mrs Timpson are pleased to announce the arrival of their granddaughter Amelia Jane 7lb 1oz born at 3.27 a.m. on Monday 25th May, 2020.* She cut out the announcement and put the clipping in one of her files then sat back and thought about what to do next. James was a daddy, she thought, and wondered how he felt about it. She was amazed at how detached she felt when thinking about him now; she was well and truly over him and knew him for what he was, slime. She quite fancied that boy she had met over near the reservoir that time but he was resisting her approaches and she was worried she was losing her charm. She could have her pick of any of the boys, they all had their tongues hanging out when she sashayed passed them but, apart from a friendly smile, the boy she wanted didn't seem the least bit interested in her.

On the way back from school one evening she decided to go to the chip shop as she was feeling peckish and took a short cut down a road she rarely used, noticing a couple of women across the road pushing prams and chatting away. She quickly turned her head as if checking out the front gardens of the houses she was passing hardly able to believe her luck; one of the chatting women was Myleen, she was sure of it. She continued walking a few more yards then crossed over the road and followed the women stopping every now and then to tie her shoelaces or pretend to admire flowers in one of the gardens she was passing. The women stopped outside one of the houses and chatted for a while longer, then the woman she thought was Myleen waved goodbye and continued down the road then turned into one of the houses further down the road. As Myleen shut the door behind her she didn't notice the girl in school uniform walking past, she was much too busy thinking about preparing her baby's feed. Her mother came out to see her and lifted the sleeping baby from the pram, waking her up in the process and causing her to cry. Myleen hid her irritation, it was no use saying anything anyway as her mother wouldn't take any notice and would just remind her of whose house she was living in and to be grateful for small mercies.

She continued down the road ecstatic, of course she already knew the road where Myleen lived, she had found that out from the file in the school secretary's office ages ago but she hadn't realised she was in the actual road where she lived until she saw her. She chided herself for not keeping the information in the forefront of her mind but thanked her lucky stars that she had taken the short cut to get some chips. No more slip-ups she told herself sternly but with a big grin one her face.

She arrived home feeling really happy and offered to make her mother a cup of tea as she looked worn out. As she gave her mother the tea her mother told her to sit down as she had some news to tell her. She sat down and waited thinking her mother was going to talk about what she wanted for her birthday, but she was in for a shock.

Later that evening she was still furious and unable to think straight. A baby, her mother was going to have a baby; what on earth was she thinking of? She had actually asked her mother why her dad didn't use condoms to avoid an unwanted pregnancy but her mother told her that the pregnancy was not unwanted, the baby was definitely wanted and would be a little brother or sister for her.

She didn't want a little baby brother or sister; she was quite happy as she was, thank you very much. The thought of her parents actually having sex repulsed her, ughh, plus the fact that they had actually done it when she was in the house, sleeping next door. How could they? It was disgusting, and if they thought she would be pleased with the news they had another think coming.

She heard her dad come in from work and the sound of voices downstairs then, after a few minutes, there was a soft knock at the door and her dad popped his head around the door and asked if he could come in. She couldn't say anything but she did manage to nod her head and he came into the room and somehow they ended up in a hug. She hadn't hugged him like this for ages and now realised how much she had missed it, her daddy loved her. She started matter of factually telling him how to go about getting an abortion and didn't realise he had pulled away from her and was staring at her open-mouthed in horror. She suddenly stopped and looked as him. "What's the matter? Why are you looking at me like that?"

"The baby will be a brother or sister for you, get used to it," he answered as he turned and swiftly left the room.

She was confused at first, not taking in what he said before realisation hit her. "You'll be a laughing stock, everyone will laugh at you and point their fingers at you and what's worse, they'll laugh at me too. I'll lose friends because you couldn't keep your cock in your trousers."

The slap across the face when it came sent her reeling across the room. Her dad undid then pulled the belt out of his trousers and wound it around one hand, quivering with rage. She stopped speaking unable to take her eyes from the belt dangling in her dad's hand, then crouched down on the floor saying she was sorry, so sorry and pleading to be forgiven. She didn't mean it. How long her father stood over her she never knew but it seemed like forever, then suddenly he was gone. Stupid bastard, she thought, but knew she had only narrowly avoided being beaten again. She needed to learn to keep her thoughts to herself and her mouth shut.

Later that same evening she lay on her bed going over what had happened and wondering how quickly things had got out of hand and gone wrong. One minute she was in a good mood arriving home and it seemed almost the next minute her father was going to punish her. She thought over what she had said and was astonished at her impudence, unbelievable that she had actually spoken out loud the thoughts she was thinking. She didn't regret what she had said, however, although she did think that she shouldn't have said what she said out loud. She believed that it was only due to her acting ability that she had not received the beating she undoubtedly deserved but part of her regretted not being punished. How could she improve as an actress if she was denied the opportunity of learning through experience? She now knew without a doubt that she was not her daddy's little treasure any more and that from now on she would have to tread very carefully.

Chapter 16
Misadventure!

It took quite a few weeks before her home life returned to as normal as it could be although something was missing, something that had been there all the time but hadn't been noticed, had been taken for granted even, until it was gone. She searched in her mind to find out what it was that was missing but try as she might couldn't put a name to it.

As the weeks flew by her mother put on a lot of weight although she was continuously feeling nauseous or being sick. Her only solitude came from lying in a dark room with a cool flannel on her forehead.

Her mother was unable to do the normal jobs around the house and therefore she was expected to pitch in and pull her weight. She found herself doing the shopping and cooking the meals and although she protested at first by saying she was still at school and shouldn't have to be made to do housework she came to enjoy the cooking. Doing the washing was a job she hated, handling all those dirty smelly clothes. How on earth had her mother done it all these years? Despite her loud protests she did all that was asked of her but refused to do cleaning. Who did they think she was, a servant, well she was having none of it.

Her mother gradually began to feel better and soon took over the cooking again but she still had to go out and do the shopping and use a trolley as well, stupid thing. Still, she stashed a black hoodie and a pair of trainers in it just to be prepared for any eventuality.

Whilst she was out she noticed a pram similar to that one Myleen had and went over and parked her trolley nearby and pretended to sort through its contents whilst studying the brake system, her plan being to find the unprotected pram outside a shop and release its brakes and hope it rolled into the road. She knew that there were a lot of cameras around and that she would need a lot of luck but at the moment she hadn't thought of anything else. The pram outside the shop didn't belong to Myleen as she found out when the young mother came out of the hairdresser's but she did manage to see all that she needed to. She wondered if Myleen was one of these mothers who left their kids outside the shops they went into or if she took her kid inside. She hoped it was the former. Things would be so much easier but she prepared a strategy in case it was the latter. All she had to do now was be patient but patience wasn't one of her many attributes and time was ticking away.

A few weeks later whilst out shopping she noticed Myleen and a friend pushing their prams along the pavement not taking too much notice of their familiar surroundings as they happily chatted away.

She watched them from across the road and had an inspired thought, all she had to do was get the timing right. She parked her trolley in the litter-strewn doorway of a boarded-up shop, took off her top and pulled on the black hoodie, substituted her shoes for trainers and she was ready. She eased out of the doorway onto the semi-crowded pavement then ran briskly down the road, then crossed over it further down and made her way back up the other side of it, slowing her pace down whilst she made her calculations. About fifty yards ahead of her she saw a zebra crossing and a few yards beyond that the two women with the prams which she hoped and prayed would be maneuvered to the edge of the pavement as they waited to cross. Still twenty yards away the women moved their prams to the edge of the pavement still blissfully happy in each other's company and chatting away. They pressed the nearby button and waited for the lights to change. As she passed behind the mothers she appeared to stumble and fell against Myleen whilst at the same time giving her a shove in the middle of her back, then kept on running, hearing shouts and screams and the screeching of brakes and a dreadful thump as a car collided with something. She disappeared into the maze of side roads and lost her jogging top in one of the many bins before she crossed over the main road further up and walked down it to see the carnage she hoped she had created.

A crowd had gathered near the crossing and was being held back by a couple of policemen. She lost herself in amongst them and craned her neck as she watched the activities and loved every second of it particularly the sad wreckage of the pram. She listened to what the people in the crowd were saying and joined in and echoed some of their comments. The police were taking names of addresses of witnesses as she edged herself out of the back of the crowd and made her way back to the shop where she had parked her trolley relieved to find it was still there. She quickly changed into her shoes and continued with the shopping.

She stood waiting at the bus stop feeling dissatisfied and not at all like she should feel at a successful outcome. That was the trouble of course, she didn't yet know if all of her planning had a successful outcome. True she had got her timing perfect but she didn't yet know if the baby was dead or even if her mother was. She wasn't bothered if it was one or the other but the not knowing had taken the edge off everything. She wished that she had seen what had happened although she knew it wasn't possible if she was to escape undetected. She decided to give herself credit where it was due and cheer up. After all she had achieved something. All she had to do was wait for the news then she could celebrate.

When she arrived home she told her mother all about an accident in the High Road that she had come across, then dutifully unpacked the shopping and hung out the washing humming a vague repetitive song as she did so.

Chapter 17
A Ride for a Ride!

The local paper reported that a young woman had been killed in a tragic incident but her baby had against all odds survived, although it was still being cared for in the intensive care unit. She knew the minute she read it that it was Myleen, just had to be, but didn't know whether to be happy or not at the news as she thought one out of two wasn't bad. She then thought of it another way; she had only been fifty percent successful and decided that that wasn't good enough; she should have done better.

She watched her mother moving slowly around the house and was even more determined never to get pregnant if that was what it did to you. Her mother stayed downstairs all of the time now, finding the stairs much too difficult and now at least the sofa-bed was put to good use.

Along with many of the school pupils she went to Myleen's funeral but gained nothing from it to add to her study. She dutifully sang the chosen hymns and, when wiping her eyes, poked a finger in them so as to show real emotions although she couldn't care less.

James was there with his family and she saw that Myleen's parents had even brought the baby along, unbelievable, fancy bringing a baby to a funeral. When she could she stared at James and couldn't believe the change in him; he looked old and beaten down. She inwardly thanked Myleen for taking James away from her. She was so glad that she wasn't stuck with such a boring little man. She couldn't believe that she had once fancied him let alone slept with him. He had crossed her and was now paying the price.

She knew many of the hymns off by heart so was able to let her mind wander whilst still looking like she was taking part in the proceedings. Her mind wandered back to the fatal accident in which no witnesses had come forward. The police had appealed for a mysterious jogger, picked up on CCTV cameras, to come forward and be eliminated from their enquiries but to date had had no response.

She had avidly watched the news reports of the accident and had seen her mother's face blanche when Myleen was named as having been killed at the site. She made a point of accessing every bit of news about the accident and couldn't believe the local storm it had produced. Apparently, the crossing was a known accident black spot and protestors had flagged it up for something to be done years ago.

The baby had spent a few days in an intensive care unit but was eventually announced fit and well and allowed home with her grandparents. She didn't envy her at all, fancy growing up with smelly old people. I mean it was bad enough that her parents had sex at their age but at least they hadn't that smell that seemed to cling to old people.

She listened to the various people who went out to the front of the congregation to sing Myleen's praises. It briefly crossed her mind that she should go out the front and tell the truth, tell everyone what a slut Myleen had been. The thought sent a shiver of excitement through her as she thought of the reactions that would follow and she almost got up but it was too late. She noticed James was sitting with Myleen's parents and wondered about that, after all Myleen had been under age when she had the baby. She would have thought that they would have wanted him shot at the very least! She stared at him feeling nothing and realised that now Myleen was out of the way she could have him if she wanted to and she briefly toyed with the idea of stringing him along but then decided she couldn't be bothered. He just wasn't worth the effort. The congregation stood up and sang the final dreary hymn as the curtains closed around the flower-draped coffin. She was appalled, the flowers would be burnt. True she didn't like cut flowers but that was no way to treat them. What on earth were they thinking?

She followed her mother's slow progress out of the church and watched as she hugged Myleen's parents and kissed the baby's forehead and dutifully lined up beside her and shook hands and bowed her head as if in respect. She took a quick glance at the baby, ughh, nasty little thing. You should be dead, she thought as she smiled and said how pretty she was and what a lovely choice of name Amelia Jane was.

Her mother made her excuses of not being up to going to the reception and she decided that she didn't want to stay either. The family quietly made their way home and her dad settled her mother in the front room whilst she made a cup of tea for everyone and put on the dinner, then sorted out the washing without being asked, thankful at not being made to go to the reception. After all she had no interest in James now. The families had paid their dues with interest and she wanted a new challenge.

At last the summer holidays were over and she was going back to school. She looked at herself in the mirror, no longer the gawky little schoolgirl and wondered where the time had flown. She was in the top year now at long last. She had decided to give in to her parents' wishes and pursue a career in maths and had already chosen what university she wanted to study in, not that she had given up on the idea of being an actress, she would just put it on hold for the time being. After all she was still young, she had plenty of time. She would have to move away from where she lived but couldn't wait. It was time she flew the nest and got away from her parents and the expected new family member. Just a few more terms at school then she could be free.

The thought came to her why did perfectly healthy people die young? She let this thought roll around her brain for a while unable to come up with an answer. Supposing she died young, supposing she never got to be an actress or something, supposing one day she just didn't wake up, it could even be tomorrow that that happened or maybe even this afternoon.

She was horrified at the thought that her life could end at any moment and that she would have no say in it because she hadn't yet explored all the possibilities in dying or finished planning what she wanted to happen to her when she died. She needed to make a will and fast so that she wouldn't be caught out if she died. She got out her laptop and typed in 'Last will and testament' and began to study how to go about what she wanted to do.

On returning home from school one day she popped her head around the living room door to say hello to her mother but noticed that the bed was empty. Funny, where on earth could she be? She checked downstairs, then found a note from her dad on the kitchen table saying her mother had been taken into hospital but not to worry, he would bring her up to date when he returned home. What did he mean when he returned home? Was he going to leave her mother in the hospital? Why would he do that and what on earth could be wrong with her mother after all she was only pregnant, it wasn't as if she was ill or something?

She put the dinner on finding it very easy to appear thoughtful, then did her homework, then settled down in her room and waited for her dad to return. When he did her told her not to worry, her mother was going to be kept in hospital under observation for a few days. He kissed her on the forehead and thanked her for preparing the dinner then went into the front room and promptly fell asleep on the sofa bed. She went into the front room and stared at him briefly then gently covered him with the duvet and kissed his forehead telling him goodnight.

Later in her room she pondered over the day's events and wondered about her mother; surprised that she missed her so much but, at the same time, realising that she missed her because she was having to do all the housework instead of her. If that was what being married was like you could stuff it, she thought, running around doing the shopping, cleaning and washing and everything else that came with it. In a way she could understand her mother looking so worn out sometimes and feeling down about being taken for granted. Of course she didn't know if her mother felt down or used at any time, she just assumed she would be, knowing that she would be in the same position. She supposed that she should be grateful to her mother for making her take on some responsibility in the house. She would find it useful when she moved out and had to fend for herself.

Try as she might she could not sleep so she took hold of her laptop and updated her notes by adding that marriage was definitely not on the cards, then read up a bit more about the wording in a will, then lay back and thought about the boy she fancied but who was ignoring her. No, she thought, he wasn't ignoring her, he was playing her knowing that the more he kept her at a distance the closer to him she wanted to be, and boy oh boy did she want to be close. She lay down and fantasized about being with him, watching him undress, seeing his manhood standing erect as he stood over her whilst she pleaded with him to love her. This was a change of roles for her, usually in her fantasies she was the one who stood stony faced whilst her man grovelled at her feet and she found it exhilarating and played and replayed the role in her head till at last she went to sleep.

Not surprisingly she was late getting up and when she went downstairs she found a note from her dad telling her that he had gone to the hospital. She thought about getting dressed and joining him there and surprised herself by making the effort to do so.

She finally found her mother in one of the side wards and barged in. "Hello, Mum," she said, as she leant over to kiss her. She saw that her mum had been crying as she pulled back and glancing at her dad she saw that he had been crying too. "What's the matter? What's wrong?"

"Your mother may have to be induced," her dad said in a quiet voice, "the baby is not doing so well."

"Induced, what's induced? What do you mean?"

"There's a chance that the baby may die so they are exploring the possibility of inducing the pregnancy, making the birth happen before it should to try to save the baby's life," her dad explained whilst holding onto and caressing his wife's nearest hand.

"What about Mum? Doesn't she have a say in all this?" She jumped to her feet hands on hips.

Her mother smiled weakly at her. "It's all right, darling, I just want what's best."

"Will it hurt you, this inducement thing, will it hurt you, Mum?" She leant forward and cuddled her mum. "I love you, I don't want you to be hurt."

Her mother weakly returned the cuddle then lay back as if exhausted and her dad said that she should wait outside as he wanted a few words in private with her mum. So she went outside and watched them through the glass thinking it was great that the baby looked to be dying, all the fuss and bother would soon be over and the household would get back to normal. She thought of what she would wear to the baby's funeral and imagined the tiny coffin being hidden by closing curtains, then wondered if that would happen. After all a baby wouldn't be worth all the effort of stoking up the furnace, would it? There was nothing of them really when you came to think of it.

Her dad came out of the room and touched her arm and startled her, so deep in thought she had been "Fancy a coffee?" then, without waiting for her to reply strode off to find the hospital canteen with her trailing behind struggling to mentally get back in the real world. They sat opposite each other in the canteen with a coffee and a sticky bun each, then both started to talk at once, laughed then she gestured to her dad to speak. "I was just going to say how nice it was of you to make the effort to come and see your mum. I know it is difficult for you seeing as how much you dislike hospitals."

She didn't have an answer so didn't give one instead just shrugged expressively and gave her dad a weak smile which immediately had the effect she wanted. He put out his arms and she fell into them and they hugged in silence for quite a long time before she came up for air and grinned at him. "I love you, Daddy." She was his little girl again, his little treasure.

Her dad was staying at the hospital so she kissed him on the cheek and made her way home determined to find out a bit more about pregnancy and what inducing was all about. She spent the rest of the day absolutely fascinated and horrified by the topic.

How on earth did a baby get out down there and what on earth made women want to get pregnant in the first place? They couldn't all be accidents, could they, could they? Had she been an accident, she grimaced as she thought of her parents having sex in order to produce her and decided that yes, she had been an accident but they had decided to go along with the pregnancy anyway, a bit like Myleen had. The thought of Myleen made her sit up and she gritted her teeth thinking how much she hated the bitch and would love the opportunity of killing her over and over again, but hold on, she smiled, she hadn't actually killed her, had she? It was an accident pure and simple.

She had her dad's dinner ready for him when he returned home from the hospital and he reminded her to make sure her school uniform was ready for the following day. She sulked and said she wanted to go and see her mum but her dad was adamant; she was not going to miss school and that was the end of it. As they sat together in the kitchen she asked about what it had been like when her mother was pregnant with her and was surprised to learn that the pregnancy was nearly the same as now. Her mother had spent a long time in hospital and she had spent three weeks in an incubator when she was induced.

Induced, she had been induced. She tried to get more information from her father but apart from him suddenly saying, "We decided not to have any more children after you as it was too dangerous." He clammed up and in the end she gave up as he was falling asleep and dutifully went up to bed to think over what she had learnt. Questions, she had so many questions and she still didn't know if she was planned or an accident and realised it would be difficult to find out, hmm, she would have to think about that one. Now, what was this thing her dad had said 'too dangerous to have any more children' or something like that. Who was it too dangerous for? Was it the baby, was it her mum? What did he mean? If it was too dangerous for the baby why were they having another one? If it was too dangerous for her mum, same question, why were they having another one? Nothing made sense and she wore herself out trying to work things out.

The next few days passed without incident and she began to settle into the new routine of preparing her father's evening meal and doing various chores around the house, finding that being kept busy made her tired and helped her sleep at night.

On the Wednesday evening she went up the hospital again and was relieved to see her mother looking so much better, there was even talk of her coming home as everything had stabilized.

When her dad left the room to get a coffee she said, "Mummy, was I induced too?"

Her mother closed her eyes briefly then opened them and said, "Yes, darling," and looked directly at her waiting for the next inevitable question.

"Did I nearly die?"

"Yes, darling, you were in an incubator for over three weeks; we couldn't take you home until the hospital were satisfied with your progress."

"Why did I nearly die?"

Her mother lay back in the bed and said, "There were complications with the pregnancy and if you don't mind I think now is not the time to talk about this."

Her dad chose this moment to come back into the room and glanced quickly from one person to another. "Have you been tiring her out?" he said to his daughter as he sat down beside his wife and lifted her hand and gently kissed the back of it. His wife smiled but said nothing more and he looked to his daughter for an answer but she just shrugged her shoulders and slumped back in her chair briefly then said, "I'm off home," and disappeared out of the door. She wandered through the hospital fascinated by the activity, then went and sat in the A&E department for a while before going on home. One of the patients in a cubicle was being put on a drip and she wondered what would happen if the drip was pulled out.

The next few days passed quickly and she really concentrated on her lessons finding the swimming sessions a welcome relief although she pushed herself hard as usual. She was used to having the pool to herself and was surprised when she saw Byron, as she had found out, also practising hard and almost matching her length for length. He was particularly good at butterfly and she had to really pull all the stops out to stay ahead. Eventually she was satisfied that she had shown him who was the superior swimmer and fluidly eased herself out of the pool and sat on the side and watched him for a while, then wandered off to the changing room putting an extra swing to her hips as she walked, all to no avail it seemed as he did not acknowledge her in the least.

That evening she returned home to find her mother ensconced in the front room surrounded by flowers. She called out, "Hi, Mum" and disappeared up to her room to think over the day. She knew she should have spent longer welcoming her mother home but it was too late for all the niceties now, she would just have to make up for it later.

She lay on her bed feeling bloated and ugly and knew her period was a few days off, horrible messy thing, she could do without it as she definitely wasn't going to have children. She didn't need them in her life. She thought about Byron. Why didn't he like her? Why didn't he ask her out? After all he must know she fancied him. She suddenly sat up. He didn't like her because she was chasing him, that had to be it, a male macho thing. She needed to back off and pretend she didn't give a shit about him. It should be easy after all she was an actress, well, nearly an actress. All she needed to do was to go out with one of the other boys. But who? she didn't fancy any of them. She would have to make it seem that she was genuine after all they would sense if they were being used. She suddenly thought of a boy she had liked briefly before her affair with James. She had seen him in the swimming pool and had noticed him because he had a huge bulge in his swimming shorts and, on top of that, he had a scooter. All right she preferred motorbikes but a scooter was better than nothing! What was his name? Ben, yes, that was it, Ben.

Over the next week she gradually upped the ante and soon had Ben lusting after her. He was obviously only interested in getting his end away but perhaps she would let him after all it had been a long time since she had sex and she had to admit that riding pillion on his scooter whilst she gripped his manhood was a totally unique experience.

Her mum was doing well but was tired all the time and she began to resent the baby for mucking up her life. As she sat with her mum with her hand on her stomach to feel the baby kicking (or whatever it was doing) she mentally told it time and time again that it wasn't wanted and that it should die and leave them in peace, all the while saying nice things out loud.

Ben stopped the bike in a deserted countryside lane to let it cool down after breaking the speed limit, feeling really pleased with himself and assured that today he was going to get a result. As he was speeding she had almost pulled his dick off and now he had a rock hard-on that she was going to get the benefit of whether she wanted to or not, and anyway if she didn't she was going to have a long walk home. As she took her helmet off and ran a hand through her tangled hair, he caught hold of her arm and pulled her close to him one hand behind her buttocks pressing them into him so that she could get the benefit of feeling his rock-hard manhood. His penis was almost climbing out of his pants and he made up his mind there and then he was going to fuck her whether she liked it or not, although he reckoned, she was up for it going by the way she had fondled his tackle on the ride up there.

He whispered, "Oh, baby, you are driving me crazy, you're so beautiful," the same old line he used every time as he clumsily groped her breasts then suddenly twisted her so that she was facing away from him telling her to lean on the bike seat that she had recently occupied, whilst his hand groped with the button and zip of her trousers and dragged them down to her knees kissing her buttocks in the process. It was all working out, all going to plan, one of his fantasies was about to come true, was about to become a reality. She meekly stayed in the position he had put her, loving the way he gripped her around her hips and kissed her buttocks as he pulled her jeans and pants down to her knees. Ben thought he was going to come before he had a chance to get his cock in her but managed to slow himself down and, taking out his mobile, took a couple of shots of her, then stashed it away in his pocket and completed 'a ride for a ride' remembering to whisper endearments every now and then as girls seemed to like that sort of thing. The first session was over and done almost as soon as he put his cock in her. He had no control whatsoever as his penis squirted his seed into her. He felt a bit ashamed of his performance but made up for it later with another more intense session where his mind was totally on his own needs and he couldn't even remember her name or be bothered to whisper endearments. When he felt ready, he took her home and dutifully gave her a peck on the cheek before driving off. She watched him go then walked the two streets to her house, after all, she was not going to let him know where she lived. As she walked, she realised she had made a big mistake with Ben, the sex had done nothing for her. She had thought that his having a big dick would make it good but she was wrong and now she would have to extricate herself from another problem of her own making.

As she arrived at her house an ambulance pulled up outside her house and her front door flew open and she saw her dad beckoning the paramedics in. She stood aside in shock not able to take in what was happening, then came to as her mother was taken past her on a stretcher and put into the ambulance. She screamed for her mother through her fingers. Her dad held her briefly then told her to hold the fort as he was going in the ambulance with his wife, and suddenly they were gone leaving a noisy silence. She stood in the front garden for a moment, then realised that some of the neighbours were watching so quickly went indoors and shut the front door behind her. The front room floor and bedding seemed to be covered in blood and she set to clearing everything up whilst wishing she had gone in the ambulance.

Somewhere she could hear a phone ringing but it took her a little time to locate it. It was not her phone, it was Ben's, she had lifted it from him on the way home and had completely forgotten all about it. She turned the phone off then made herself a drink and sat down to look through it and found the photographs of herself leaning butt naked over his scooter as if waiting to be serviced. She was fascinated and found the photographs of herself strangely erotic but decided to delete them as she didn't want anyone else seeing them.

So that was his game, was it? Well, she would have to come up with some suitable punishment. He was a naughty boy and naughty boys should get punished.

Chapter 18
Just Deserts

When Ben arrived home he searched through his pockets for his mobile but couldn't find it in any of them. Shit, he must have dropped it when he was shagging her. He was feeling really pleased with himself and couldn't wait to tell his mates, although that would have to wait as all their numbers were on the lost mobile.

Meanwhile the object of his thought was busily cleaning the house from top to bottom. She did not know what had got into her but at last, exhausted she slumped down on her bed and fell asleep. A few hours later her mobile rang and when she picked it up she saw it was her dad calling. She sat up and answered it and listened as her dad, almost crying it seemed, told her that she had a baby brother now and that her mother had been touch and go for a while but was now pulling through. In that moment she hated the baby for putting her mother at risk almost as much as she hated her mother for nearly dying. So lost in her thoughts was she that she nearly missed her dad saying that her brother was being kept in an incubator for a while and that her mother would be kept in for observation.

Baby brother, she had a baby brother, was that a good thing? She didn't know what to think but suddenly she burst into tears and cried herself dry.

The school day came and went without incident without her paying attention to anything and in the evening she bought a pot plant and went to the hospital. Her mother lay ashen against the white sheets with her eyes closed. She was not sure if her mother was asleep or not but thought that she looked dreadful. She noticed that she now had a drip attached to her arm and sat quietly and watched the fluid dripping into the suspended bag for a while, careful not to make a noise to wake her mum or dad who was fast asleep in the armchair provided for visitors. She wondered if she would be able to go and see her baby brother before he died. He was bound to after all her mother looked dreadful so, she reasoned, he must be ten times worse. She borrowed a piece of paper from the help desk and wrote a note to her parents then returned home.

This became her routine for the following week which she followed as if in a dream. On the Thursday evening she was allowed, with her dad, to see her baby brother for the first time although she could not see much of him what with the incubator and all the tubes coming out of him. She couldn't believe how tiny he was. How could something that small survive? As she walked back with her dad to her mum's room she watched her dad cry, tears rolling down his face as he told her that her little brother was doing well, he was a fighter like she had been. She thought that he was just kidding himself but said nothing just squeezed his hand very tightly.

On Friday at school she noticed Ben for the first time that week and went over to him and asked him if she could meet him after school and although he was offhand at first he eventually agreed. When she met him she told him she was sorry she had not seen him that week but that her mother was in hospital and she was worried. She asked him if he would take her for a ride on his scooter that evening to the same place as before and perhaps this time, she suggested, they could stay out all night! Ben thought all of his dreams had come true and couldn't believe his luck. He immediately agreed and arranged a time to pick her up and suggested a quickie there and then to tide him over. She almost refused but then thought why not and quickly removed her underwear as he pulled her behind some green bins, where she then leapt up and curled her legs around his waist and hooked them behind him with her ankles as he fumbled with his zip to free his penis, then bounced her up and down on it until he climaxed.

Later that evening she met him outside the house two streets away wanting to appear eager and managing to do so. Ben suggested somewhere nearer but she said that the first place they had gone to had become special to her and could they please please go back there. He was putty in her hands although the joke was that he thought he was running the show.

As soon as they had arrived she stripped off her jacket and blouse and let him undo her bra. He stood behind her roughly fondling her breasts and nuzzling her neck telling her how much he wanted her. She giggled and pulled away then opened her rucksack and took out two bottles of wine which she waved in front of him. He told her that he didn't drink that shit and, for a moment, it looked like he was going to force himself on her but she broke away giggling and said that she had found that only real men drank red wine, nobody else could handle it as it was so strong. He took up the challenge and without any finesse whatsoever glugged down half of the bottle, then triumphantly held the bottle aloft, then drank the rest and threw the bottle down on the ground then reached for her, but she managed to avoid his outstretched arms and said she wanted to get naked for him and started to undo her jeans.

She was not sure how long the date rape drug that she had ordered on line took to have effect but before long Ben was flat out on the floor, occasionally mumbling incoherently and definitely with no idea as to where he was. She took out the manacle she had bought and manacled his right wrist to his left ankle. She had spent time selecting the manacles wanting to make sure that they could not be easily undone without the right key. She stood back and stared down at him, then took some photos with the mobile she had found in his jacket pocket whilst it was still light, then put it in her jeans pocket and took some more on her own mobile, then put his helmet in the compartment of the scooter, picked up and stashed the empty wine bottles in her rucksack and did a quick recce of the area before driving the scooter home. She loved the sense of freedom the ride gave her and was surprised at how quickly she arrived back to where Ben lived. Turning off the scooter engine in the next street and silently pushing it to Ben's house she parked it on his forecourt narrowly missing being seen by a group of inebriated people meandering around the streets. She breathed a sigh of relief as she cleared his neighbourhood realising that that part of her plan had been the weakest and walked the few miles home and fell into a deep sleep without bothering to undress.

She awoke mid-morning Saturday and had to really concentrate to remember what she had done the previous evening. She wondered what Ben was doing now, then giggled to herself, not much at all if she remembered rightly. She felt happy, justice had been done and serve the little perv right, then completely forgot about him and did some housework, got the washing on and made brunch after which she went to the hospital and found her mother in the process of being examined by a doctor so had to wait outside. Her dad looked as if he had aged a thousand years during his wife's stay in hospital and she vowed to help out as much as possible so that he could finally relax. She longed for things to be like they used to.

Chapter 19
The Canal

More than a week had gone by and the school was buzzing about why Ben had not made an appearance. She felt eyes on her as she walked through the corridors but didn't react to them using it as a means to improve her acting skills but she did find the day tiring and was pleased to go home.

She wandered around the house not sure why she was feeling a bit down. In the kitchen she noticed a hot cup of tea on the table and going to the window she saw her dad in the garden talking to their next door neighbour. She wandered outside into the garden and said hello to him then continued down the garden and went into the garden shed. She had left the window open a fraction the last time she had been in it and was pleased to see that there were no remains of insects present as she loved them and couldn't bear to see them dead and dusty. She heard her name being called and, on poking her head out of the shed door, saw her dad beckoning her from the kitchen doorway. Intrigued she went back up to the house and found two policemen in the kitchen, their size actually dwarfing her dad.

The policemen asked her name, then said that they were checking the whereabouts of Benjamin Rush who had been reported by his mother as being missing. They had been informed by several of his known associates that she was his girlfriend and wanted to know if she had seen him recently or if he had made any sort of contact. She looked at her father then shook her head then said in a soft voice that she hadn't heard from or seen him recently. The police then asked her when was the last time she had seen him and she said that it was at least a week. She had spoken to him at school and had arranged to meet him after school then, with a little catch in her voice she said that he had waited for her after school and she had told him that she thought it best if they broke off their relationship for the time being, as she couldn't give him her full attention seeing as her mother and new baby brother were extremely ill in hospital.

She paused for effect and looked away and wiped away an imaginary tear, then smiled bravely at them and continued speaking after getting the nod to do so from her dad. She took a deep breath then said Ben had laughed at her and told her no worries there were plenty more fish in the sea and had simply walked away from her after informing her that he had a hot date that night and that was the last time she had seen him. She hadn't wanted to break-up with him, she had just wanted space to concentrate on her family and she was so sorry that he was missing. He must have been more upset than he had shown her. If she had just known he would react like this she would never have broken up with him.

The police thanked her for her time and left and she threw herself into her father's arms and cried that it was all her fault that Ben was missing. Her father reacted to script and held her fiercely and stroked her hair as he told her over and over again that Ben's disappearance was not her fault, that she couldn't possibly have known how he would react when she broke up with him, she was not responsible and shouldn't feel guilty.

She didn't feel guilty but allowed her father to calm her and persuade her to go upstairs and rest and he would bring her up a drink. She kissed his cheek and meekly went upstairs then, when safely ensconced in her room, allowed herself to smile and congratulate herself on her performance. Seeing the police in her own home had momentarily scared her but her training had stood her in good stead and she had responded like the true trouper she thought she was.

True to his word her dad brought her up a drink and sat with her for a while before leaving her to sleep but sleep eluded her and eventually, she got up and silently left the house and walked the dark streets until she reached the canal. She sat quietly beneath a bridge listening to the water rushing by and feeling totally relaxed. Her head fell forward as she dozed but shot up suddenly as there were sounds of anger nearby. She looked around her momentarily disorientated then peered around the corner of the bridge and up the bank where she saw two figures struggling, then all of a sudden one of the figures tumbled down the bank and lay still. The other figure at the top of the bank shouted, "I told you to leave her alone," then twirled around dramatically and staggered back towards the pub.

She turned her attention back to the figure who had fallen down the bank but he wasn't moving. She lit and smoked a cigarette and tried to regain the feelings she had had before the shouting had commenced but, in the end, gave up, flicked her butt end into the flowing water and pushed herself upright and walked over to where the figure lay.

She managed to roll him to within a foot of the edge of the canal when he started to groan then opened his eyes and clearly said, "Hello sweetheart." She rolled him the final foot and watched him slip almost silently into the canal water then stood and watched to see if there was any sign of him. There wasn't so she gave a final glance up the bank towards where she knew the public house to be then walked home and this time she went straight to sleep.

Chapter 20
Back to Bite You

She found that time was slipping away from her and longed for her mother and baby brother to come home so that they could be a family again. Her little brother was defying all the odds at the moment and was putting on a little weight, not much but any weight gain for him was a step in the right direction. She whirled through the house making it spic and span wishing that she hadn't let the housework slip, much better to do it little and often than have to do it in one big go. She finally lay down on the grass in the back garden and soaked up some sunshine and wondered what it was going to be like to have a new baby in the house although Alfie was over a week old now. Fancy calling him Alfie, she wanted a strong name like Marcus or Ryan but her little brother, if he survived or even if he didn't, was going to be named Alfie and all the sulking in the world wouldn't change that.

She had put the cot that she and her father had purchased in the small bedroom but her father had moved it into their bedroom much to her annoyance. Bloody kid was already pushing her out. Why hadn't it died? Life would have been so much easier if the little bastard had died. In her heart of hearts she knew she didn't actually mean that. During the week of visiting him in intensive care he had become so much more than a thing in a ventilator. She had watched him fight for his life against all odds and she admired this trait in him. He was her little brother and she would defend him against the world though possibly not from herself!

The school was holding mock exams at the moment and all of the top year seemed to spend their spare time with their heads in books. Not her though, she knew she was clever and anyway she had a retentive memory which helped a lot.

At dinnertime she decided to give swimming a miss and went into the school canteen and found an empty table to eat her meal. She had only had a few mouthfuls when, to her surprise, Byron sat opposite her and placing his tray on the table started to eat. For some reason she felt uncomfortable and thought he was staring at her but, every time she managed a covert glance in his direction, he was simply looking at his meal.

Finally she caught his glance and smiled sweetly at him and said, "Hi."

"Hi yourself."

"How you doing?"

"Okay I guess."

She fiddled with her fork searching her mind to continue the conversation but all she could think of was how hot he looked and how much she would like him to be busy between her legs. She flushed up at the thought and quickly took a sip of water then looked across at him and found he was looking at her with a strange expression on his face. He suddenly said, "Where's Ben?"

"Wha, what did you say?"

"I said where's Ben?"

"How should I know, I haven't seen him in over a week."

"Nor has anyone else it seems. Funny how he's just dropped out of sight."

"We broke up, I saw him after school that Friday and we broke up."

"That's not what I heard."

"I don't care what you heard and anyway what's it to you?"

"Mate of mine said he saw you both humping behind the school bins," Byron said with a big grin on his face.

"Well he's wrong it wasn't me behind the green bins," she hissed at him, then realised she had given herself away and hoped he hadn't noticed but of course he had.

"I saw you on the back of his scooter about half six that evening, you had a rucksack on and were holding on to his dick."

"Well it wasn't me. He told me he had a hot date that evening so it must have been her you saw."

"How do you know it was a girl?"

"I didn't, I just assumed it was."

She shifted in her seat wishing she had gone swimming and looked for a way to end the conversation when Byron said, "Oh, by the way, Clive sends his regards."

"Clive, Clive who? I don't know any Clive," she responded momentarily out of kilter, her mind still reeling about being seen on the scooter.

"Your cousin Clive. Come on, you must remember your cousin Clive, he moved a while back."

"Oh him, he tried to rape me you know, in my own room. It was lucky my dad was at home as I don't know what would have happened."

"Course you know what would have happened, exactly what you wanted to happen."

She stood up and hissed at him, "How dare you, how dare you say that, you don't know, you weren't there," as she turned to leave, the actress in her taking over.

Byron reached over and pulled her back down into her seat saying, "His dad gave him a beating because of you."

"Well serve him right, he deserved it."

"I spoke to him on the blower last night. He said he couldn't sit down for at least three weeks afterwards."

"Well, good," she responded, "I hope he learned his lesson; I just wish I'd been there to watch it."

Byron pulled a face at the remark. "So you like seeing people get hurt. That's your game, is it?"

"No, I don't like seeing people get hurt," she blatantly lied. "He needed to be punished and I needed to see it so that I could get closure."

"Clive's coming down to see me at the weekend, said he'd like to see you as he owes you one."

"Well, I don't want to see him, and if he tries anything my dad will sort him out."

"Oh I think your dad is far too busy to be your knight in shining armour again, don't you think? what with your mum and new brother."

"How come you know so much about me?"

Byron ignored the searching question. "Seems to me that a bloke has to be careful around you, first Clive and now Ben and we haven't even mentioned James yet."

Now she was frightened. How did he know so much? Her mind reeling, she got up to leave again then realised she couldn't, not just yet anyway. She had to hear what he had to say about James so she sat back down. "Okay then, Mr. Knowall, what is it about James you think you know so much about and which particular James are we talking about? This school is absolutely full of boys called James," she said in a tone that dripped with sarcasm, then realised she had taken the bait he had proffered and inwardly cursed her stupidity.

Byron didn't reply immediately, just gave her that half smile she was so crazy about then said, "He's a mate of a mate, his dad recently married into your family if I am not mistaken and you and he had a session at the hotel reception." She didn't answer but couldn't prevent blushing. He watched her then said, "You really should have checked the room out first you know. You had a nice little audience from what I'm told."

That did it, she got up and glared at him then swept theatrically out of the canteen and continued out of the school, whilst her mind worked overtime trying to work out what his game was.

Chapter 21
Lost and Found

By the time she eventually arrived home she was worn out having walked the streets for miles whilst trying to get her head in order but she hadn't succeeded. Her mother was baking and had flour up to her elbows and was humming along to the radio. She stood watching her for a moment until her mother caught sight of her and smiled. "Hello, darling," she said, and pushed one cheek forward to be kissed. She dutifully kissed the proffered cheek then asked her mother if she wanted any help before escaping to her room.

Why was Byron so interested in the boys that had been in her life and how dare he question her? It was none of his business. He could of course know nothing at all and had just thrown out a line to see if she hooked onto it. Yes of course that must be it. He knew nothing but was pretending to know something to get a reaction from her. Sly bastard, how dare he play her but the trouble was she had been hooked and now he would know that she knew more than she was saying. She thought herself clever but he had easily got the best of her.

She got up and walked around her room holding her fisted arms stiffly down by her sides. She didn't like to be bested in anything but Byron had got under her skin and she was making stupid errors.

Had Byron told the police he had seen her on the bike because the police hadn't said anything that time that they had come around to interview her but of course they wouldn't, would they? Perhaps he had told them and they thought that she was a liar but were getting more evidence against her. Who would they believe? It was her word against his. She was a decent, middle-class girl whilst he was a scruffy yob.

For a little while she felt better but the feeling did not last for long. Perhaps he hadn't told them because he was going to blackmail her! What did she have, apart from the obvious, that he could possibly want? He didn't fancy her, she knew that, so what was his game?

She had been checking all the papers since she had left Ben and to date there had been no news of him although there had been a couple of speculative comments as to his disappearance and his mother had also made a plea for him to return home on local television. She said for him not to worry, whatever he had done they would sort it out together and that they loved him and wanted him home safely. She greatly enjoyed their distress and, for a while, sat and pictured him as she had left him. It was ten days since she had seen him. The time had flown quickly for her but she wondered if it had flown as quickly for him.

The answer was, of course that no it hadn't. It had taken him quite a while to recover his senses and realise his predicament. He wasted a lot of time swearing and cursing and telling his girlfriend what he would do to her when he caught her but eventually realised that he was wasting time, he needed to move. He had one inspirational thought and searched as best he could through his jacket pockets but screamed in frustration when he realised his new mobile had been taken, although he did find a bottle of water which he foolishly drank all in one go. He pulled and shook and twisted the manacles but they were made of sturdy stuff and resisted all his efforts to undo them, then finally got to is feet and, like a toddler learning to walk, swayed and wobbled along the beaten track and made a good couple of hundred yards before collapsing from exhaustion.

Over the next few days or so he managed to cover a couple of miles having learnt to balance and maintain a rhythm in his movements. His manacled ankle and wrist had open wounds that bled every time he moved and caused him excruciating pain. Every now and then his inner voice would scream at him to give up, to just lay down and accept the fact that he was going to die, accept the fact that nobody would find him, but something in him wouldn't give up. His need for vengeance was burning brightly; he wanted to live so that he could get his own back on the bitch that had caused him to suffer. He promised himself that when he found her his suffering would be nothing to what he would do to her. He passed the long cold rainy days and nights picturing his revenge taking place, hearing her scream for mercy, and so he kept on torturing himself. When he could no longer walk he discovered how to roll although he found it difficult to maintain a certain direction at first and wasted a lot of time and energy going off in different directions to the one he wanted. Whilst recovering from yet another futile attempt he noticed a tall tree about fifty yards away and decided to use it as a landmark and, after many attempts eventually reached it.

Feeling at once he had achieved something positive, he looked for another landmark not too far away and aimed for it and, upon reaching it, looked for another landmark until he came to a bank at the bottom of which a small stream flowed. Water, he had to have water, but as he tried to navigate himself down the bank, he couldn't control the speed he was doing and tumbled the thirty feet or so down into the stream below, knocking himself unconscious on the rocks that lined the bottom of it.

He was in luck, though it was doubtful he would have seen it like that, for the following day a couple of intrepid power walkers stopped on the bridge to admire the view and saw him lying in the stream below. They had no idea where they were so their mobiles were tracked and before long help had arrived and Ben, though barely alive, was transported by helicopter to the nearest hospital.

His discovery made the news and although his name wasn't given out, she just knew it was him. She happened to be watching the news with her parents who both aired their gladness that, through providence it seemed, someone had been found alive. She said nothing but went online to find out what she could which, frustratingly, was not enough. Over the next few days she scanned the newspapers for updates but surprisingly little information was given out, all the papers seemed to be saying the same things in a different order!

In a morning assembly news was given out that Ben had been found and was being looked after in an intensive care unit. The headmaster said a special prayer for him and his family and said that he knew the good wishes of the school for a quick and speedy recovery would be sent to him and his family.

She spent her dinnertime in the swimming pool steaming up and down the lengths trying to work off her frustrations at the lack of further news. Quick and speedy recovery, I don't think so! She worried what she was going to say if he recovered and cursed the fact that he hadn't died as he was meant to. The swimming didn't do anything to ease her mind and she went to get out of the pool, not realising that Byron and a few of his friends were blocking her way. He pushed her roughly back in the water and she briefly went under the water before resurfacing and realising he was there. She went to get out again but was pushed back again and, as she went backwards into the water, she saw the grinning faces staring down at her. She swam across to the other side of the pool but as she put her hands on the side to heave herself out of the water they were stepped on and, as she pulled them away, she fell back into the water. She got angry and shouted at them all to, "Fuck off!" as attempt after attempt was blocked. She swam up to the stairs at the deep end but was pushed back into the water. She started to scream and curse at the boys who only grinned back at her, until finally she stood in the middle of the shallow end and threatened them all to no effect. Byron got down on his haunches so that his head was on a level with hers and smiled, although his eyes weren't smiling. "Aren't you happy that Ben's been found?" he said, as he looked around at his mates then back at her. "Let's hope that he comes back soon, eh?"

"Yes, yes of course I want him to come back," she responded whilst thinking die, die, you bastard. Just die.

"It's not funny is it, being on the receiving end for a change, is it?"

"I don't know what you mean. When I get out, I'm going to report you all." This remark was accompanied by her glaring at them and raising and waving her fist. "You think you've got the better of me, well let me tell you," and here her voice rose a few notches, "you will never get the better of me, ever."

If she expected them to be impressed by her speech, she was sadly mistaken, as they stood by the pool side laughing down at her. She was exhausted and couldn't think of anything else to say so said nothing and just stood there in the shallow end with her head bowed. She had no idea how long she had stood there but her shivering made her look up and she found that they had gone, she was alone. She pulled herself out of the pool expecting at any moment to be shoved back in and cautiously made her way to the changing rooms. It was empty.

As she sat in the shower the tears came, mixing with the shower water, then eventually she got changed and returned late to class ignoring a comment from the teacher. She kept her head down but was sure that all the pupils were staring at her, was sure that they all knew what had happened in the pool. She sat at her desk and vowed revenge but deep down she was well and truly scared of what would happen next.

He had a sister; Byron had a sister. In fact, if she remembered rightly, he had two, one older and one younger. The older one would have left school by now but the younger one must be in one on the lower classes. Suddenly she felt a whole lot better. She would get back at him through his younger sister, then he would find out not to gang up on her.

She asked her mother when Alfie would be coming home after all he was two weeks old but her mother said that he wasn't yet strong enough but soon she hoped, real soon. She went with her mother to the intensive care ward, then left her mother and went and sat in the A&E department and people watched whilst thinking about Ben being in intensive care and wondered if he was full of tubes like her brother. It was a pity, she thought, that he was in a hospital so far away. After all she would love to visit him and tell him to die and save everyone a lot of bother.

She was sitting next to a woman in a wheelchair dressed in a hospital gown supported by a carer. She watched fascinated as the carer fussed over the woman. Alice, she called her, and made sure that the drip she was on wasn't tangled and that she was warm and comfortable, and thought how nice she was. She wondered what was in the plastic packet hanging on the frame connected to the woman's arm by a clear plastic tube. The woman in the chair dozed off and the carer checked she was all right before picking up a magazine to read. After a while she got up to talk to a receptionist then left the room. When she returned five minutes later, she found the drip was no longer attached to Alice's arm; it was hanging free dripping merrily onto the floor. The thought that there might be foul play afoot never crossed the carer's mind as Alice often gave involuntary movements where her arms and legs were flung wide and it was thought that the drip had been tugged out during one of these episodes.

Back in the intensive care unit she watched her little brother and asked her mother when she would be able to cuddle him properly like other mothers did. Her mother simply smiled a sad smile at her and gave her a quick hug and said, "Soon, darling, soon."

She travelled back alone as her mother was going to stay at the hospital for a couple of days. She gazed out of the dusty window of the bus, her mind back in the A&E department. She had no intention of killing the lady in the chair, she just wanted to see how easy it would be to pull the drip out of her forearm. It was funny, she had thought the woman was fast asleep but whilst she was trying to find the edge of the tape something made her look up and she found the woman looking at her with a big smile on her face. "OK nurse," she said before closing her eyes again. She played the actress to the hilt and smiled back, then carried on with what she was doing. It wasn't as easy as she had thought it would be. She had seen countless films where it came out just like that. She thought that perhaps she could have cut it with scissors or pierced it several times with a needle. She mulled over her thoughts, then decided that she would put a packet of needles in her bag to pierce the tube if the need arose, rather than cut it as that would make it obvious it had been tampered with. Pleased with her line of thinking she turned her thoughts to Byron's younger sister who was not going to be as easy a target as she thought. Rumour had it she was a brown belt in some form of karate, Wado-ryu, she thought it was, whatever that was, and that meant she had to be on top of her game if she was going to get at her. She wished she had done something like it when she was younger although she was pretty much occupied with swimming she had to admit. She would just have to target the girl when she was most vulnerable. After all everybody, even she, was vulnerable sometimes.

The rest of the week passed quietly and there were no more incidents in the swimming pool although it took her a few sessions before she got back into her regular training rhythm. Her mum had returned home sometime during the day on Friday and was surprised and pleased at how clean and orderly the house was. Over dinner she said that Alfie was making good progress and that she had been able to hold him briefly. Her face shone as she spoke of her little son and her daughter wondered if her mother had shone like that when she spoke of her as a baby.

The following day whilst her dad went up to the hospital, she and her mum went to visit a distant cousin who was feeling poorly and needed a bit of family support. She wondered about that on the journey. Why now? Why suddenly visit her out of the blue when they had not bothered to for ages? Was she dying and wanted to say a last goodbye? Was she rich and going to leave them lots of money? They had only met up at funerals which wasn't the best way to cultivate someone socially and anyway they were running out of relatives. She wished for a moment that she was part of a large family so that there would be an opportunity to attend more funerals, then shook her head. She had liked being the only child up to now and yes she had a little brother but she soon would leave the nest and then her parents could dote on Alfie as much as they wanted.

She hadn't thought about her distant cousin for ages so busy was she getting on with her life, but now all her previous plans had come flooding back and she remembered researching the brakes on the wheelchairs that some disabled people used with the intention of greasing them up so that they wouldn't hold and would then freewheel into the road or collide with something. She didn't really care which after all it was the end result that mattered.

The cousin lived in a ground floor maisonette which was surprisingly roomy and well maintained. There were cats lounging everywhere of a variety of colours and breeds. She told them her favourite was a large male manx cat who spent most of his life sitting on her lap or curled around her neck. She carried with her a gadget that controlled everything from closing the curtains, raising the bed to turning on the television.

They all settled down briefly in the front room then she volunteered to do some shopping and left her mum and cousin chatting away, both of them lounged on by cats. The shopping did not take her long but she was glad to get out and do a recce of the area for when she returned. She had taken the spare door key hanging up beside the front door as a fail safe in case the carer lost hers, and had a duplicate made before she returned surprised at how much the duplicate key had cost when it only took a few minutes to cut. She wondered briefly if she should train to do the job as there seemed to be an easy fortune to be made but eventually dismissed the idea. There was no way she was going to be stuck in a shop however skilled she was at key cutting! On her return she made sure the key she had cut opened the front door, then returned the spare key to its hook.

Whilst her mum and cousin were discussing a knitting pattern she had time to examine the remote control having taken it with her to the bathroom. She saw what batteries were used in it and made a mental note before putting the cover back on and returning it. After all, you never know when such information could be useful! Her cousin was feeling around her many pockets and patting the sofa nearby as she talked about the pattern and was visibly relieved when her fingers touched the replaced remote. After all she saw it as her lifeline. The rest of the visit passed smoothly and before too long they were on their way home, with her mum saying how pleased she was with her for doing the shopping for her cousin. She soaked up the praise then sat quietly and let her mind meander whilst she touched the spare key in her pocket and ran her thumb down its smooth edge.

The journey home seemed to take much longer than the journey there and she was glad to finally get home. Her dad was in the kitchen whistling quite happily and, she stopped still for a while to listen, deciding she liked the sound and wondered if she could use it at her funeral. Whistling after all seemed to be a happy sound and she wanted people to be happy at her funeral. Not happy that she was dead of course, just happy celebrating a celebrity.

Later that day she sat back and looked at what she had typed knowing that it was not yet right but unable to take it any further. She was amazed at how difficult writing a will could be! She had started off all right and then, instead of sticking to her notes had added random thoughts as they came to her and the end result was messy. She had even made the mistake of repeating a fact in a different format, though why she had done that she had no idea. Usually she didn't have a problem with prose. She got up and without thinking opened her bedroom window to let a fly out and watched it go, wishing she could fly and suddenly feeling trapped. She put her hands on her chest as she struggled to breathe, panicking that she was dying, gasping for that last precious breath of air. She sat and rocked herself back and forth on the bed as her thoughts got darker and darker. She hated herself: she was ugly, she was too thin, she was too fat, her teeth were crooked. She was useless, a waste of space, she didn't deserve to live. She lay down and pulled the duvet over her, overwhelmed by her vicious thoughts, but in the darkness under the duvet her thoughts seemed to multiply and whirled around and around her head taunting her, telling her to end it all here and now. If other people had shouted or said these things to her, she would have just shrugged them off but now, on her own, she felt the whole world crushing down on her, alone, so alone.

Her mother came upstairs and knocked gently on the door, then popped her head around it and saw that her daughter seemed to have gone to bed. She was just turning away when she heard a muffled sob and went over to the bed and pulled a corner of the duvet back and saw her daughter shivering and shaking beneath it. She sat on the bed and called her daughter's name whilst holding out her arms and, before long, she had her daughter safe in her arms, rocking and kissing her, stroking the hair from her tear-stained face, whispering that she was loved, she was safe. They stayed locked together for a long time until at last her daughter fell asleep. Her mother lay her gently down, kissed her forehead and quietly left the room.

As she came downstairs her husband came out of the kitchen. "I was just coming up to see if you were all right you were gone so long," then, seeing her face said, "What's the matter, what's wrong?"

"I think she had a panic attack or something," as she described how she had found their daughter. "Perhaps she's doing too much what with all this swimming and the mock exams and the like. Perhaps I should take her to the doctor's."

"I think she's old enough to go to the doctor's on her own but by all means suggest it to her and see if she wants you to go with her."

Pleased to have a strategy of sorts they then talked about Alfie. They had both planned on visiting the following day but now they decided that their daughter should not be left on her own so her father said he would stay home. They held each other enjoying the closeness, truly happy in each other's company but both worried about their children.

The following day she got up feeling on top of the world with no memory of the previous evening. She threw on her dressing gown and thumped down the stairs into the kitchen for her breakfast. As soon as she entered the kitchen her parents stopped talking and, in unison, turned to look at her before smiling and wishing her, "Good morning, sweetheart."

She guessed that they had been talking about her for some reason but shrugged off the thought. Of course they talked about her. After all that's what parents did all the time, talked about their kids. She felt warm and happy as she sat down to eat her breakfast, life was oh so good.

The small television in the kitchen was on and she saw an image of Ben flicker on to the screen. She stopped and stared at it then signalled for her mother to turn up the volume. She had obviously missed some of what the newscaster was saying but was in time to hear that Ben, after struggling to survive, had died in hospital the previous evening. The headmaster of her school was pictured saying, during a brief interview, that Ben had been a model student and that the thoughts and prayers of all the teachers and pupils of the school would go out to his parents at this sad time. The local police chief said that the circumstances prior to his death were suspicious and an investigation was ongoing, and they appealed for witnesses to come forward, even if they thought the information they had was insignificant.

She arranged her face to a sad profile and pushed her breakfast away from her. "Oh Mum, oh Dad, how awful. Poor poor Ben," she cried, as inside her she danced a jig. He had tried to get the better of her and had come unstuck and she hoped he had suffered in the process. She cried for her parents' benefit and gave a polished performance.

Chapter 22
Recovery and Revenge

The autumn term came and went and she buckled down to the mock exams and swimming schedules. None of the students challenged her to her face about her relationship with Ben and one or two of them had even given her sympathy which she lapped up.

She had got into the habit of going around to Ben's house and though the relationship was strained at first she worked really hard at it and managed to wend her way into the family and be invited to attend the funeral.

She arrived at Ben's house bright and early and watched his mother swing between sadness and elation that the day was finally here. She helped his mother put the final touches to her dress suit and pinned on a brooch before they moved out to the waiting cars.

She dressed in a bright yellow trouser suit that showed her figure to perfection, telling everyone who asked that it was Ben's favourite colour when, in reality, she hadn't the faintest idea what his favourite colour was and couldn't care less anyway. She noticed that there were a few reporters outside the church and she managed to get into a lot of shots without seeming to be trying to do so.

His mother had asked her to give a talk about him seeing as she was his last known girlfriend but she refused saying she wasn't confident enough in front of all those people, and adding that she had only felt confident when Ben was around to support her. Even as she was saying it, she wondered if she was pushing her luck too far with such a sickly comment but it seemed to be accepted. Now as she sat in the church, listening to what she could only describe as a lot of drivel, she wished she had got up and said something, at least it would stop her from being so bored. She had noticed that there weren't any flowers, apart from buttonholes, which seemed a stark omission until she was told that Ben's mother had specifically asked for donations to be sent to the hospital that had fought to save him. She quite liked this idea and stored it away in her memory to add to her notes.

The church was packed, mostly with sixth formers from school who had been given compassionate leave to attend. She wondered why so many were there when most of them would hardly have known him. Then her thoughts drifted to her own funeral and she decided that she would include people who didn't know her when she was alive. After all it would boost the numbers and give her greater kudos.

She started to fidget, feeling eyes boring into the back of her head, but willed herself not to turn around to see who it was. After all she had dressed in a bright colour to stand out, she wanted to be noticed. She realised that the feelings flooding her were not those that came from kind thoughts. Someone out there was giving her the evil eye.

At long last it was time to file out and she got up with the family holding the mother's arm as if to give her support. As she walked slowly down the aisle, she perused the crowd but no one person stood out. She noticed Byron and his friends towards the back of the church but thought that they were too far away from her for her to feel their threat as strongly as she had.

The reception was packed and though she tried hard to keep away from Byron she seemed to keep bumping into him and his pals. The last time she had tried to sweep by him he had leant forward and whispered in her ear, "Fancy a quickie?" She had gone to slap his face but he had easily caught her swinging arm and given her a peck on the check at which she coloured up momentarily feeling embarrassed and confused. She roughly pulled her arm away and swept off in the direction of the toilets with the comment, "See you by the green bins," following her. She nearly stopped but decided to carry on as if she hadn't heard it, fuming that they were laughing at her, making fun of her.

At long last it was over and she returned home with Ben's family, hugged each of them in turn then left for home insisting that she was all right to catch the bus on her own, she was quite capable of looking after herself. As she got off of the bus and turned into a deserted side street, she didn't see the dark shadows that came out of the alley and dragged her into it; everything was a blur. A pad or something like one was thrust into her face and within seconds she had passed out and therefore didn't see or feel her lower clothes being stripped off her and the repeated forceful rapes. She was found in the early morning huddled up against the alley wall and before long she was transported to hospital and, because her injuries were so severe, kept under sedation.

She awoke in a hospital bed attached to a drip which she idly watched for a time as she became more and more aware of her surroundings. She suddenly screamed and tried to pull the drip from her arm but a nurse, alerted by her screaming, prevented her from doing so and almost immediately she stopped struggling and fell back into a troubled sleep mumbling incoherently.

The next time she was aware she saw her parents standing by her bed and felt her mother stroking her arm. Their faces were distraught and although they tried hard to put on a brave face they failed miserably as they watched their beautiful daughter struggling to make sense of things.

The days and weeks passed and she began to ask questions about why she was in hospital, had she had an accident or something. She was initially surprised at how weak she felt and was initially ashamed to be given a walking frame to help her build up her strength. She moaned and groaned and put up resistance to no avail as she was encouraged to follow a recovery programme.

She was eventually told about the rape by a doctor with her parents present but, as she had no memory of it, she refused to believe them. When the doctor told her that she would no longer be able to have children she laughed outright and said she didn't want to have any anyway. She started seeing a woman counsellor but at first refused to talk to her as she didn't think that talking to a total stranger would do her any good. She knew and accepted by now that she had been raped multiple times and that because of the severity of the attack she would no longer be able to have children but, to her, this was a blessing. During a counselling session she suddenly grew angry. If she didn't want children that was her choice but now, she couldn't have them so she had no choice at all. Try as she might she could not remember anything at all about the rape; she kept coming up against a brick wall. She could remember going to a funeral and leaving Ben's house and getting on a bus but after that remembered nothing at all except an overwhelming feeling of panic.

Physically she made good progress but mentally she was in denial, she could not remember being raped therefore she deduced she hadn't been, even though everyone told her she had been and thought she had accepted the fact. She couldn't relax as her mind kept castigating her. It was all a nasty plot meant to keep her in hospital. Yes, her body was covered in bruises, especially the inside of her thighs, but that just meant she was beaten up by some pervert. The police interviewed her in the presence of her parents but she had nothing to tell them so she told them nothing.

One day she started screaming and couldn't stop and was eventually sedated to help her rest. Her parents were called in and it was decided that she should return to Ward 3 as they had the expertise to aid her recovery.

When she woke in Ward 3, she immediately recognised where she was and felt safe. She used the frame provided to walk to the doorway but had to return to her bed as weakness threatened to overtake her. She was astounded, it had only been four or five steps to the door that had sapped her energy. What had happened to the years of physical training?

The counsellor she had seen in the ward continued to give her daily visits and, to her surprise, she began to look forward to them.

Sometimes she spoke to the counsellor and sometimes she listened to her and it was through these sessions that she gradually realised that she was in denial and had tried to bury what had actually taken place. She cried buckets the first time she admitted out loud that she had been raped but it took a lot more sessions for her to be able to accept the facts and try to move on. She clearly remembered getting off a bus, then the feeling of panic though why she did not know, the memories stayed locked away.

She was angry at the people who had done this to her. How dare they violate her! The sessions seemed to be getting nowhere now as she poured out her anger in the form of vile threats but eventually she moved on. The people who had done this to her weren't going to win, she couldn't let them drag her down but the stumbling block for her was that she didn't know who her attackers were or how many there had been. Progress was being made though it was slow. Learning to forgive people she didn't know, at least out loud to the counsellor, was difficult.

Her parents visited her daily throughout all this time, whilst Alfie was left with a babysitter, and attended the counselling sessions with her permission. She felt removed from them, as if they belonged to someone else, but she wanted them to bring her baby brother so as she could be distracted from the intense sessions.

Christmas came and went and by now she could walk without the frame and make it to the games room as she had decided to call it. She looked in vain for the boy she had seen there years previously but many of the staff were new and didn't know of whom she was asking about. She thought about him a lot as she sat in the games room doing puzzles. She remembered she had even written to him for a while until she had suddenly stopped writing. She thought she had a lot to thank him for as he had shown her the inner workings of the system.

She suddenly stopped doing the puzzle and sat upright. How come she could remember so clearly something that had happened years ago yet not be able to recall anything about her attack? She closed her eyes and concentrated, not allowing herself to avoid facing the truth, she would remember, she would remember and suddenly she did.

She could see herself getting off the bus as if it was actually happening. She could actually see the pavement as she stepped down on to it. She walked a few steps to a corner then turned into a side road, then felt a surge of panic in her chest, then a feeling of having her face smothered. Try as she might she couldn't breathe, and that smell, that awful smell. What was it? She put her hands to her mouth trying to breathe as silent tears coursed down her face. The memory became clearer, someone had smothered her face from behind her before she was raped, that was why she couldn't see him or her. Try as she might she couldn't see anyone and suddenly she started biting her forearms and screaming obscenities.

She spent a couple of days under heavy sedation before she was stable enough to go back into the games room and mix with the other patients. Once upon a time she would have thought they were all loonies and kept well out of the way but now she realised they all had genuine reasons for being there. She laughed at herself for going soft, feeling that the place was getting to her. She carefully examined her new memories with the counsellor until she could finally admit that she wasn't at fault. She had been anesthetized and raped. It wasn't that she was refusing to remember what had happened to her, she was out of it when the rapes occurred and therefore would have no memories to aid recall.

She was allowed home for a few daily visits, then at last she was allowed home for good although she still had to keep up the counselling sessions.

Walking into her own front door felt strange. As she took her coat off Alfie came crawling out of the front room and grinned at her and suddenly she felt better. She sat down on the floor with him much to his delight and played peek-a-boo games and tickly spider.

All of a sudden, she tired and went up to her room. Everything was as she had left it all those months ago, familiar yet strange. She sat on the dressing table stool and brushed her hair over and over watching herself in the mirror as she did so. She had been violated but it was all her fault. She had made herself vulnerable by travelling home on her own but someone was going to pay dearly. There were people out there who had used and abused her and they were laughing at her. She could even pass them in the street and not know them but they would know her. It could even be boys from her school watching her knowingly as she walked past. A thought suddenly occurred to her, supposing photographs had been taken, not of her being naked but of someone in the process of actually raping her, perhaps even a video was taken. She was horrified of these possibilities and tried to calm herself down using the strategies she had been taught but it took a long time. The police had no clues apart from various semen samples and no witnesses had come forward.

She didn't leave her room unless it was to go to the bathroom or have her meals and frequently snapped at her parents when they tried to tempt her out of her room. Eventually she got into the habit of walking to the park with her mother when she took Alfie out for a walk in his pushchair and began to relax back into a home life. Alfie was doing his best to walk and she delighted in him trying to maintain his balance then take his first few steps.

Her first few days back to school after the Easter break took every ounce of strength but she did it, she kept her head down and worked hard. Dinner time was difficult because she didn't feel able enough to be able to swim, so she buried her head in a book to pass the time.

Every morning she had to steel herself to go to school and every evening she would collapse in bed exhausted, but she got into the routine and finally began to feel better until she finally felt strong enough to start her swimming sessions again although, by her usual standards, they were soft sessions.

One evening she returned home to hear Alfie grizzling and went into the kitchen to see why as he was usually such a happy little chap. His little cheeks were bright red and his cheeks were tear-stained. Teething her mum said. She felt sorry for him and tried to cheer him up but eventually went up to her room and closed the door and put her earphones on so that she couldn't hear him.

Later that evening she quietly slipped out of the house and, dressed all in black clothing, melted into the night. She had been checking out the red-light district approximately four miles from where she lived and knew the girls who ran that edge of the district by sight. She waited until the girls were busy with a client then stripped off her hoodie to display a skimpy top which accentuated her ample cleavage. She swayed back and forth keeping an eye out for the girls to return and was rewarded when a car pulled up and the window wound down.

She had no idea what to say and hadn't actually given it much thought but mumbled something and got into the back seat of the car which quickly picked up speed as it pulled away then pulled into a murky alleyway a few minutes later. The quietness, apart from the clicking of a cooling engine when the ignition was turned off, was overwhelming. A train rushed by over the nearby bridge then the man spoke. "What happened to the regular?"

She said the first thing that came into her brain which seemed to satisfy him. "I don't know, busy fucking someone I suppose."

He laughed then stared at her through the central mirror "Ok, I'm ready, you can start."

Start what, she thought, I can't do anything if I'm sitting in the back seat. Perhaps he wants me to get in the front with him. She wrinkled her nose in disgust at what that might mean but opened the car door as if to get out.

"What you doing? Close the door," he shouted and she immediately slammed the door closed as hard as she could so that he would know she had complied with his wishes then he said, "Same price as always?"

She had no idea so said the first figure that came into her head. "£30."

"£20 and not a penny more."

"£30 and not a penny less."

He was quiet for a while then said, "I'm telling you bird, this had better be worth it or you'll be sorry," as he handed the money over to her.

"Go on, start," he said then gave her some clues as to what he wanted her to say. "Tell me what a naughty boy I've been and what I can expect to happen when my father gets home, go on tell me," his voice rising as he finished speaking.

She started slowly at first. "Just look what you've done. Haven't I told you to leave it alone more times than I can count."

"Yes, yes, that's it, go on, go on."

She slipped into role play. "Well I can't save you now even if I wanted to. You just wait till your father gets home and gives you the good hiding you deserve." The man in the front of the car was becoming more and more animated, his breathing sounding harsh and she realised that he was masturbating as she spoke to him. She continued, "There's no getting away with it this time, young man, your father will be very very angry with you and will pull down your trousers, pull you over his knee and give your bare bottom the spanking of its life."

She was enjoying herself immensely. She could see at first-hand how an audience, (the man), responded to her subtle manipulations as she called it.

The man's breathing was becoming quicker and his movements more animated so she knew he was getting close to ejaculation. "He will smack your bottom so hard that you won't be able to sit down for a fortnight, you hear me. You will be wriggling and screaming at him to stop. You will keep telling him how sorry you are but it won't do you any good at all. He won't stop until you hurt so much you can't bear it any more, and even then he might continue."

The timing was perfect and the man climaxed, shuddering and groaning with the effort in the front seat. As his moans died away, she raised herself up and looped a tie around his neck, crossed the ends then fell back into the seat bringing up her legs to rest behind where his shoulders would be and exerted as much pressure as she could, pulling hard with her arms whilst pushing as hard with her legs.

By the time the man realised what was happening it was already too late although he did try to live.

All was quiet as if listening. She climbed out of the car and almost reverently closed the door, then walked under the railway bridge and pulled on her black hoodie, slipped her gloves and the tie in her pouch, blew a kiss at the car then ran home.

Once indoors she reviewed what had happened to see if she could improve on her performance. After all, that's just what it was, a performance. It had only taken her thirty minutes to run home and she realised that at last she was getting back to full strength again. She had initially been caught out expecting to have hands on and thanked the man for giving her an easy introduction into what life on the streets was like. She didn't envy the people who lived that way and wondered briefly how they had come to be in that situation in the first place.

She suddenly realised what she was doing, sympathising with people she didn't know and shook her head to rid herself of the thoughts she was having then lay down and thought through the past evening evaluating her performance in the minutest detail to see if she could improve in any way. She then thought back to when her dad had punished her and how she had later masturbated whilst thinking about it and realised that she wasn't the only one who got sexual gratification through punishment. She had actually helped someone else go out in a blaze of glory.

She heard Alfie crying and one of her parents getting up to attend to him. Poor little sod was teething and she didn't envy him one iota but thought it strange that no matter how painful it was you couldn't remember it being so when you got older. She heard her mum singing a lullaby to soothe Alfie, little did she know she was soothing her daughter to sleep as well.

Chapter 23
Observations

Her results from the mock exams had been good by anybody else's standards but not by hers so she really applied herself to get up to the standard she was used to. She spent time after school studying with her maths tutor as Alfie's constant grizzling at home distracted her and she found herself ready to scream at him to shut the fuck up.

She found time to go to the mother and baby classes held locally and looked in amazement at all the different mothers, some of them a lot older than her own mum! She watched Alfie toddle around chatting happily to himself and kept getting up to defend him when another child snatched something from him or pushed him over, although her mum told her to leave him alone; he had to learn to socialize by himself.

At last she could stand it no longer and left telling her mum she needed to go home to study whilst thinking, socialize, socialize, more like bullying. A couple of times she had come within seconds of giving a child a resounding slap and knew she had to get out of there double-quick before she blew it. She wandered into the local park and on the spur of the moment took a boat out on the lake. Her co-ordination was good and before long she was in the middle of the lake, alone at last. She sat still listening to the lapping of the water and watched the ripples as she ran her hand through it, so cool, so clear. The gentle rocking of the boat made her sleepy so she pulled the oars into the boat and lowered herself to the base of the boat and leant back against the wooden seat and soon she was sound asleep.

Her dream was vivid, she was in a thick pea-soup of a fog and, dropping down to her knees she found that it was floating a foot above the pavement. She crawled on her hands and knees to a brick wall and watched the feet of people passing by feeling how weird everything was. Suddenly the fog dropped to ground level and for all she could see she may well have been blind. She suddenly felt small and insecure and screamed for someone to find her, help her and awoke to find that she was still in the rowing boat which had somehow managed to earth itself against the bank under a huge weeping willow. She scrambled out and made her way home worried about the dream but not sure why she was, then had second thoughts and detoured to the library and looked up dreams and their meanings but found nothing to salve her anxieties.

Her mum was already home by the time she got there with Alfie fast asleep in his pram in the garden. She went out to look at him then continued down the garden to the shed to check that no insects were trapped in it. Her dad kept moaning at her for keeping the shed window open as he had some bedding plants on the go but, to his intense irritation, it made no difference.

She went into the kitchen and began to prepare the vegetables for dinner whilst watching her mum kneading pastry prior to making a pie. She turned suddenly to her mother and said, "Does it matter that I won't be able to give you any grandchildren now?"

Her mother stopped kneading, momentarily taken aback by the remark out of the blue then responded, "Of course not, darling. Why? Whatever put that thought in your head?"

"Isn't that what all parents want, to be grandparents?"

"I don't know, darling, maybe some do, maybe some don't. I can only say that it doesn't matter to us."

"Doesn't matter because Alfie will have kids when he grows up so you still have a chance to be grandparents."

"Oh, darling, it's early days to talk about the future like that, Alfie is only a baby."

"Supposing he can't have children, what will you do then?"

"Enough. This conversation is going nowhere. We love you both the way you are and that's all there is to it. We will deal with what happens when it happens."

She opened her mouth to make another comment then saw the set of her mum's mouth and knew that, for the time being at least, this conversation was closed. She put the kitchen radio on and before long they were both humming along to the current pop music.

After dinner her mum helped her to braid her hair and she found herself actually feeling quite fond of her mother whom she was watching in her dressing table mirror as she stood behind her with hairgrips in her mouth. She examined the feeling and decided she quite liked it.

After the evening meal she went up to her room, then soon after ten o'clock she slipped out into the streets dressed in her black hoodie and leggings and jogged along the empty pavements not sure what she was looking for or where she was going. She climbed the railings into the local park where earlier she had taken a boat out and sat at the base of a tree for a while enjoying the space and solitude. After a while she could make out talking nearby and realised she was not alone. She crawled slowly on her hands and knees towards the sounds trying to see who was there and then made out a couple who were busy having sex whilst chatting away to each other.

She remembered the only time she had seen people having sex was when she had seen Clive in the girls' changing room but he had been standing up. These people were lying down and she had never watched people lying down making love. She settled down to watch and make notes. She was surprised at how long they were taking; she had thought that it would last only a few minutes but the boy had been bouncing merrily away on top of the girl for the last twenty minutes or so. They were obviously enjoying themselves and had obviously, so she thought, done this before. She wondered what they would do if they suddenly found out someone was watching them perform and almost shouted out to them but managed to bite her lip. Supposing someone had watched her when she was having sex, making love as people called it. Would she be devastated or would she play to an audience? She remembered that Byron had said something about her being watched the first time she had sex with James at that wedding reception, said something about checking the room out first. She realised her mind was drifting off and pulled herself back into the moment. She was part of an audience who had gone to see a play, maybe Romeo and Juliette, and thrilled at sharing their experience, sharing what they were doing and thought that this must be what audiences would feel when she was on stage.

The tempo of the couple suddenly changed and an air of urgency hung about them. As soon as this happened, she silently rose to her feet and edged closer, gently distributing her weight on each footfall. The couple were not communicating in any known language now, only the sounds of people climbing to ecstasy, however brief. Grunts, groans, gasps with an occasional, "Oh yes, yes," pierced the atmosphere.

She was standing right beside them now but, so lost in their mission were they that they had no idea she was there. Balancing on one leg she carefully lifted the other over the bouncing couple and placed it down on the other side of them. Still she remained undetected. She looked down at the now frantic action between her legs and waited, and waited. Suddenly the boy shouted out something as he climaxed and this was her cue to act. She reached forward and cupped one hand under his chin whilst the other hand was placed on top of his head and suddenly lifted and twisted his head sharply thereby breaking his neck. The boy was dead before his body landed on top of the girl but his penis still managed to squirt the last of his semen into his girlfriend.

As soon as she had twisted his neck she had let go and stepped over the couple in one flowing movement, and had moved swiftly away listening out for realisation to hit the girlfriend but there was no sound for a few minutes and it was not until she was climbing the railings surrounding the park that she heard screams piercing the night. Some lights came on in houses surrounding the park but by this time she was streets away running smoothly. On reaching home she glanced around, then quietly went indoors stripping off her top and placing it in the washing machine. She looked out of the kitchen window into the black garden for a moment and the darkness stared back at her. Some moths were outside the window fluttering to get in to the light so she turned off the kitchen light and went upstairs to bed.

She thought about the couple in the park and mentally thanked them for increasing her knowledge for when she would become an actress, then settled down to a dreamless sleep.

The following morning her mum was in one of her disorganised moods, at sixes and sevens she called it, so she offered to take Alfie out for a walk to the park to give her mum time to sort herself out. When she reached the park, she found a small crowd of people gathered outside the gates and the way barred by a policeman and lots of police tape stretched around the entrance, some of which had come unstuck and was waving merrily in the morning breeze. She listened to the gossip of people who had no idea what had happened but were filling in the gaps anyway. They all knew that there had been a murder but nobody knew who. There had, apparently, been heartrending screams (some with vivid imaginations said blood curdling screams) in the early hours of the morning and soon after the police were seen bringing the park keeper to open the gates, and not long after that an ambulance was called. Those were the facts; the rest was gossip.

Alfie wriggled in his pushchair wanting to get out and into the park and screamed his frustration as she turned and walked away from it, his arm stretched back pointing to it, his head craning round the side of the pushchair as they walked away. "Park, park."

She took him for a walk by the canal and for a while played Pooh Sticks with him, delighting in his obvious joy then bought him an ice cream and returned home to find it neat and tidy and back to normal. She lifted the sleepy Alfie from his pushchair and put him in the baby pen in the garden making sure he had enough shade, then got out the reclining garden chair and sat beside him watching him as he slept.

She dreamt about the fog again, another pea-souper. She could actually see bits floating about in the dark grey mist. She felt she was choking, she couldn't breathe, she was ripping at her clothing, too tight around her chest her pounding heart beating louder and louder until it was all she could hear. She was going to die she knew it; she was going to die and no one would know, she would be lost forever in the choking fog. She then saw her body rotting on the pavement as people walked by within inches of her complaining of the awful smell. She screamed for someone, anyone to find her, to help her as the mists closed around her then suddenly, she felt her mum's arm on her shoulder, shaking her, calling her name over and over again. She opened her eyes and saw her mum's worried face inches from her own and threw her arms around her, crying how much she loved her and thanking her for coming to her rescue.

Later in the kitchen she discussed the dream with her mum. What did it mean? It was the second time she had had this dream although this time it had moved on further, this time she was dead and rotting on the pavement as people walked by. Her mum was suitably horrified by the dream and held her daughter close and rocked her gently whilst crooning to her. At first she had gone to pull away but then she relaxed into her mother's arms and allowed herself to be soothed.

Over dinner that evening she told her parents about what had gone on at the park gate when she had tried to take Alfie in there and her mother said that it was no wonder she had had such an awful dream with a murder happening within miles of their doorstep. They put on the radio and listened to the news and learnt that a body had been found in the local park and a female had been taken in for questioning. They looked at each other in horror. What was wrong with the world? What on earth was going on?

Chapter 24
A Thief and a Cheat!

She returned home from school worn out and wanted to do nothing but collapse on her bed, so was less than pleased when her mother asked her to take Alfie out in his pushchair and go into town and buy a baby gate to put at the base of the stairs, which Alfie had developed a fascination for and insisted on climbing at every opportunity. She changed from her school uniform and moments later was pushing Alfie along the road towards the bus stop with Alfie chatting away quite happily and pointing to various things along the way.

The ride into town seemed to take ages with the amount of traffic there was about and she was pleased when they finally reached their stop and got off the bus.

A group of people on skate boards rolled past just as she stepped down and bumped into her and the pushchair knocking it over, but didn't stop. She heard their laughter as they continued down the road as she righted the chair and soothed a frightened Alfie. She decided to get him a lolly to help him calm down and found that her purse had been snatched from her bag. She looked around her to see if it had dropped on the pavement and luckily found her keys in the gutter but of her purse there was no sign.

She slowly made her way home wishing she had kept her bus pass separate from her purse and cursing the group of people who had bumped into her. How could she have been such an easy target? She castigated herself for not being on her guard, whilst at the same time knowing that everybody was vulnerable sometimes, even her.

When she arrived home she told her mother what had happened and even cried a few tears in the process, which, to her surprise, were genuine tears. She had been made, in her eyes, to look a fool and somebody somewhere was going to pay the price.

The local paper was full of the local murder and even had a picture of where it had taken place but offered no new evidence. Frustrated she threw the paper down and searched through the daily paper looking to see if the man she had strangled in his car had been found but there was nothing. She screamed in agitation. What was wrong with people? Why hadn't he been found yet? Mind you she didn't envy the person or people who did find him. The hot balmy days would ensure that he smelt like a sewer, or worse. She didn't know what rotting dead people smelt like but she was sure it would not be pleasant.

Perhaps, she thought, the police had found him but were keeping the discovery quiet in order to flush her out. Well, she was not going to fall for that one, no way was she stupid enough to be caught!

Her bedroom door slowly opened, then Alfie toddled through the door. "Alfie, what are you doing upstairs?" she asked him as she scooped him up and carried him struggling downstairs. Her mother was cleaning out the refrigerator and she was asked if she would give Alfie his evening bath and bottle and settle him for the night. To her surprise she thoroughly enjoyed bath time, with Alfie screaming in delight as he tried to catch the bubbles she blew for him. Later she sat nursing him as he sucked contentedly on his bottle and then she started singing to him. Every now and then he would reach up his hands towards her face and try to chuckle even though the bottle was still in his mouth. At last he fell asleep in her arms and she took him to his room and laid him down gently into his cot and kissed him goodnight. For some reason she felt fulfilled and full of love for him.

School the following day brought new challenges to her. She had been called out of her class to go and see the school nurse and had bumped into Byron on the way and all her old feelings for him had flooded back. She behaved like a besotted little schoolgirl instead of a mature sixth form pupil. She had worked hard to push him from her mind and had really thought she was doing well but this close contact with him showed her that she wasn't doing well at all. With her face flushing she stammered apologies accepting the blame for the collision even though they were both at fault and quickly made her way to the nurse's office, where the nurse gave her a form to take home to get permission to have a vaccination. She thrust the form in her bag and returned to class.

From that moment it seemed that Byron was everywhere she was. She couldn't avoid him and wondered if he was getting in her face deliberately. She told herself over and over again that she hated him, despised him, he was not fit enough to clean her boots all the while knowing that if he gave her the slightest inclination of being interested in her she would be there in an instant.

She punished herself with an intense swimming session and almost gave up on the last length whilst pushing herself to the extreme. She had decided that in future, to test herself even further, that she would finish her swimming session in the deep end, thinking that when she was tired she would have to fight and overcome the tiredness in order not to drown. She held onto the side rail panting with the effort she had put into the session but still unable to escape from her thoughts. Should she kill him? she wondered, for if he was dead then she could get on with her life, and she had not forgotten that she owed him and his friends big time for humiliating her in the pool that time. It had been a long time ago and she had almost forgotten but now everything was fresh in her mind. Something niggled her as she showered and changed then she had it. He had a younger sister. She could pay him back through her. She wondered if some of the other boys had siblings; it was time for her to do some homework.

She was the first one to finish the maths exam and be allowed out of the room and was thankful for the empty corridors as she moved through the school. As she was passing the year 9 cloakroom, she glanced behind her, then started examining the names on the pegs until she found the one she wanted, then started searching coat pockets and transferring the contents. When she was satisfied she had done enough she left and travelled home.

The bell rang signalling the end of the day and the pupils spewed out of the classrooms to collect their coats and go home. Sally put her hands in her pockets to check her keys were still there and found her pockets empty and soon other children found that they too had items missing. Their teacher came out of the class to see why the children hadn't gone home yet just as Mirelle put her hands in her pockets and pulled out items that weren't hers. Sally saw her keys in Mirelle's hands and said, "You've got my keys you thief, give them back," as she snatched them. Other children found that their possessions were in Mirelle's hands and started shouting, "Thief, thief, thief," until they saw their teacher and became silent.

The teacher looked at Mirelle and asked her what she had to say for herself but she was in shock and although she tried to speak nothing came out of her mouth. Sally said, "She's a thief, she stole my keys," and other children joined in to pointing out their possessions in Mirelle's out-stretched hands.

The teacher sent the children back into the classroom and sent the others home apart from one who took a message to the headteacher.

One by one the children identified their possessions then Mirelle finally found her voice. "It wasn't me, I was with you all the time. I didn't do anything, I just found things in my pocket."

Mirelle's parents were requested to come into the school where they found their distraught daughter. It was decided, after a long discussion that no further action would be taken as all the items had been returned to the rightful owners but she received a severe warning.

From that moment on her life changed for the worse as former friends shunned her. She spent all of her time alone and was even dropped from the school hockey team as pupils refused to play with her in the team. Everywhere she looked she felt that people were talking about her and she began to make excuses to avoid going to school until one day she found herself standing by the canal watching the brown water rush by and simply collapsed into it and was swept along and out of sight, her body being recovered two days later by a lock.

The school was in shock at the discovery of her body and suddenly her former classmates began to feel ashamed of themselves and wished that they had been kinder. Unfortunately all the wishing in the world was not going to make a difference; she was dead and that was all there was to it.

At the same time the school bag belonging to Byron was found to contain copies of an upcoming test and he was suspended whilst investigations were carried out despite his protests of innocence. He claimed that the papers had been planted on him and that he didn't need to cheat, he knew all the answers anyway. His sister had been branded a thief and now it looked like he was a cheat. The family weren't having a good time!

One person was though, the person who had gone through the coat pockets to exchange the contents, the person who had put the papers in Byron's bag and left it where it could be discovered. She was amazed at the complexities of people, of how only doing one little thing such as taking things from pupils' pockets could start a ripple that could end in a death. She hugged herself with glee and swung around her room laughing and thinking, that will teach them to make fun of me, as she suddenly laughed out loud. Boy, oh boy, did she feel good.

The daily paper named the person who had been found dead in a car and appealed for witnesses and she rolled his name around her tongue wondering if she could go to his funeral, then decided she wouldn't as she had been to enough funerals during her lifetime and had learned all she needed to know. The only funeral she needed to attend now was her own but first she needed to become famous then she would be all set.

The whole school attended Mirelle's funeral and her parents were overwhelmed by the multitude of flowers and the soft-spoken words of comfort. Byron stood beside his parents and she was shocked at the change in him; gone was the cheerful friendly young man replaced by a haunted young man who couldn't look anyone in the eye. She decided then and there that she was over him, he was boring, she needed someone new and exciting!

At last the exams were all over and it was the last day of school. She could hardly believe it and suddenly, for a brief moment, she didn't want to leave as she looked around her at the familiar surroundings. However this feeling soon passed and she was leaping around in celebration with the rest of the students. There were hugs and promises to keep in touch even from people she didn't know and then at last she was on her own. She walked past a corner supermarket then, on second thoughts went back and looked around and bought herself a drink and some sweets, although sweets were not usually her thing and continued the journey home.

Alfie didn't like the baby gate one bit and screamed his protests as he gripped and shook the steadfast gate then eventually gave up and went in search of another stimulus.

Her mother was busy hanging the washing out, so she helped by holding the washing basket so her mother didn't have to keep bending then went up to her room. Something was niggling her but try as she might she couldn't pin it down. There was a loud clatter from downstairs and Alfie started to yell so she got herself up to see what was the matter and found that Alfie had managed to pull the baby gate on top of himself. She picked him up and checked him over but found no visible injuries so surmised he had just frightened himself. She took him into the garden to hand over to her mother who was busy chatting to a neighbour and explained what had happened before returning indoors.

She lay on her bed wondering what people looked like when they had drowned thinking that they definitely would not look as beautiful as fish. Drowning was another form of suffocation she thought. Amazing how many forms of death ended in suffocation of one sort or another.

Her mother called up the stairs to ask her if she would mind going to the shops for her and to take Alfie with her. Her first thought was to refuse but then she thought she had nothing else to do so why not and twenty minutes later she was in and out of the local shops with Alfie demanding this and that at the top of his voice.

With the shopping finished she made her way home wondering what she was going to do with her life now she had left school. If she told her parents that she wanted to work in a mortuary they would be shocked and horrified. She could just hear them now telling her that she was throwing her life away and she amused herself for a while imagining she had put her life in a plastic bag and was chucking out with the rubbish. Sometimes she wondered if she was weird. Did other people her age have the same sort of thoughts that she did? But she then decided so what if she was weird, everybody else could go jump.

Once back home she settled Alfie then started unpacking the shopping and putting it away. For some reason she thought of Aunty Jean although she had been dead for ages. She wondered if she would end up like her, lonely and frightened to go out but easily manipulated to do things against her will. Was she going mad? Was Aunty Jean mad? Why couldn't she get her out of her head?

She saw her parents off on their fortnight's holiday at the coast and celebrated by making a mess everywhere she went. It was so good not to have to clear up after herself or put her dirty washing in the bin. She got up late and went to bed even later and it was only when she ran out of milk and cereal that she realised the honeymoon was over. She had just two days to get the house back in some sort of order before her parents returned. As luck would have it, when she decided to do the washing the weather decided it wasn't going to play ball and chucked it down so, on top of everything else, she had to go to the laundrette to get the clothes dried although she had to do some fast talking as the launderette didn't usually allow people to only dry their clothes.

She finally got the house neat and tidy and the only tell-tale sign of a last-minute clean-up was the number of black bags put out for collection. She prepared a meal for her parents, then went into the garden and fell asleep in the lounger which luckily was in the shade, the weather having decided to be nice again.

The fog was smothering her, choking her, and this time when she fell to the ground there was no clear space beneath it. She had a scarf over her mouth to filter out the debris floating in the fog but she was gagging as lumps of slimy greenish phlegm appeared out of the dark grey mist and seemed to head straight for her mouth!

Her movement to avoid the phlegm entering her mouth caused her to fall off the lounger and she awoke with a start just as her parents appeared at the kitchen door. She hadn't realised how much she had missed them until she saw them and got up and hugged them both. Alfie wasn't interested in hugging; he wanted some water play so she sorted a bowl out for him and the three of them watched him.

Her exam results were all that she could wish for and she was offered a place at the university she had wanted to go to. Pity it was at the other end of the country but for some reason unknown to her she had always felt drawn to Scotland and now she had a chance to go there. Everything was a whirlwind as arrangements were made and instructions given, though they mainly went in one ear and out the other. During her last week home she went shopping by herself and bought a present for her mum, a nice little locket.

"What's the matter, daring? You seem preoccupied," observed her mum at the dinner table and although she shook her head and gave a brief smile to show that everything was all right it wasn't. Something was wrong, badly wrong. She had slipped up somewhere but for the life of her she couldn't think what. She offered to clear up after dinner and do the washing up so as to keep herself preoccupied saying it was maybe the last time she would have to do it for a long time. Her parents looked at each other then, thankfully, went out into the back garden with Alfie and left her to it. She watched them out of the kitchen window for a while then went up to her room and opened her bedroom window. Her suitcases were already packed and lined up by the wardrobe door. This was going to be her last week in the home she had known since she was a baby but she felt neither excited or sad. Her world would be perfect if only she could work out what was worrying her.

Chapter 25
Punishment to Fit the Crime!

It must have been the middle of the night when she suddenly sat up and said, "Aunty Jean," then suddenly everything fell into place and she knew what she had done. She had been so busy congratulating herself, patting herself on the back and thinking she was so clever when the only thing she had done was prove herself to be a fool, a stupid fool. She gritted her teeth and bunched her hands into fists and screwed up her face whilst making soft growling noises in her throat.

Pride before a fall, more like pride before a fool. Oh how could she be so stupid? She had sent a parcel to her distant cousin who was wheelchair bound and although the address was right she had addressed the parcel for the attention of Aunty Jean and, as if that was not enough she had sent sesame biscuits to her distant cousin when it was not her who had the allergy, it was Aunty Jean and she was already dead! Her distant cousin might not even open the parcel she had sent thinking there had been some mistake and that it was for someone else. What if she phoned her mum and told her about it? Her mum would recognise the name, Aunty Jean. What then?

She decided she should be punished for making such a grave mistake but what was to be her punishment? What was it that she detested that she would make herself do or do to herself even? She could go to the red-light district and give someone a blow-job. Her face wrinkled up in disgust, she couldn't do that, even if she was forced to, she couldn't do it but what then? How could she make sure that she would never make the same stupid mistake again?

She decided she would beat herself and, after she had locked her door and stripped naked, she took a thin belt out her bedroom drawer and wound it around her fist as she had seen her father do years before, and stood in the middle of her room the belt dangling from her hand, feeling frightened yet excited. How many times should she do it to teach herself a lesson she would never forget, how many? She thought that five strokes would be enough, then shook her head and doubled it to ten then doubled it again, twenty strokes, that should do it.

At the contact of the first stroke across her back she almost cried out and hurriedly got a pair of socks from her drawer and stuffed them in her mouth and bit down on them as hard as she could as she swung the belt again then again, then again. The pain was unbearable and she begged herself to stop telling herself that she had been punished enough, that she forgave herself for making the mistake and she breathed a sigh of relief as the hand holding the belt dropped to her side then suddenly, as she was relaxing, it became animated and swung backwards and forwards across the front of her delivering half a dozen vicious lashes to her back and buttocks. She was shivering with pain and briefly took the sodden socks from her mouth to regain her breath. She called herself a coward, a wimp, a waste of space, she was only halfway through her punishment. She promised herself that if she stopped again she would add ten more strokes although her brain screamed out that it was too much she couldn't do it. She widened her stance and stared at her reflection in the glass pitying the wimp she saw there then. Finding resolve from somewhere she stuffed the socks back into her mouth and delivered ten lashes to her body without stopping, then dropped the belt to the floor and sank to her knees as she wet herself. She had never in her life felt such awful pain, even when she had rigorously stuck to a harsh swimming schedule, she had never experienced pain. She keeled over onto her side and spat out the socks then lay in a foetal position whilst her body shuddered and shivered uncontrollably. She dragged herself to her bed and after many attempts managed to at last climb into it and cover herself up.

She slept late the following day and at first couldn't understand why it was so painful to move but then the memory of what she had done to herself flooded her mind and she felt ashamed. Nobody knew she had received a just punishment for her mistake, nobody had watched her suffering. She didn't have to mix with the family knowing they had heard her being punished and feel the shame of that. She tried to get out of bed but found she couldn't no matter how hard she tried; it was just too painful.

Her mother popped her head around the door. "Hello, lazy bones," she said, then stopped and came into the room and stood by the bed. "You look terrible, what's wrong?" as she placed the back of her hand against her daughter's sweaty brow. "You're burning up."

"I don't feel well," she managed in a small weak voice that wasn't stage-managed for in truth she felt dreadful, giddy, sick, hot, cold and aching all over.

"No getting up for you today, young lady," her mum said in a cheer-you-up sort of tone (which went straight over her head). "I'll bring you up a cold drink in a moment or two," and with that left the room.

The room spun and the bed felt like it was rocking up and down and she suddenly threw up all over her clothing and bedding but was too weak to do anything about it and just lay in the vomit as it slowly slid off her neck to soak into the surrounding bedding. She had no memory of her mother finding her in such a state and calling for her father to help, or of their horror as they helped her from her bed, thereby exposing the self-inflicted lash weals across her back and buttocks.

Eventually she was back in a clean bed though she wasn't aware of it and her parents talked in shocked tones of why their daughter would do such a thing to herself. She had seemed so happy just lately especially since getting a place at the university she had applied for. What were they doing wrong? Why was their daughter hurting herself in such a dreadful way? They held onto each other for support, neither of them able to come up with an answer but both of them feeling guilty although they couldn't work out what they had done wrong. They were just a normal family with just a normal family's problems. Surely this couldn't be happening to them. After all they were just ordinary and happy to be so.

As soon as she opened her eyelids she recognised where she was but was too weak to keep them open for long. It was nearly two weeks since she had been admitted to Ward 3 not that she was aware of being transferred there or of any of the subsequent treatments. In the brief moment she had had her eyes open she had noticed a drip tube by the bed and that image stayed in her head, gradually turning into a snake that slithered up her arm and gradually began to coil itself around her neck getting tighter and tighter. She could see its flickering tongue, could feel its bulging eyes on her as it slithered round and around her neck. She felt herself choking, felt her eyes bulging out of their sockets. She scrabbled at her neck to try and pull the snake away then, suddenly, it was gone as if it had never been.

Some weeks later she wandered along the passage to the games room and sat in the corner and watched the other inmates. She had been in the ward for nearly five weeks now and had relaxed into the familiar routine. She actually quite liked it there, she felt safe and beginning to come to terms with the fact that what she had done to herself was wrong. Nobody deserved to be punished like that. She thought back to the counselling session she had just come out of and the endless probing questions, thinking that although she quite liked the counsellor she was seeing she had to be careful as they were tricky people, seeming to ask perfectly ordinary questions to get her relaxed then suddenly asking her questions she did not know the answer to such as "Why do you feel the need to punish yourself?" and "What did you do to make you want to punish yourself in such a way?" She felt the questions were all the same just put together in a different way and prided herself that she was too smart to be caught out. She would tell them what they wanted to hear as long as it was nowhere near the truth.

She had nearly finished a thousand-piece jigsaw when one of the other inmates thrust it off the table and started cursing her for making the place untidy. In one swift move, without thinking, she rose to her feet, gripped the girl's ears and headbutted her in one swift movement, then sat down as the other inmate fell to the floor. She watched them take the girl out of the room but couldn't understand why she also was taken back to her room and locked in, so protested her innocence all the way to her room using the foulest language she could think of, managing to work herself up into a blinding rage in the process where reason had no place to be.

It was dark outside when she woke although the light was permanently on in her room. She thought back over what had happened and realised she had bitten the bullet, the girl had been a test for her, a chance to show how much she was progressing and she had blown it big time. She could see it all now, could actually watch the staged performance and see herself walking into the trap like an innocent. She decided she hated herself, she needed to be punished for being so stupid and this time it should be permanent, she didn't want to wake up feeling like she had the last time, she just couldn't go through that again. Although she was the innocent party to start with, she had responded with violence and needed to be punished, she hadn't started it but she had certainly finished it. She felt her rage building then realised what she was doing, she was playing their game not hers. The more she displayed childish tantrums the longer she would stay, and they were childish tantrums she was displaying without a doubt, the phrase 'it's not fair' being, to her, a typically childish response.

Little by little in her therapy sessions she began to express feelings about how she felt when her mum became pregnant, how she blamed the baby for nearly killing her mother. As the sessions continued she embroidered her story some more saying how her parents didn't seem to have much time for her any more now that they had a son and that she suspected that they had always wanted a son and that there wasn't room for her in their hearts any more. She told them that she had chosen a university in Scotland as it was far away from them, so that they could forget her and live their lives without her.

She began to look forward to her therapy sessions and spent hours thinking what she could say next.

Her parents visited her regularly sometimes bringing Alfie to visit and she would sit with him on her lap and chat to him until he wriggled to get down. She knew her parents were told much of what she said in sessions as she had given permission for her counsellor to do so and she watched them during visiting time as they tried to come to terms with what she had said. They kept telling her how much they loved her and how much they longed for her to be back home with them. She said, "How can you want me back home when you keep putting me away?" and watched her parents recoil from the remark and almost felt sorry for them. None of what she was saying was true, she was just making it up as she went along. They were silly to get so emotional when all she was doing was putting on a performance!

Christmas was fast approaching and there was talk of allowing her home for some day visits so that she could spend the celebrations with her family. During one of the visits home, she suddenly thought about the university in Scotland and couldn't believe that she had forgotten she should be going there. She remembered she had mentioned the university once during her counselling session but it hadn't dawned on her then that she should be going there. Her mother showed her a letter they had received from the university showing that she had forfeited her place by non-attendance. Could they do that? Were they allowed to do that? She had been ill, it was not her fault she had been ill, it wasn't fair. She tried to build up a full head of steam but in the end couldn't be bothered, she had lost her place, so what, she would get a place somewhere else. Her parents watched her as she seemed to calmly accept the rejection and marvelled at the change in her and saw a light at the end of the tunnel.

Her mum had meanwhile written to the acting college in the hope of there being a vacancy giving the name of her daughter's drama teacher as a reference and had received a large envelope in return which she gave unopened to her daughter.

As she tore open the envelope of acceptance and quietly read the contents she felt overwhelmed and suddenly got up and hugged her mum telling her, "Thank you, thank you so much."

She sat in her room hugging herself with delight and amazed at how everything had worked out. She was going to acting college, she was actually going to acting college, how wonderful was that! She was going to be famous and people would love her and send her fan mail and she would be rich, so rich she would not know what to do with all the money. She laughed out loud and twirled around her room as she did so. She only had a little time until the start of the January term and she had to get her bag and books sorted out. She had been given a reading list although she didn't understand what reading had to do with acting but her mum promised to go to the library to see if any of the books on the list were kept there or they would have to go on the web to get them.

Christmas came and went as it does and she felt that the anticipation of Christmas was better than the actuality of it and soon she was on her way to college travelling on public transport. The total journey took her fifty minutes and on arrival she stood and looked at the façade of an ordinary run of the mill building. She didn't know what she expected but certainly she didn't expect this and felt disappointment for a moment then went up the stairs and into the reception. She was taken through the processes that new students go through and collected her student card then was given a timetable and shown into a room in which a tutor was conversing with a dozen or more students. She was waved into the room then waved to sit down without the tutor stopping what he was saying. She looked around at the other students then back at the teacher and wondered when they would start to act so that she could show them what she was made of.

So deep in thought was she that she didn't realise that the tutor had stopped speaking and was looking directly at her. "Pardon, sorry, I didn't hear you."

There was some tittering amongst the students as the tutor said, "Your name, I asked you for your name." She told him her name and was welcomed to the class and she asked him when the real acting would start. There was a startled hush then he cleared his throat and said, "Real acting?" and held his arms wide as he looked at his students, his audience, then said, "is there such a thing? I thought it was all a pretence, a work of fiction if you like," at which he got the response of laughter from the students that he was pressing for. She was embarrassed and looked down into her lap as he said, "Class dismissed and don't forget I want two thousand words on this play," he waved the book at them, "by Friday at the latest," and, picking up his briefcase he swept out of the room. She trailed out of the room following the other students and found herself in the dining hall and finding a table to herself she sat and looked at her timetable not being able to make head nor tail of it.

"Hello, my name is Roseen, I'm supposed to show you the ropes for the next two weeks."

She looked up and said, "Why?"

"School policy."

"Oh, OK, you can start by showing me how this timetable works."

Roseen sat opposite her and explained the timetable and said, "Don't worry, everybody had the same problem when they first started, you'll soon get used to it," then, after looking at her watch, "Hey, come on, we'll be late for the next class," as she picked her bag up and turned to go.

"What is it, I mean what are they teaching?"

"English."

"English! You're kidding."

"Nope but actually it's poetry and prose."

What the hell is prose she thought as she trailed behind Roseen, admiring her long black silky hair as they went. She soon found out and actually enjoyed the lesson although she had no idea what it had to do with acting.

The next few days went by in a blur as she struggled to get a mental map of the college and get her head around what they actually wanted from her. On Thursday she was late having overslept and walked into the class to see the chairs had been arranged in a circle and their tutor standing in the middle of it. She dropped her bag on the floor and hurriedly took a seat aware of the eyes of the rest of the students upon her. The tutor said, "I'm going to call out a word and I want each of you in turn to stand where I am now and act it out. One rule, no speaking, the days of the silent movies have long since gone but for now we will hone our skills as they did." He must have said this to his students hundreds maybe thousands of times but he left space for their response and was rewarded with the laughter and smiles that he expected.

"Joy, despair, excitement, jealousy, hate, puzzlement, anxiety, greed, stupidity, love, remorse."

Nobody was allowed to hog the floor for more than a few minutes but she found the time in the centre of the room seemed so much longer. Some of the students had no problem displaying their talents and one or two even got a round of applause though she was not one of them. She couldn't understand why she couldn't convey an expression to the rest of the students when she felt she had been acting all her life. Perhaps there were many different forms of acting but she had to find out and soon as she didn't want to be the one seen to have no talent whatsoever and maybe be asked to leave because of it!

At home in her room, she practised in front of her mirror again and again, she just had to get this right and she wouldn't rest until she did.

On Friday she teamed up with Roseen and they went to the library to do some research before they were due at the next lesson where they were learning how to criticize someone's work in order for them to learn and grow from it. She found this very difficult, not the criticizing someone else's work but accepting criticism for her work, she felt that they were just being spiteful and getting at her.

The tutor asked if there was anyone else who had forgotten to hand their work in and she realised with a start she hadn't done it. Her mind ran over lots of things she could say but, in the end, much to her surprise, she told the truth. "I'm sorry, I forgot."

The tutor asked her to stay behind after class had finished then sat on a desk in front of her and looked down at her. She knew what he was doing, stamping his authority without words but she kept her face open, her eyes wide as she looked up to him. He smiled. "I know that you are playing catch up at the moment as you are two terms behind your fellow students but I will not tolerate laziness. Do I make myself clear?"

She wasn't sure if the space he left was to be filled with words or actions so she did nothing except wait. "I will give you until Monday morning to finish the assignment given and I want it on my desk first thing, is that understood?" She nodded. "All right then, you can go."

The tutor sat on the desk and watched her collect her bag and leave the room whilst twirling his thumbs in his lap as he ran his mind over the day's events. The class door opened and closed and he saw Roseen standing just inside the doorway. He nodded his head and she turned to lock the door then slowly undid her blouse and dropped it to the floor. Then she reached behind herself and undid her bra and brought her hands around beneath her breasts whilst giving him sultry looks allowing her bra to slide to the floor and stretched her arms above her head and grasped her hands as she threw her head back and swayed her hips, her black hair reaching down to the top of her legs. All this time her tutor hadn't moved, his eyes rivetted on Roseen. He suddenly licked his dry lips and shifted his position on the desk, his rock-hard penis making his position on the desk uncomfortable. Roseen hooked her thumbs over the waist band of her skirt and slowly, oh so slowly pushed it down until he had a glimpse of her lacy white underwear and groaned with longing but still didn't move from the desk. He was under her spell and waited for her to indicate when she wanted him to get closer. She crooked an index finger at him and he threw himself at her feet looking up at her adoringly as she glanced disdainfully at him, then looked into the distance whilst her supple body worked its magic. "Kiss my feet," she commanded and he instantly obeyed then looked up and watched her slide her panties down her hips and pleaded with her with his eyes to not tease him any further. Their performance was one they had enacted many times over and they had, over the months, honed it to a fine art. It was after all one of their favourite performances. It ended, as it always did with a frenzied coupling, their cries of ecstasy ringing through the empty college.

She worked hard on her homework and was pleased with the result and couldn't wait for Monday morning when she would put it on his desk. She packed it in her bag straight away to make sure that she didn't forget it and sat and thought about her tutor. She had decided she didn't like him; he was a little creep although she did admit that when he performed in front of them, she couldn't take her eyes off him. That was what she wanted, what she craved for, that ability to switch on and have people begging for more. She shook her head and laughed coming out of her dream world. She had a lot of hard work to do before she reached that peak even if she was a natural.

Alfie was having a bad time with his teething and her mother asked her to take him out to the park to see if he would settle. It took a while for her to get him in the pushchair as he held himself stiff and refused to go in it but in the end, she managed to relax him by tickling him and finally secured him with the straps. Alfie didn't like being outwitted and screamed," No, no, no," at her as he tried to wriggle out of it and for the first hundred yards or so she had difficulty pushing the swaying chair. She knelt down in front of him and told him quite firmly to sit still but she had put her head too close to him and he managed to grip her hair which took time to release without hurting Alfie or removing too much of her hair.

Alfie calmed down at the park and started to point at things. "Doggy," or "duck, duck, quack, quack," happy to be somewhere different to take his mind off things. She pushed him past the place where the murder had taken place and wondered why there was nothing at all in the news these days; it seemed to have been forgotten somehow.

All to soon Monday morning came around and she almost skipped out of the door looking forward to handing in her homework. Her mother watched her leaving and breathed a sigh of relief. At last her daughter seemed happy, seemed settled and that could only be a good thing. Sending her to college had been the right decision. Alfie had not yet woken up so she put on some washing and settled down for a nice cup of tea humming along to the wireless as she made it.

Once at the college she walked straight to the classroom and went up to the tutor's desk and waited for him to notice her but in the end had to give a little cough. He looked up then signalled her to place her work on his desk without saying a word and went back to what he was doing. She stood there nonplussed for a moment then turned and went to a seat.

The tutor finally got up and said, "Today we are going to study form then for homework we are going to discuss how it is that people can look at the same thing but express it differently." He looked over the head of his students to the classroom door and waved his arm. "Come in, come in," he said, and everyone turned to see a lady clutching a blanket around her enter the room. The tutor told his students to stack the chairs at the back of the room and get out the easels whilst he placed a chair on the small platform at the front of the room but the lady waved it away and once on the platform the lady dropped her blanket and lay down.

Most of the students started sketching straight away but she was mesmerised by the naked form displayed in front of her. The woman must have been middle-aged and had bulges on her body that nature had never intended her to have but her face was glorious. Ordinary but glorious.

She stood behind her easel staring, her first reaction when she had realised that they were to sketch a nude was what the fuck has it got to do with acting but now that thought was forgotten.

"Having problems transferring thought into action?" the tutor said standing far too close to her for comfort. She gave a small smile then picked up the pastels and started to draw.

All too soon the lesson was over and the model was being helped from the floor. As the model left the room she wanted to protest that she hadn't finished, that she had hardly started in fact as she looked around at the work displayed on the other easels.

"Name your work and put it on my desk and don't forget the assignment of 2,000 words due in tomorrow morning without fail." This comment was greeted with groans from all the students as they stacked the easels away and made their way to the canteen. Roseen was behind her in the queue and followed her to an empty table. "How you doing?"

"OK I guess, although I thought I was at acting college not art school." Roseen laughed and said, "You'll like the next lesson, it's all about stage lighting."

"Stage lighting!"

"Yes, and before you say what has that got to do with acting the answer is everything."

She smiled briefly at the comment as she stirred her coffee and dunked her biscuit in it. "You're a dunker too, oh brilliant, so am I," said Roseen as she started doing the same.

"I hate that prick," she suddenly spoke her thoughts out loud, surprising herself as well as Roseen.

Roseen looked at her then said, "You mean there's more than one prick?" with a half-smile on her face and they both burst out laughing.

"Our tutor, he thinks he's a somebody but he's a nobody, I hate him."

Roseen was pleased to hear this. She did not want another female on the scene, the tutor was hers and hers alone and nobody was going to get in her way. It was good to know she didn't have a rival.

The lesson on stage lighting was fascinating, she loved it. She hadn't realised how important it was in a production until she saw what the effects of bad light positioning could be. The lesson was over before she knew it and she left for home to prepare the homework for the following day.

She had been up most of the night working on her homework and woke late and had to rush in to college. As she walked into the classroom, the tutor looked up and said, "So nice of you to join us," eliciting a ripple of laughter from the class. She sat and noticed that the pictures from yesterday's lesson were displayed on the wall.

The tutor moved from one picture to another sometimes praising the work and sometimes admonishing it. When he reached her work he stopped and faced the class whilst pointing at the picture. "The college went to all the trouble of hiring and paying for a nude model and this student has just drawn her face, interesting."

She stood up. "Everything that was her was in her face and I looked to capture it."

Some of the students nodded agreement and she sat down satisfied with her retort. The tutor looked at her for a moment then said, "Come and see me after class," then continued assessing the art work.

What the fuck did he want to see her for, she didn't want to see him that's for certain. She thought of ways to avoid seeing him but all too soon the class was finished and she was alone in the room with him.

"Have you finished the assignment I gave you yesterday?" he asked holding a hand out to receive it. She was caught unawares for a moment then fumbled in her bag and handed it over to him. "Here's your previous assignment. I have been kind to you and not deleted marks for handing it in late, you may go."

She left the room with her tail between her legs and hurried to the dining room to grab a coffee before the next lesson with steam coming out of her ears. Roseen came over to her table and sat down "You all right?"

"No, I'm not," she said through gritted teeth "how can he make me feel so small?" She took out her homework, then threw the book down in front of her in disgust. C-, I have never in my life got C-. What is he playing at?"

Roseen was very happy, her beloved obviously didn't think too much of the new girl even if she was pretty. She twisted the knife innocently. "Oh dear, if your marks don't improve you'll have to leave the class," then, "come on, we'll be late for the next lesson."

"What is it" she asked as she thrust her work into her bag and got up to follow.

"Costumes."

At the end of the day Roseen checked that there was nobody around, having a good excuse for being there ready just in case she bumped into anyone but she didn't need it, the coast was clear.

She sat and bounced on the tutor's lap, then threw her arms passionately around him and told him all about the conversation she had had with the new girl. As she told him she watched his face carefully to see if he gave away any indication that he was interested in the girl but was satisfied that he only cared for her. She went down on him and he absentmindedly stroked her hair and whispered endearments whilst wondering how he could withdraw his affection from her and end the relationship. The new girl thought he was a little prick, did she? he thought, shifting himself to a better position on his chair. Roseen looked up at him and renewed her efforts to please him and eventually she did if only for a little while longer.

C-, it was there in front of her but still she found it hard to believe. Her lowest mark ever had been a B+ but she had been unwell at the time and really should not have sat the exam. Everything else was A or A*. The stupid tutor at college had it in for her she was certain but he didn't know who he was dealing with. She would just bide her time and watch and wait then he would find out that he had picked on the wrong student! She sat in her room and stared at her marked homework with red writing scribbled in the margin and comments followed by exclamation marks and the finishing comment, 'Must do more research' followed by the C-. She threw the book down in disgust. Research, when did any of them get time to do any research? She realised that she would have to get in his good books in order to make progress and decided that if that was what it took on her road to becoming a great actress then that was what it took.

The class sat in a circle each holding a script, all having been designated a role. The tutor talked to them about timing, about how the space between words was just as important as the words themselves but, if there was too much space, too much of a pause, then all was lost, the result would be a shambles.

She noticed Roseen was not happy, as she kept fidgeting and looking daggers at another student who had been given the prime role in the play and wondered what was going on.

Chapter 26
It's a Crime!

Roseen was not at college for the rest of the week and she had to admit that though she didn't like her much she missed her. Ashly, on the other hand, was on cloud nine, at last the tutor had begun to recognise that she had great talent and was giving her the lead roles. It had taken her many months to usurp Roseen and now she was at the top of the tree she was going to stay there! She didn't see any rivals at all in the group, even the new girl, the one who had started after Christmas didn't faze her. Sure, she was pretty enough but this game was cutthroat and she would gladly cut throats if that was what it took.

To know that Ashly thought of her as the new girl would have amused her greatly. It was now half term and she had it all planned out, do all the college assignments in the first few days and then have the rest of the week to herself. That was the plan but somehow it didn't quite work out that way. To start the assignments in the first minute became putting them off until the last minute and she cursed herself for not sticking to the plan. Alfie had been as good as gold all week but now that she wanted some peace and quiet in order to concentrate, he was screaming his head off. She finally finished during the early hours of Monday morning and even remembered to set the alarm which she happily slept through four hours later.

The class was already in progress by the time she arrived. She had wanted to slip in unnoticed but the tutor stopped the class and introduced her to them. She hurriedly sat down within the circle of chairs and avoided eye contact with her fellow students for a while.

"As I was saying, before we were so rudely interrupted by a latecomer, this lesson is about word association. I will explain it to you for the benefit of those who weren't here earlier and for those who still seem to be struggling." He stopped and cleared his throat before continuing, "If I say the word fine, then the next person in line could say for example guilty, weather, money etc., and then the person next to them will say another associated word. Understand?" He moved out of the centre of the circle of chairs and started patrolling around the outside of the circle. "Ashly, reward."

She quite liked this lesson although was not certain how it could benefit her acting ability. She didn't like the fact that the tutor was on the outside of the circle for it meant that for a time he was directly behind her and she didn't like the feeling at all. She noticed that Roseen was not in class and wondered where she was and decided that maybe she was catching up on her assignments and would be in later.

In the dining hall she couldn't help looking at Ashly who was in the midst of a group of friends laughing and joking. She wondered what they had to laugh and joke about. She bet that they didn't get C- for their assignments. In fact, when she came to think about it, she bet she was the only one who did. Did they know about her low marks and thought she was a bit of a dunce? Is that why they were laughing? She missed Roseen being in class, at least when she was there she looked like she was fitting in.

After break they returned to class and were welcomed by a lady they had not met before, a Miss Shonord. She had them stack their chairs at the back of the class then got them to gather around and explained what she wanted them to do and why. Singing chords for the next hour made her throat sore and, although Miss Shonord had explained that it was preparation for when they were in Year 2 of their course, nobody could see the purpose of it and some of the students even put a complaint into the student's union.

Her marks were improving and now she was consistently getting B's and once even a B+. She couldn't believe her change of attitude. Once upon a time she would have been appalled to get less than an A and now she was grateful to get a B.

Alfie's second birthday meant that the house was full of his friends from playgroup so, after giving him his present she made sure she was well out of the way. Two years old, her little brother was two years old, where on earth had that time gone!

On the Friday coming the class were informed that they were visiting a local amateur production and that some of them would be allowed backstage to talk to the performers. A buzz of excitement went around. At last they were going to mix with actors and actresses. They were told to concentrate on the stage lighting aspect as this would be included in part of their end of year exams. This announcement briefly took the edge off their excitement but by the time Friday arrived they were at fever pitch again. Only four students were selected to go backstage and she wasn't one of them but she wasn't that bothered, reasoning she could learn more about stage lighting from out front anyway. Ashly and three of her friends went backstage and met the actors and got signed autographs even though they had been told not to.

The following Monday she returned to class to find Roseen present but such a different Roseen from the one she thought she knew. This one looked lifeless, dull even, her once black glossy hair dull and straggly, her face gaunt, her shoulders drooped as in defeat. She made a point of sitting next to Roseen in class and in the dining hall but got no response from her although every now and then she saw Roseen staring at Ashly. She put two and two together and came up with four. Of course, Ashly was the new kid on the block and now Roseen was used unwanted goods. She bet the tutor would have told her something along the lines that he had to stop seeing her as he was getting too involved and that she was too young for him. He was letting her go so that she could find someone her own age. No wonder Roseen looked the way she did. That bastard needed a lesson to teach him respect and she was just the person to teach him.

Her birthday filled her with dismay, not the presents but the fact that she was getting old. She tried to smile and look happy for her parents' sake but once in her room she examined her face closely to see if she was getting wrinkles or things that old people got. She sniffed at herself wondering if she was beginning to smell like her grandparents had, for although they had been dead for quite some time, she still remembered their smell.

On Monday morning the class was in for a shock. Out of the whole college they had been chosen to do a performance at the local theatre in three weeks' time, so they no time to spare. The tutor handed out the scripts to the chosen performers and the rest of the class were given various roles such as makeup, costumes, lighting etc. When he stopped in front of the two of them, he barely glanced at Roseen as he said, "You two are in charge of the costumes. You'll need to ask the advice of Mrs Hibbitt in the upper sixth and for goodness sake don't upset her, we have too many prima donnas in this school anyway." He moved away designating various roles then raised his voice to ask for silence. "The play," he stopped and waited for the noise to die down, "the play is about twins separated at birth who later meet up and swop roles." He stopped speaking to allow the chatter to die down. "The gist of it is the rich sister who swops roles finds happiness but the poor sister who swopped into a rich lifestyle doesn't. Right, those of you who have been given roles sit in a circle and we'll run through the script."

She watched the chosen few talking through the script for a moment noting that Ashly and her friends had key roles in the play, then asked Roseen about the costumes but Roseen was in no mood for talking and simply shrugged her shoulders so she went to the secretary's office to make an appointment with Mrs Hibbitt, then came back to the classroom and helped the groups who were organising props. There was a buzz of excitement in the air with rumours that a local celebrity would be attending and a lot of hot air was wasted discussing who it could possibly be.

By the end of the week, they transferred to the hall so that they could get familiar with working on a stage. Sitting in the hall and looking up at the stage was a lot different from standing on the stage and looking out into the hall. All of a sudden they felt extremely small and vulnerable. The group in charge of lighting managed to highlight everyone except the ones they were supposed to whilst the person who had to raise the curtains managed to break the automatic winder so had to draw the curtains up winding a huge handle which had the trait of trying to unwind itself.

Halfway through the second week she was given the role of understudy to the rich sister who became poor and tucked herself away to learn her lines when she could. She went with Roseen to see Mrs Hibbitt and spent useful moments with her in the wardrobe department. A lot of the costumes needed minor repairs so the college's seamstress was kept really busy.

On Friday they had a full rehearsal. By now all the scripts had been taken in and the performance they gave was appalling as hardly anyone remembered their lines and the student who had been given the role of prompt was overwhelmed. Everything that could go wrong did go wrong and the tutor castigated them and made them practise over and over again, telling them they only had one more week before they made themselves and him look like utter idiots. At one point Ashly burst into tears and ran off of the stage so the students had time to regroup before the tutor returned with her as she smiled bravely at the class.

During the lunch break some of the class practised relaxation techniques to help them focus. She watched Ashly sitting in a group all with their eyes closed and humming, their fingers in the gyan mudra but refused to join them and instead left the premises to have a smoke and found Roseen outside doing the same. "Bad for your health," she offered but Roseen simply shrugged and drew deeply on her cigarette. She tried again. "Do you think they'll be ready by next week?"

Roseen ground her cigarette under her heel and said, "I couldn't give a fuck one way or the other," and got up and went back into the building.

She stood there for a moment watching the retreating figure whilst chewing on her bottom lip, then followed her back into the building. She exchanged glances and a quick smile with a clean-shaven man coming out of the building and missed a step and would have slipped and fallen if he hadn't put out a hand to steady her. His eyes were startling as he gazed into her face for a moment, then continued on his way. Who was he? Who was he? She had seen him before somewhere, but where? She turned to look for him but he was nowhere in sight and had seemingly vanished leaving her breathless with a thudding heartbeat. How could he do that to her? They hadn't said anything and yet she was shivering in anticipation. She told herself she was a fool but that didn't alter how she felt. If this was how it felt to be a fool then she wanted to be one. She hurried back to the hall realising she had taken too long a break.

During the afternoon they took a trip out to the local theatre and were told that that was where they would be meeting up from now on.

Full of expectation on their arrival they were soon dismally disappointed as a disinterested caretaker showed them around the premises, for although they didn't have any experience of what to expect the dark and dingy little theatre looked to be on its last legs. The tutor gathered his class on the stage and set everyone to work sweeping and cleaning. The group in charge of the lighting had worked out the system. The group in charge of sound put on some music and all of a sudden everything looked and felt a whole lot better.

The dressing rooms were checked out and spruced up, the props checked and repaired or replaced as necessary and the curtain mechanism checked so that by the end of the day, although they had not put in any performance practice, they had worked hard and all wended their weary ways home.

The following Monday they rehearsed over and over again, the tutor seeming to be in a foul mood and cracking the whip. The pamphlets advertising the play had spelling errors but as it was too late to get them redone they were posted out anyway. As far as the tutor was concerned his students were "a bunch of idiots" and the rehearsal was "a shambles" and would make him "a laughing stock."

She had managed to keep a low profile and keep out of the way by staying in the stalls, wiping down the seats and clearing rubbish from the floor. Every now and then she sat down and watched the performance on stage glad she was out of it for the time being. She had no idea where Roseen was although she had glimpsed her earlier walking across the back of the stage with an intent look on her face. She hated to admit it but saw that Ashly somehow managed to transcend herself and become the person she was pretending to be, not all the time, but the indications that she had star quality were there.

A break was called for and two students went out to fetch take-aways in. Most of the students lounged about on the stage or went out for fresh air or a smoke whilst waiting for the food to arrive. Halfway down the steps in the seating area was a small doorway that led to the toilets and continued on down to reach the back of the stage area. She now slipped silently through that doorway and felt her way along the murky passageway and down the steps until she came out into the backstage area. All was quiet. She moved along the hall and found the room she wanted and ever so slowly opened the door and slipped inside then pushed the door closed. She waited, listening, then slowly moved forward hardly daring to breathe. The 'Stars' dressing room she had entered had nothing in it to show it catered for a star. In fact, apart from it being the biggest of the backstage rooms, it was really quite dowdy. As she moved forward, she could hear a faint humming sound and gentle melodic music.

Ashly was sitting on the stool in front of her dressing table, legs crossed, eyes closed, fingers in the gyan mudra position as she meditated before lunch. She had worked extremely hard but was unsatisfied with her performance. She knew she could do better but she was having trouble tapping into her reserves. She felt she was letting herself down as well as her beloved tutor so she had taken time out to try to calm herself and help her refocus. At last she felt a calmness descending upon her and she floated on a carpet of inner peace. Ashly never felt the plastic bag go over her head and tighten behind her neck and only partially became aware enough to claw at her face before she died.

She kept the bag over Ashly's face longer than she should have just to make sure, then peeled it off and scrunched it into a pocket, then arranged Ashly's forearms on the dressing table and placed her head sideways on top of them to make it look as if Ashly was asleep. She had had a little bit of trouble arranging Ashly as she had gone floppy, so spoke quite sharply to her about behaving herself. Once satisfied she took a step back to take an overview and her heightened sense of hearing picked up the slight click of a door handle turning. She looked around her then crouched in the only hiding place the room had to offer and waited with baited breath.

Time seemed to pass slowly with no indication that someone else was in the room and she was just about to stand when she saw a shadow pass over a small beam of sunlight. She froze but try as she might she didn't hear anything else though she knew someone else was in the room. Who was it? What did they want? Had they realised Ashly was dead? Were they stalking her?

She was beginning to get cramp and knew she would have to move soon. If she was caught so be it. She eased herself upright and peered through the space between the mirrors of the dressing table but saw nobody. She stepped out from behind the dressing table then gasped, her hand flying to her mouth for there in front of her was the apparently sleeping Asley with the handle of a knife protruding from her back. She glanced around the room but there was no one else in it. Whoever it was had left without her hearing them go. She carefully opened the door and looked up and down the passage, then returned to the passageway that led up to the toilets and seating area and sat in one of the seats staring down at the stage. She closed her eyes for a moment then felt a hand shaking her shoulder as one of her fellow students called her name and told her her take-away was getting cold. She mumbled a thank you and followed him down onto the stage and sat a little apart from the group and ate her lunch.

Five minutes or so later one of Ashly's friends asked where she was and received shrugs in reply then Cilla said, "Still meditating I expect. I'll go and get her," and disappeared off the back of the stage in the direction of the dressing rooms.

Although she knew what scene Cilla would be confronted with she was still taken by surprise when shrill screams sliced through the air. The tutor told everyone to sit still and stay where they were and hurried out of sight but returned a few minutes later his arms around the shoulders of a sobbing Cilla. He told Martin to take a register of everyone present and to make sure they stayed where they were as he led Cilla away from the group and sat down with her at the back of the hall.

Two hours later the group were still sitting on the stage although Cilla was nowhere to be seen and the police were taking charge, having set up in the manager's office.

When she was finally called into the office, she was confronted by two officers. The woman officer was young but efficient. She checked the name on the register, introduced herself, then sat back and smiled openly. "So where were you during the rehearsals then?" she asked.

"I was cleaning the stalls."

"Cleaning the stalls?"

"Yes, wiping down the seats and picking up rubbish."

"Unusual for a company to take their cleaner along."

"I'm not a cleaner, I was doing it to help out, make the place tidy."

"That was kind of you I must say. Why weren't you on the stage?"

"I didn't have a part; I mean I was an understudy for one of the roles but I wasn't needed."

"So out of the kindness of your heart you decided to clean the stalls. Was anyone else with you?"

"No, I was on my own."

"So you have no witness to say where you were then?"

"Witness? What would I want a witness for? All I was doing was cleaning the seats."

There was a moment's silence then, "Where did you get the water from? You must have needed to change it now and then."

"From the cleaner's cupboard next to the toilets. Look, why are you asking me all these questions? Has somebody said something?" As soon as the phrase left her mouth, she knew she shouldn't have said it.

The officers in front of her smiled. "Why, what on earth could they have said?"

"I don't know, I was just saying." She suddenly remembered the scrunched-up polythene bag she had suffocated Ashly with was still in her pocket and one of the policemen must have sensed a change in her as he studied her curiously. She flicked her hair back and quickly recovered her composure and gave him her sweetest smile.

One of the officers rose to her feet and said to show her where the cleaner's cupboard was so she duly led her up the stairs and along the small passage to the toilets and cleaning cupboard. The officer noticed that the passage way continued and asked her where it led but she feigned ignorance and after a moment or two they returned the way they came back to the manager's office and she was left by herself as the officers discussed evidence to date.

They returned into the room. "What was your role in this production?"

"I didn't have a role to start with, I was responsible for the costumes. Well, when I say I mean we, me and Roseen were made responsible for costumes."

"Roseen!"

"Yes, the tutor told us we were responsible for costumes, it was only later he made me an understudy. We were told to liaise with Mrs Hibbitt."

So where is this Roseen now?" the inspector said running her finger down the names of the register. "There is definitely no Roseen listed here. Now why do you think that is?"

"I don't know, I didn't do the register. She was here earlier. I saw her walking across the back of the stage. She looked upset."

"How very convenient for you, pointing the finger at someone who is not on the register and who no one else saw!"

"Look, I don't know what I am supposed to have done. You're try to make me say things that are not true. I'm not blaming anyone. What's happened to Ashly? Why don't you let us know what's going on?"

"You can go for now but we will want to see you again." She left the room and returned to the stricken group on the stage some of whom were beginning to protest at being held so long. The class tutor, looking paler than she had ever seen him, cleared his throat. "Everyone has to return to their homes and talk to nobody. Ashly has been found dead which is why you have all been questioned." A shocked clamour from the group was silenced. "Do not return to college until notified," and with that he turned away and left the stage.

She mentally gave him a slow handclap thinking he could do a lot better and made her way home. She was excited beyond words. Who had killed Ashly? Well yes, she knew she had initially but who had made doubly sure? Which of the students was a killer? She had to admire them; she hadn't heard a sound. She thought back over the questioning at the theatre and wondered if she had done enough to avoid suspicion. Nothing for it, she would just have to wait and see, exciting though.

Chapter 27
Two Down, Let's Try for Three!

She awoke late on Tuesday morning thankful that she didn't have to go to the dingy theatre. The previous evening she had told her parents about one of the students dying and that there being a police investigation and enjoyed their horrified faces. She thought it was far too early to hear any news but was surprised when the event was briefly broadcast on local news. Someone obviously couldn't keep their mouth shut. She wondered if it was the killer, the other killer who had spilled the beans, but couldn't work out why he or she would say anything and perhaps draw attention to themselves. She lay back on her bed ignoring her mum's call to go downstairs and help with Alfie and went through each of the students but in the end, she had to admit that she had no idea who the other killer was. Perhaps she was next in the list. Oh, it was just too exciting. She decided she had better start transcribing her notes so that if she was killed her parents could follow her 'Blaze of Glory' guidelines. She could see it now, see the headlines. True she hadn't yet become famous but she could perhaps work on the 'cut off in her prime before reaching her true potential' guidelines.

She eventually went downstairs to find mayhem as Alfie during a tantrum had somehow managed to open the washing machine door mid-wash and flooded the laundry room. Alfie was, at the moment, sitting in his playpen happily engrossed with his toys whilst her mother was mopping the kitchen and looking stressed beyond words, so she took over the mopping up after making her mother a cup of tea and settling her in the kitchen. A few minutes later her mum called her into the kitchen and she saw a news broadcaster outside the local theatre interviewing the caretaker who was saying he knew nothing, he was only the caretaker but he was aware that a college group had been going to put on a performance soon (here the camera zoomed in on a poster displayed on the billboard) but now, of course, that wouldn't be happening. There was a lot of activity in the background and pictures of fluttering police tape but no one else was available for interview so the solemn-faced reporter gave his name then the picture changed back to the news desk. She looked at her mum and her mum looked at her then said, "You are not going back there, promise me you won't go back there. It could have been you. Do you realise that? You could have been lying in the morgue now and…" she suddenly stopped speaking and started crying. "Promise me you won't go back."

She sat and looked at her mother in astonishment at the display of emotion, then said, "Mum, mum, it's all right, I'm here, I'm safe," and got up and threw her arms around her mother in a display of affection all the while thinking I hope she doesn't blubber like this when I do die. So much for it being a joyful occasion. She could spoil everything, all these years of planning for nothing.

She had to get out even if it was only for a little while. She had hated cleaning the seats and clearing up other people's mess but now she found she missed it. They had all been working towards something and now they had nothing to focus on, nothing to work towards. She sat in the local park with Alfie in his pushchair and stared unseeing around her and cheered herself up with thoughts of attending Ashly's funeral. She wondered what type of funeral she would have and hoped it would not be a run of the mill one. It would make a nice change to attend something different, something unusual. She thought about what she would wear and decided that she needed to go on a shopping trip in the next few days. After all she didn't know when the body would be released and she didn't want to be unprepared.

The local paper and the nationals showed a picture of the run-down theatre, giving it more notoriety than it had had in years but gave no new information. She wondered if the police would want to question her again and so lost in her thoughts was she that she was halfway home before she realised she had left Alfie behind at the park. She ran back the way she had come cursing her stupidity. Supposing something had happened to Alfie, supposing his pushchair had rolled down into the water and he had drowned, supposing someone had taken him. She tormented herself as she ran the short distance back to the park and found the pushchair with Alfie fast asleep in it beside the bench she had been sitting on. Her fears had worn her out and she sat and wondered how easily fictional possibilities assumed a reality that stopped her from thinking rationally.

The headlines on the evening news gave her a lot of answers to questions she had been raising but also raised more questions. A girl had been found hanged in the wooded area of a local park and investigations were ongoing and it was believed that the girl was from the same acting college as Ashly who had been found dead at a local theatre the previous day. She had been to the park with Alfie. Supposing the girl had found Alfie all alone and had killed him instead of herself! They had walked past the wooded area, maybe she was already hanging there waiting to be discovered. Shit. She had missed the chance to see the corpse, missed the chance to find out who the girl was. She was reported as being from the same acting college as Ashly, but who was she and why had she hung herself? Surely she couldn't have hung herself on her own. Perhaps someone else had hung her but why would they do that? Was it to keep the girl quiet or some other reason she hadn't yet thought of? Was the girl who had hung herself or who had been hung one of the students in her class? Could one of them be the person who had murdered Ashly? So many questions, so many blind alleys. She thought it was a wonder that any criminal was caught. Two and two made four. She finally became certain that the girl in question had killed Ashly and then had managed to hang herself in remorse. Perhaps she had climbed the tree, tied a rope around a branch, put a noose around her neck and then just fell off the branch, that would work. Silly bitch. She ran through the names of the girls in her class but apart from Roseen, no one else had a motive that she could see. Roseen had been usurped in the affections of the form tutor but she didn't think that she was the killer. After all it was too obvious and Roseen was too stupid by half.

The headlines screamed out in the local paper and the nationals with pictures of Ashly. As she looked at the pictures of her she was almost jealous that Ashly was getting so much notoriety. Though she perused the paper from cover to cover she found very little mention of the girl who had hanged herself in the park. She threw the papers down in disgust and mentally went through all the girls in her class but still could not identify who the other killer was. She would just have to wait but it was so frustrating. Was she that stupid that she missed the obvious?

She managed to get a part-time job stacking shelves in the local supermarket thinking all the time how ironic it was that she had taken such a lowly job. She wasn't at all thankful to have a job thinking that it wouldn't do her career any good if it was discovered when she became famous.

She was most put out when she found that Ashly's parents had decided on a private family funeral. She had even bought something to wear for it and now it would be wasted. She wondered about having a private funeral for herself but soon dismissed it. After all her fans, her 'public' would demand to be present at her passing. She smiled to herself as she pictured the adoring fans reaching out to touch the golden cloth draped over her as the cortege passed, calling her name, promising never to forget her, telling her she was a legend in her time.

She was so lost in the moment that it took several more moments before she realised her mum was shaking her and telling her that she would be late for work. She asked her mum to phone in for her to say she was sick but her mum just gave her one of her old-fashioned looks and refused, saying she must face the consequences; it was the only way she would learn by experience. She momentarily forgot herself and screamed at her mum saying everybody else's parents would phone up and why was she the one stuck with a parent who wouldn't support her when she needed it? Her mum left the room without a word, her mouth set firmly, refusing to be drawn into an argument.

When she finally got to work, she was given the sack and no amount of acting on her part could change the decision. She was furious and blamed her mum for not waking her up on time, ruefully thinking that she now desperately wanted the job that she had thought beneath her. On her return home she found a letter from the college informing her of the starting date for the second-year students. She had thought that the college would have given her more information about what had happened but, apart from the starting date, there was nothing else in the envelope.

She tried for other jobs thinking that it would be easy as she had not had a problem getting the one she had just lost, but she was in for a shock and couldn't find work of any kind.

She searched the columns of the papers looking for an indication as to when the funeral of the hanged girl would be but couldn't find it in any of the papers. She didn't even know the name of the girl who had been found hanged in the local park. She would just have to wait until she went back to college and find who was missing. She was sure she hadn't missed it. She had read every paper and watched all the news broadcasts. Why was the hanging being shrouded in mystery? Surely it was a straight forward case of suicide? One thing she knew for sure though, she didn't want to die by hanging, not if the descriptions she had found on the web were anything to go by. Hanging, she thought was not so much about the person who took their life but about the person or people who found them. She was sure the image would haunt them forever.

As the days passed and the police didn't come knocking on her door to ask more questions, she put them out of her mind completely thinking that she had been clever enough to fool them, to put them off the scent.

She was glad to get back to college and sign in and have her photograph taken for her student pass. She saw one or two of the students who had been in her class but not to talk to. It was strange to be back there, it almost felt like another lifetime had passed in the meantime and perhaps it had, she thought. After all, two students had died, their young lives nipped in the bud. Such a shame!

She found they had got a new form tutor, a Miss Prichitt, a rather stern old-fashioned sort of lady with tightly permed grey hair who wore half glasses, over which she continuously peered at them and didn't so much speak as command.

The number of students had dwindled so the thought of finding out who had hanged themselves by their absence was useless and no one else talked about it, at least not with her and, in the end, she decided to let it go. What did it matter anyway? The girl was dead and the police possibly thought that the girl who had killed Ashly had then committed suicide. It was all very neat, too neat really but there you go.

The second year of college passed in a whirl, she had never been so exhausted. They were expected to stay late and practise, practise, practise and the students often thought that their new tutor would be better off working in a prison. She did however, begin to mould them and they felt themselves developing into the actors and actresses some of them would eventually become.

The class put on several productions during the second year and even had a write up in the local paper. Her favourite lesson of all was learning to throw her voice and she worked so hard she even had mild praise from the tutor. The more she learned the more she realised what she didn't know. It was so much more than keeping a straight face and pretending as she had done as a child, and the thought of how she had been, so full of herself but in actuality knowing nothing, made her squirm. One or two of the students got bit-parts in one of the soaps broadcast on television and although she pretended she didn't care less she cared very much. It was obvious to her that she was the best in class by a long shot and she was frustrated that no one else could see it too.

She often wondered what was the matter with her. Since her exploits with James and Ben she had lost interest in having a boyfriend although she had had several offers from the boys in her class. She had let them down gently not wanting to make enemies, although she knew she could handle it if she did. She wondered at this softer more thoughtful side to herself, perhaps it had developed through acting or perhaps it had been a part of her all the time but had only just surfaced.

Alfie's third birthday came and went followed, soon after, by hers but she didn't celebrate getting older, she hated it, in fact, and every day she examined her face for wrinkles and applied various creams that were fashionable at the time. She was glad it was the end of term and pleased with the results she was getting from the tutor. Her retentive memory had stood her in good stead throughout the term but something was missing from her life though she couldn't put a name to it. Her parents were proud of the way she was applying herself but were anxious that she was too hard on herself but when they mentioned it their daughter simply told them they didn't understand her and that they were too wound up in Alfie to even think they had a daughter! Even as she said it, she knew she was being unfair, that they would be hurt by what she was saying but so what, life wasn't kind all the time, they should get real.

During her early part of her third year at college her tutor called her into her room and discussed her progression and asked about any problems that she could help with. She wanted to tell her tutor about her fears of getting old but something stopped her. She didn't want to appear vulnerable and unsure of herself especially in front of a tutor she had come to admire. Miss Prichitt said that a local company were looking for a young actress for a few months and had asked her to recommend someone.

She left the office with her mind in a whirl wishing that she had said yes immediately instead of going away to think about it. She mentally slapped herself for the fact that she could have seemed unwilling and the part offered to someone else!

Instead of going straight home she called into a pub and treated herself to a couple of beers. Halfway through the second pint a beer was put down, rather clumsily, on the table in front of her and a familiar voice said, "Well, well, well, if it isn't the rising young starlet, let me buy you a drink," and with that turned without waiting for a reply and went to the bar. She got up the minute he turned away and made her way to the door but stopped when a hand gripped her upper arm. "Leaving so soon, that's not very nice especially when I've just bought you a drink." She looked into the face of one of the last people she wanted to see, her tutor from the first year in college, removed his hand with some difficulty and said, "Another time maybe," and left. The minute she reached the street she ran as fast as she could then calmed down enough to check around her and make sure he wasn't in sight. She was relieved when she didn't see him realising that the sudden sight of him had really upset her, him, of all people, him. She hadn't thought about him at all but now memories of him and the way he belittled her by marking her down and the way he walked about as if he was a gift to women came flooding back. As she calmed down, she realised how stupid it was of her to run. After all he would know where she lived, their addresses were on the register he had used. Well, she would just have to deal with it, and not act like a silly little schoolgirl. She had once vowed that he needed to be taught a lesson and now it looked like the time was ripening.

She didn't have to wait long before she knew he was following her. She made it look like she wasn't aware of the fact but all the time she was enticing him into a trap. She would leave the house after dark and once around the corner would sashay down the road leading him a few blocks away. She got on a bus and almost laughed out loud at his attempts to remain unseen as he got on it too. She deliberately left it until the last minute to get off the bus leaving him trapped on it until the next stop and realised she was enjoying herself immensely.

She had dressed herself entirely in black for this occasion as she felt it was fitting after all many people still dressed in black to go to funerals whether they were going to burials or cremations. She left her long hair flowing down her shoulders so that her stalker could easily identify her on these dark nights and led him into the trap. Her stalker was in a panic, having lost her on the bus and had run all the way back to the stop she had got off at, panting heavily and sweating profusely. He caught a glimpse of her turning into a side road not too far away and ran over to it, not thinking it strange that she should still be in sight, not realising that she had waited until she saw him before moving.

Once around the corner she tucked her hair in and pulled up her hoodie then crouched down behind a parked car and waited. She could hear him long before she could see him, as he was not making any effort to be quiet. She was amazed that he was actually humming to himself as he walked past her then he stopped, just a few feet away from her and listened before continuing down the road. She slowly breathed out then, keeping on the outside of the parked cars, stalked him.

He stopped again and said, "Where are you my beauty, come to Daddy," before suddenly turning and walking back the way he had come and taking her unawares. She took the baseball bat she had secreted down her trousers and moved up swiftly behind him and swung it at his head with all the force she could muster, then once more as he was falling to the ground. She stood, legs braced, over him, feeling powerful whilst she stripped the cling film off of the bat and rolled it into a ball then, slipping the bat back into its hiding place and the cling film into a pocket she turned back into the road she was in and ran home through a maze of side roads and alleyways, only slowing down long enough to dispose of the cling film in one of the many dustbins parked outside the houses.

On reaching home all was quiet so she hand-washed her clothes and put them on the line then sat in the garden and stared up at the full moon. It was beautiful, so clear, so close, she spoke to it reverently with tears rolling down her face. It would be here, she thought, shining its reflected light on people yet to be born when she was long since dead and gone and suddenly she felt small and insignificant.

The following day she awoke early, feeling refreshed and full of hope, had her breakfast then left for college determined to see her tutor and accept the part offered. A new girl had joined the class, transferred from a college up country and she straight away decided that she didn't like her, she sensed a rival.

Her tutor was pleased with her decision to try for the role offered and made her responsible, as was college policy, to see the new girl, Olive, settle in. She had difficulty holding in her mirth when she heard the new girl's name. Poor sod, fancy being lumbered with a name like that.

Olive though was not a new comer to college life and quickly settled into the system so that after a week she no longer needed to be chaperoned. She showed her flair in the performances they put on for the rest of the college students and quickly became a popular member of the class.

Miss Prichitt took her to a meeting with the owner of the company that had approached her in the first place. He owned several such enterprises and Miss Prichitt had called him an entrepreneur, a word she had never heard before but one which she looked up and studied so that she would not be caught out and look a simpleton.

The restaurant they entered was amazing and dripping with wealth. She had never stepped foot in such a place but kept all her feelings hidden and acted as if she was used to such luxury, surreptitiously watching how other customers in the restaurant acted. She wasn't included in the conversation initially although she knew the director, Mr Bainridge, was watching her. There was something familiar about him and she cast her mind back to when she could have seen or met up with him previously, something about his eyes. Halfway through the meal she remembered why he looked so familiar. That young man she had bumped into on the college steps all that time ago looked just like him except he had cropped hair and Mr Bainridge had a crop of black wavy hair and was distinguished by greying sideburns. By the end of the meal she had been invited along with Miss Prichitt to a performance at the company and from then on to attend rehearsals. She almost curtsied as they said their farewells but managed not to by sheer will power.

They had a seat in one of the boxes and the theatre, nothing like the dingy little theatre they had gone to in her first year, was packed to capacity. The performance was electric and she was, in turn, moved to laughter or tears. Miss Prichitt watched her and almost envied her her youth, her experiences yet to come, her lowest moments of despair, her highest moments of joy, the range of people she would meet. She was glad to help where she could but knew that nothing improved an actress like her experiences. The young girl beside her was extremely talented, gifted even, but major roles were hard to come by as she entered the cutthroat world. She wished her luck, but knew that luck wasn't enough by a long chalk.

Christmas came and went with its usual excitement of anticipation followed by its usual low of despondency. Spending more than you had and plunging yourself into debt year after year never seeming to learn. Alfie had made it bearable with his unbridled excitement at everything as he kept pulling the decorations off the tree in search of something edible. He chatted non-stop about Father Christmas and his reindeer and she spent time with him at bedtime reading him stories about the incredible adventures of a white Rex rabbit called Legolas and her ginger brother called Gideon. He would follow the words in the book as she read it to him, giggling at what they got up to. He kept plaguing everyone to buy him a white rabbit but seemed happy enough with the toy rabbits he was given.

From now on her time would be spent differently, two full days with the new company and the rest of the time in college. If she thought she had worked hard before she had to re-evaluate the thought. Her two days spent at the company exhausted her. She had thought she had gone there to show off her acting skills but found that instead of acting she was the general dogsbody rushing around at everybody's beck and call. She brushed shoulders with many people she had seen on television, ordinary people who were extraordinary on stage. Some of them treated her kindly and some didn't and she quickly learnt whom to avoid.

The rest of the time at college was relaxing to her whereas previously she had found it difficult. She kept Miss Prichitt updated on what she was doing with the company and found that Miss Prichitt was not at all surprised at how she was treated and told her to hang in there, she was being tested, pushed to the limit. Many young actresses thought that talent alone would get them fame and fortune and, truth be told, some did strike it lucky, but the rest had to keep their noses to the grindstone and get by on whatever was offered and hope to be discovered through their bit parts. Some had agents and some didn't but she couldn't afford one and took Miss Prichitt's advice that many of the agents were out there for their own ends and that she should bide her time.

She realised that wherever she went in college she was being stared at, especially by the first years and realised that, in the college at least, she was becoming famous as she was seconded with a well-known company. The students had no idea that she rushed about obeying orders and generally cleaning up after people; they saw her quite differently and she wasn't going to let them learn any different!

She was given a minor part in the current production out of the blue due to someone being sick and she read through the script avidly so that she did not make mistakes but was mortified when she was continually castigated for being in the wrong position or in the way of someone else. She suddenly realised that not only did she have to learn her lines she had to learn the lines of everybody else as well so that she knew where they should be and where she should be and what was going to happen next. Learning the whole script to her was no problem as she had a retentive memory but she wished she had been told about the importance of it in the first year for by now it would then be second nature.

Although she was one of the performers she was still regarded as the general dogsbody and was continually put in her place so that she didn't get any grand ideas about herself. Humility was not one of her prime characteristics but she would get nowhere fast if she didn't adopt it.

The opening night, the night they had worked towards for months, was finally here and she couldn't believe how agitated some of the actors and actresses were. She saw Mr Bainridge milling amongst the performers, shaking hands or kissing both cheeks of the actresses, and following close behind him was the young man she had met on the steps of the college. Mr Bainridge smiled in her direction then moved away amongst the performers and she made sure that she kept the young man, obviously his son, in sight.

The opening night was a huge success, bigger than they ever imagined, and all the cast felt excited and relieved that everything had gone so well. There was a huge party atmosphere and bottles of champagne were popped and platters of food appeared as laughter and chatter filled the air.

She was totally caught up in the atmosphere and drank far too much champagne for her own good and as she weaved her way back from the ladies', she saw Mr Bainridge walking towards her, broadly smiling and the next minute she was in a small room just off of the corridor his hands clasped around the back of her neck as he thrust his tongue down her throat. She was taken by surprise at the initial approach then, as she felt his hard groin press against her crotch, and, after a brief moment of hesitation, she was kissing him back just as hard. She felt his hands drop to her sides dragging her dress up and she pressed herself hard against him, rotating her hips and rubbing his rigid manhood against her crotch. She threw caution to the wind, wanted sex and she wanted it now. As he kissed her she undid his trousers and placed her hands on his ample crotch hearing him groan as she did so. He kissed her neck, her ears, her eyes as he whispered things to her in a language she didn't understand and, at the time, made no difference. He pushed his boxers down freeing his manhood and suddenly her hands were full of his hot rigid penis. Without thinking she bent down to kiss it and suddenly he was thrusting his penis into her mouth, his hands clasped behind her head as he moved. She was shocked, she had wanted him, but not like this, she wanted him properly. She somehow managed to twist her head so that his penis was no longer in her mouth and cupped his balls with her hands then gripped, twisted and squeezed them causing him to squeal in pain. "No one does that to me, you hear me, no one," as she released them.

"You bitch, I can destroy you," he said through the intense pain that gripped his groin, "I'll make sure you never work again."

She laughed up at him. "I don't think so. You may be used to fucking all the young actresses that come your way knowing that they are using their bodies to promote their careers but with me you have come unstuck." She paused for breath as she rearranged her clothing, then continued, "You WILL help promote my career or I will spread rumours of you being a sexual predator, preying on vulnerable people that you should be caring for as they are making your company successful. Without them you are nothing. I will also tell them of how tiny your penis is." This last remark wasn't true but she knew how vulnerable men could be about their tackle and wanted him to squirm whilst she had him on the hook.

She watched him pull up his trousers then reached up and kissed him on a cheek then bit him hard. He shouted and pulled away, a bloody bite mark in evidence on his cheek and placed a hand to the area whilst looking at her in horror.

"Something to remember me by, my dearest," as she threw her head back and swept out of the room and barged straight into the young man who she thought to be his son.

"This is getting to be a habit," he said as he reached out to steady her. "I'm looking for my father, have you seen him?" he asked whilst still holding on to her arm.

She looked up at him then pointedly down to where he was still holding onto her, then back up to his face. He flushed and murmured, "Oh, sorry," as he let her go.

She took a little time to steady herself long enough to say, "Your father is in there," waving a hand in roughly the right direction, "busy playing with himself." She put a hand up to her mouth saying, "Oops, I shouldn't have said that," then turned and weaved her way down the corridor whilst chatting away to herself. The young man watched her for a moment then entered the room she had just come out of.

She couldn't remember the last time she had had so much fun mixing with loads of people who were still acting as if they were on stage. She felt a hand on her upper arm and turned to see the son again looking concernedly into her face. He said, "How are you going to get home?"

"None of your business and anyway I have a limo outside."

"A limo?"

"Yes, a limzine."

"Really."

"No, do I look like someone who has one?"

"How are you getting home then, shall I call a black cab for you?"

"Puberlic transport. Good old puberlic transport if you must know."

"I'll drive you home, get your coat."

Moments later she was sitting beside him in a small BM with the world swirling about her. The son, Matthew, only just managed to run around and get the door open and pull her out as she threw up. She stayed down on all fours for a moment groaning as she stared down at the sick she had just ejected and wretched again. A little while later she found herself back in the BM apologising profusely. She felt a lot better than she had but still felt awful. She told Matthew her address and heard the engine start up but could remember nothing more until she woke up in bed the following morning with a pounding headache.

Alfie was screaming his disapproval of something and the sound went right through her head even though she covered it with one of her pillows. She eventually made it downstairs for a coffee and was greeted with grins from her parents. What the hell were they grinning at, she felt irritated by their expressions and was about to make a sarcastic retort when her mum said, "So, who is this Matthew then?"

Matthew, Matthew, she didn't know a Matthew, What the bloody hell was her mum going on about? "I don't know any Matthew. Why are you asking me about someone I don't know?"

"Matthew was the nice young man who brought you home last night slightly the worse for wear. Such a nice young man, really polite and concerned about you."

The penny dropped; Matthew was the name of the son of Mr Bainridge. She suddenly started giggling and said, "MB drives a BM, isn't that a scream?"

Alfie, who had stopped his tantrum at the sight of his bedraggled sister started up again hitting the high notes with ease. She glared daggers at him then took herself upstairs for a long hot bath and went back to bed thankful it was the weekend.

Late afternoon as she was sitting in front of her dressing table looking at the mess created by her brother, who had obviously been in her room again, evidenced by the creative makeup drawings on her dressing table and mirror when her mobile rang and she answered it with her mind elsewhere, "Hello."

"Hope you don't mind my ringing you, just wanted to know you are OK."

"Who are you?"

"Matthew."

Matthew! I don't know anyone called Matthew; I think you've got the wrong number."

"I gave you a lift home last night though I doubt if you would remember."

"Look Matthew, or whatever your name is…"

"Call me Matt."

"As in door mat?"

He laughed. "No, as in Matt with a double t."

"Well, Matt with a double t how did you get my number?"

"Your parents gave it to me. You don't mind, do you?"

"No, no," she lied, her eyes becoming slits. "I shouldn't be surprised."

"Well that's all right then." He paused. "Look, I'm sorry about my father."

"I don't want to talk about it, thank you."

"I just wanted you to know that I am not like him."

"Oh, so you know what he's like then. You know what he's like and yet you did nothing to warn me."

"I didn't think he would try it on with you. You are different from the others."

"Others!"

"Look, I didn't choose my father, I love him but I don't like him at all."

"Well, that's not my problem really, is it?"

"Can I make it up to you, a meal or something."

"I'll think about it," she said then cut him off and turned her mobile off in case he phoned back. She stared into the distance nodding her head as she sorted through her thoughts. She had the father bang to rights and that promised a boost to her career and now, if she worked it properly, Matthew would be her little lapdog. Feeling a lot happier she went downstairs and complained to her mother about Alfie ruining her makeup again but her mother was focused on baking and didn't pay too much attention to her, so she took Alfie out to the park. Her mother gave her a bag of cooked rice to feed the birds and she and Alfie had the most enjoyable time, at times, she thought, she almost loved him as long as he didn't use her makeup like crayons.

On her return home the delicious smell of baking pervaded the house. She just loved baking days. She remembered when she was little she used to be allowed to lick the bowl out and now she watched Alfie being allowed to do the same thing. Initially she found it sweet, then her mood changed and she went up to her room. She decided to get one of those sensory cameras she had seen advertised, one which took recordings. It took her a few weeks to get the positioning right and get in the habit of checking the film footage and replacing the batteries. The first tapes she reviewed were disappointing. She could hear activities going on in the room but didn't capture images that she could recognise, even of herself. Finally it all clicked and she got the results she wanted, clear identifiable images with the date and time on the recording.

Chapter 28
Revenge!

The Easter term approached and she was looking forward to some well-earned rest away from loud self-opinionated people. She hadn't realised that being an actress was such hard work and wondered not only how they chose the profession but why they stayed in the profession when they found out how heart breaking it was.

It took her a little while to realise she was being followed and then she realised that her senses had been warning her that something was up over the last day or so, she had just been too busy to take notice. She had gone up town to buy Alfie a birthday present when her animal senses kicked in through her thoughts. She didn't make it obvious that she was aware but she started using the reflection in shop windows or the windows and mirrors of passing or parked vehicles to try to flush out whoever it was.

They were good, she thought, she could not identify anybody who was intent on following her but she knew her instincts were sound. She went into shops then out the back way, stopped dead as if suddenly remembering something and turned back the way she had come, sat by the window in the coffee shop and people watched but still could not identify who was tracking her.

She called into college to meet Miss Prichitt who told her that the company at which she was working two days a week were drawing up a contract for her and that she would be employed full time by them when the term ended in the summer. Normally she would have been overjoyed. She put on an act of happiness at the news for the benefit of Miss Prichitt whilst thinking the news was no more than she deserved. They were lucky to get her.

Alfie's birthday came and went and she was pleased to see that the colouring book and crayons were put to good use. In a fit of madness she had bought him a bike without pedals but began to regret it as he continually barged into people. He was going to playschool now. She couldn't believe it, one minute he was a desperately ill baby in an incubator and the next he was going to school, all right, not big school, but still, he was growing up fast, too fast.

She was back at college full time now, her acting future secured but she wasn't satisfied, she felt she deserved more than a contract even though such contracts were incredibly hard to come by. The feeling of being stalked stayed with her even at college and she began to wonder if her animal instincts were laying a false trail. She began to relax checking out if she was being followed and, as the days passed, she grew more and more careless.

She casually got on the bathroom scales and her eyes nearly popped out of her head, bloody scales, always giving the wrong reading. She suddenly realised that she hardly did any physical exercise at all these days, not like she used to when she used to swim nearly every day. The thought brought her up short. When did she stop swimming, she couldn't remember? She had always thought herself fit but now she began to wonder. Early evening she decided to go on a half marathon run having no doubt that she could do it but knew her parents would try to stop her as it would be getting dark by the time she returned. Around half eight she complained of a headache and said she was going up early and went up to her room where she changed into her running gear, stuffed a pillow in her bed to make it look like she was in it and crept downstairs and out of the front door. She was so relieved to get out of the house without being detected that she ran too fast for the first seven miles finding it relatively easy. She had turned back for home at the halfway mark and immediately her mind was telling her she couldn't do it, enough was enough, best to walk even if only for a little time. She pushed on, her once fluid movement dissipating with every step, her feet hurt, she couldn't breathe, she needed a wee, she needed to stop. She didn't stop though, she couldn't give up, it wasn't in her nature to do so and when she finally made it home she staggered indoors, drank far too much water and fell asleep on the downstairs sofa, too exhausted to make the stairs.

In the early hours of the morning she didn't know what woke her and although she listened intently she heard no sound other than a car starting up nearby. She pushed herself upright grimacing at the stiffness and soreness of her muscles and made it to the downstairs toilet. She blinked in the sudden light as she turned the switch and was appalled at her dishevelled appearance then shut her eyes, had a wee and a quick face splash then gingerly climbed the stairs.

As she reached the top of the stairs, pulling herself up the last stair by gripping on the bannister her warning instincts kicked in. She stopped still and held her breath as she looked around and listened. At first she could see nothing out of place, the early dawn light coming through the skylight highlighted the familiar landing then she noticed that her bedroom door was wide open and she knew it shouldn't be. Her eyes narrowed to slits and she silently moved towards her room , aches and pains temporarily forgotten.

In one swift move she reached around the door and turned on the light as she stepped into the room whilst reaching out with her left hand to pull the door closed so checking that there was nobody hiding behind it.

The room was empty but still her senses were heightened, she looked slowly around her room and suddenly her eyes were rivetted on her bed for sticking up from the middle of it was the handle of a dagger. She had left a pillow in her bed yesterday evening so that her parents would be deceived into thinking she was in bed asleep. She gripped the duvet either side of the dagger and lifted it and after a little show of resistance the dagger came free. Without touching it she examined it then, careful so as not to smudge any prints that might be on it. She wrapped it in a towel and tucked it at the bottom of her wardrobe before she sat down on her bed to think.

Someone had tried to kill her, and not only that someone had come into her house to do it. The thought occurred to her that perhaps the person didn't want to kill just her, perhaps her whole family had been massacred and were lying bloodied and murdered in their beds! Her fantasies ran away with her until she realised she was panicking and made herself breathe slowly and deeply then got up and looked in on Alfie and was relieved to see that he was sleeping soundly, making tiny snoring sounds. She carefully opened the door to her parents' room and heard their gentle breathing so pulled the door to and returned to her room.

If she hadn't gone for the run, if she hadn't pushed herself to the limit so that she was too exhausted to go up to her room she'd be dead. She found the thought exciting yet frightening. She had been having feelings of being followed and now this proved that she had been. Someone out there had followed her, someone out there wanted her dead but how had they known where she lived? What room in the house to go into? She remembered that as she had woken up downstairs she had heard a car start up soon after, coincidence, or did it prove that the person who had tried to kill her drove a vehicle of some sort?

She lay under her duvet and imagined what it would have been like if her parents had come into the room to wake her and found her stabbed to death. She drifted off to sleep as she imagined their despair, trying to wake her, calling her name, unable to believe that their precious daughter was dead.

The following morning she was woken by Alfie breaking her hand mirror as he bashed it on her dressing table surface. She shrieked his name and shouted at him to get out of her room. He slid off of the stool and beat a hasty retreat out of the room as her mum peered around the door.

"He's smashed my hand mirror," she shouted furiously as she threw the duvet back and got out of bed.

"Careful," her Mum said looking at the shards of broken glass on the floor. "I'll get the dustpan."

She sat back down on her bed until her mother reappeared with the dustpan. "Leave it, I'll do it." Her mum left the room pulling the door closed after her and took a wailing Alfie downstairs, talking soothingly to him as she did so.

She listened to her mother going downstairs and thought that her little brother would never learn right from wrong if he was soothed all the time he did anything and decided that when she got a chance she would bat the little sod around the earhole to teach him some manners.

She swept up the pieces of broken mirror, then ran herself a hot bath whilst her mind meandered through the events of the evening. Who wanted her dead so badly that they were prepared to risk being discovered in a strange house? Could it be a male? Could it be a female? She didn't know. True she had made some enemies from years ago but why would they suddenly make an attempt on her life now? What about Mr Bainridge, now he had cause to want her dead for if she spilled the beans his reputation and all he had worked for over the years would come to nothing. The more she thought about it the more she thought she was right. Now all she had to work out was what to do about it.

An attempt on her life had been made. For all they knew they had been successful and she was dead. Perhaps she should lay low for a couple of days whilst she thought how to respond and realised how she had changed as she was getting older. Once upon a time she did things spontaneously and now she was planning a response. Oh for the carefree days when she was younger.

She realised that she didn't have the luxury of a few days, she had a few hours at most. Whoever had 'killed her' would be waiting for a reaction from her parents or the police. They could even now be waiting for news of her discovery and perhaps they might even be nearby watching the house.

The police, she was a fool, she could have started screaming blue murder when she saw the dagger and her parents would have come out and called the police. The police would have given her police protection she was sure but for how long, after all she was always reading about how undermanned they were. She should have left the knife where it was but no good crying over spilt milk. She had to think what to do now and anyway if the police were called the person who had tried to kill her would soon realise they had not been successful and perhaps try again.

She didn't like the thought of her family being vulnerable. She knew that once the police came around all their lives would be changed for ever, they could no longer play happy families, her family would be living in fear. Perhaps they would be moved to one of those 'safe houses' she had seen on some television programmes but wasn't sure if they were fact or fiction. They could move, sell the house and move to somewhere nobody knew them but she didn't want to be forced to move, she wanted to move when she was ready to and not before.

Thinking back over the years she realised that she had left some loose ends that possibly needed tying. Clive for one, yes he had moved away but there was nothing to stop him moving back and he knew where she lived. Byron was another, the one she had fancied for quite some time until she had grown out of him and he was a friend of Clive's. Hmm. She had thought Byron such a nice kind boy but he had shown another side to himself when he and his friends wouldn't let her out of the swimming pool that time.

James, what about James, could he be capable of trying to kill her, capable of breaking into her house and murdering her in cold blood. She realised she was being dramatic with the phraseology but felt it was called for. She wondered if James would have the balls to try to kill her after all he was a single parent, he had a young daughter of his own, what was her stupid name, Amelia Jane was it? or something similar and anyway it didn't matter what she was called, little bitch would do as well as anything. She remembered him at the funeral of his girlfriend though she couldn't for the life of her remember her name. He had looked shabby and ugly and she couldn't believe what she had ever seen in him. She decided it wasn't him, he was a nerd.

Mr Bainridge, now he was a possibility, he had plenty of reason to want her dead. He was a nasty piece of work who thought he could get his way because of who he was. Well, she had shown him he couldn't. She didn't think he would have the balls to try to kill her himself, he was the type who would hire someone else to do his dirty work. The more she thought about it the more she became convinced that he was the mastermind but wait, what about his son, Matthew, could he have been persuaded to help his father get rid of her, after all blood was thicker than water!

Her head was spinning with so many possibilities as she heard Alfie crying and her parents moving about. There was a slight knock on the door and her name was called but she kept quiet and simply stared at the door until she heard her parents going downstairs.

The camera! She had forgotten the fucking camera placed discreetly across the other side of the room. She had bought it to catch her brother poking about in her room but hadn't actually told her parents about it. Perhaps she was going over the top a bit after all Alfie was only four, she could easily have put a lock on the door. She felt a bit silly; it was obvious now what she could have done but she couldn't see it at the time. Oh well, let's have a look at the tape.

She ran the tape over and over again not believing what she was seeing but there it was right in front of her, the damning evidence. All that time spent thinking about who it was who had tried to kill her when the evidence was there, waiting to be found. She had heard his voice calling her name, not once but twice before he appeared as large as life on the screen. She replayed the footage over and over at the part where he plunged the knife down and smiled as he turned away. She zoomed in on his face still trying to come to terms with what she was seeing. All this time trying to work out who it was, who had deliberately left the knife thrust into her bed. Were they smiling because they realised she wasn't in the bed at all she thought, after all there must be a difference between plunging a knife in a pillow than in a body. She had been taken by surprise and hadn't given the person depicted on the tape a second thought. Well, you wouldn't, would you? I mean, after all, who would suspect their dad?

Chapter 29
Missed the Train!

By the time she went downstairs the house was empty with Mum having taken Alfie to playschool and her dad having gone to work. She wondered what life would be like without a father and if her mum could cope. She could always move out she thought, always go to pastures new but she didn't want to, there was no way she was leaving. She expected her father to be waiting at work for a phone call from her mum telling him the awful news and then, of course, he could hurry home and play the distraught father. He might be concerned when he did not get a call from his wife and perhaps would casually call on some pretence or other to find out what was going on at home. She wondered what her father would say to her when he came home from work, knowing that by the time he saw her she would have found the knife in her bed. He had no idea about the camera, no idea that she had evidence that could get him put away for a long time if she decided to use it.

She waited by the side of the steps on the crowded platform examining the ornate ironwork made by a different generation. She hated the rush hour, so many people hurrying to get home or go somewhere, not in the moment as their minds thought in future tense.

She saw her father coming down the steps as a train came into the station and crowds of people tried to get on before crowds of people could get off. The next few trains coming into the station were packed and only had room for a few people. The crowd on the platform were used to such things but it didn't mean that they were happy about it.

Finally a relatively empty train arrived and carried away a large portion of the crowd. She kept her father in sight whilst she did her best to remain out of sight. Her father finally got to the front of the crowd and stood behind the yellow line reading *The Metro*. She managed a quick upward glance to the arrival screen and saw that the train was one minute away. She counted the seconds in her head whilst edging closer and listening for the train. She heard it coming but waited a bit longer then poked a rigid finger into her father's back causing him to exclaim and turn to see what or who was prodding him. He caught sight of his daughter just as she pushed him into the path of the oncoming train and although it must have only taken a split second the sight of his surprised face, recognition stamped all over it, seemed to hang in front of her for ages and she relished every second of it knowing that he would take her image to his grave. She thought that if ever anyone discovered how to take images from the eyes of the dead she would be in a lot of trouble as would be many other people. But, as far as she knew, there was no such technology. So, for the time being she could relax, she was safe. As soon as she had pushed him she melted out of the back of the crowd, hearing the screams of horror and the screech of brakes as the train tried desperately to stop.

Keeping her head down she joined the throng of people rushing up the stairs to get away from the horror some had seen and most had heard. She got on the first bus that came along then another. She used her mobile to phone her mother to tell her she would be late as she was going to town. Then she went shopping and changed her clothes into something colourful to celebrate and discarded the receipt and her old clothes.

When she got home, she saw nothing unusual, no police cars, nothing. As she walked towards her front door, she decided that of course there would not be any activity just yet. After all they would have trouble identifying the bits of him that were left. As far as she knew he never carried anything that could identify him, always buying a new train ticket each day. He did have an oyster card for the buses he used to travel on though she didn't think he could be traced on that and anyway chances were it was destroyed in the accident.

Humming quietly, she entered the house and heard her mother upstairs. She called up to say hello then went into the kitchen to see if she could find a snack before dinner, boy was she hungry. She took her coffee up to her room and peered around the bathroom door to see Alfie giggling as her mum blew bubbles for him. Might as well enjoy it whilst you can, she thought, as she went into her room and shut the door behind her. Alfie had obviously been in her room again as her makeup was scattered all over the floor. She clenched her fists and smashed them together a few times whilst screaming through a clenched teeth then, when she had calmed, sorted through her shopping.

"Sister, sister," Alfie said as he pushed her door open and came into the room with his arms wide looking for a hug. She indulged him and swung him around loving the smell of him. He giggled and wriggled and she put him down as her mum peered around the door and called him out of the room telling him it was time for bed.

"Where's Dad, in the garden?" she asked innocently as her mum turned away to follow Alfie, then turned back to answer her saying that she thought he was working late. She picked out a scarf from her shopping and handed it across to her mum. She was engulfed in a sudden hug, a "thank you, darling" then her mum ran out of the room as clattering and banging could be heard coming from Alfie's room. She hadn't bought the scarf for her mum, she had bought it for herself, and even now was regretting her decision to give it to her mum. She hung up her new clothes in the wardrobe and sat down to think what would happen next. Oh yes, an announcement of the death would have to be put in the papers but first one of them would have to go to the funeral parlour to make arrangements. She nodded her head at these thoughts, thrilled to be experiencing at first hand the before and after of when someone close, a parent even, died.

The thought occurred to her that her father had been stupid, really stupid. After stabbing her he had gone back to bed and had slept soundly by all accounts as she had not heard him, or anyone else for that matter, moving about. He must have known that her body would soon be discovered. What sort of plan did he have in his head? Perhaps he was thinking that an intruder would be blamed or perhaps blame a burglary gone wrong. The police would find the camera when they searched the room and would have all the proof they needed to bang him up for a very long time. She smiled as she thought of the shock on his face when the camera evidence was discovered, then realised she was wasting time thinking like that. She was glad she had reacted the way she had. After all, just think of the shame and humiliation her mother would have had to live with, with her husband being a murderer.

As she went downstairs to help with dinner she suddenly thought, hold on, can't do anything until we get the body and there won't be much body to get! The thought made her laugh and she was still giggling as she went into the kitchen. Her mother looked back and smiled at her, pleased to see her daughter in such a good mood. "What's so funny?"

"Oh nothing, just something I read in the papers," she lied as she went over and helped her mother prepare the meal.

They had finished their meal and were drinking coffee when her mother anxiously glanced at the clock then her wristwatch. "Your father's late."

"You said he was working late, Mum."

"I don't know if he is working late, I just said that because he wasn't here."

"Oh."

"I think I'll phone his work, do you think?" her mother said indecisively standing up and rubbing her hands down her apron. Alfie chose that moment to tell the world that he was not tired and didn't want to go to bed, the cries of indignation spilling downstairs.

"You phone, Mum, if it makes you happy, I'll go up and see to Alfie." As she moved out of the kitchen Alfie was standing in his doorway furiously shaking the baby gate that stopped him from coming out of his room. He held his arms out to her calling, "Sister," hoping that she would pick him up and take him out of his room. She stood glaring at him and told him, in a fierce whisper to just shut the fuck up as she wanted to overhear what her mum said on the phone.

Alfie sat down. "Fuck," he said loud and clear. She looked at him in horror then decided she would have to miss out on hearing what her mum said on the phone and get her brother to bed and read him a story. She was really good at reading stories and bringing characters to life and she spent nearly half an hour with her brother before his eyelids got too heavy for him to hold open. She loved this time between being awake and going to sleep, having tried for years to feel that split second moment between them but failing miserably. She never thought about trying the same thing in the morning, being aware of that split second of being asleep and becoming awake. It just never occurred to her.

She looked down at the peaceful sleeping face of her little brother and felt a strong urge to pick him up and hug him with all her might but she resisted the impulse and instead just bent down and kissed him gently on his forehead before going downstairs.

Her mother was sitting at the kitchen table wringing her hands in her lap. "Mum, what's the matter, what did they say?" as she sat on a chair across from her mum. "Mum, Mum, listen, I'm talking to you."

"Something has happened to him, I know it," her mother said as tears poured down her face. "Something dreadful has happened to him, he would never be this late, never."

She got up and went around to cuddle her mum, stroking her hair and talking in a gentle soothing voice "Everything will be all right, you'll see, Mum. What did work say?"

"There was no answer so I just left a message."

"What message?"

"I don't know, I think I said for him to phone home as we were worried or something like that. Anyway what does it matter what I said?"

"Just asking Mum, just asking,"

They stayed entwined for a long time, rolls reversed as the child comforted the mum, crooning to her, rocking her, reassuring her and it was well into the night when they finally went upstairs to bed. She fell asleep almost at once well satisfied with the day's events and looking forward to a brand-new day.

She woke to hear Alfie crying and came out of her room to see him standing at the baby gate sobbing his little heart out. "Daddy gone, Daddy gone," he said over and over again. There was no noise from her mum's room so she gave Alfie a wash and took him downstairs for his breakfast. He was not in a co-operative frame of mind and his spoon flew through the air one way as his bowl flew the other. She was ready to shout at him but the look on his little face stopped her. She wondered if he was clairvoyant or something, wondered if he could sense that his daddy was dead. She made him a drink which he decided to have whilst she cleared up the mess he had made without a murmur. She wanted to take a breakfast tray up to her mother, a boiled or poached egg or something so that she could watch her and see what she was like before she found out that her husband was dead but she didn't want Alfie trailing after her so, in the end, decided not to.

She dressed Alfie and took him to his playschool and spent a few minutes there watching him as he socialised with other children and staff. She told a staff member that he was a little upset as his daddy hadn't come home the previous night and he was missing him, missing the usual night time routine of his daddy tickling him, reading him a story and staying with him till he slept.

Her mother came with her to collect Alfie and they went from there to the local police station to report that her dad was missing. The police took down notes and a recent photograph but said that he hadn't been missing long enough to go on the missing persons list yet. On the way home they stopped off at the newsagent to get a newspaper then continued on to the park.

She couldn't make her mum out, one minute she was acting as if everything was all right and the next tears were pouring down her face. She realised her mum was struggling and longed to tell her that her husband was dead so that at least she could get on with grieving. All this waiting for news wasn't doing anybody any good. On the way home they collected fish and chips and the rest of the day went fairly smoothly. Her dad's work phoned to see if he had returned home and said that they had asked all the staff but that nobody had seen her husband after he had left the office the same time as he usually did.

That evening she sat in her room feeling exhausted with all the running around and she almost wished her father was alive. At least if he was here, she thought, I could have some time to myself. It was only going to get worse though as soon she would have to make all the funeral arrangements. Bloody parents, who'd have them. She smiled at this thought and fell peacefully asleep.

The following morning, she put Alfie in his pushchair, called over her shoulder to her mum that she was taking him to playschool and walked up the passageway. There was a loud knock on the door just as she reached it which startled her. She opened the door to find two police officers standing on her doorstep. "Mrs Bailey?" they enquired. She called over her shoulder to her mum that the police were here, then went to move past them as her mum came out of the kitchen and came up to the front door.

"I'm Mrs Bailey. What do you want? Have you come about my husband? Have you found him? Oh please say you have," then, "what am I thinking off keeping you on the doorstep come in, come in," as she moved aside and ushered them into the house then turned to her daughter. "You'd best be moving, don't want Alfie to be late, do we?" she said as she planted a wet kiss on one of Alfie's cheeks which he immediately pulled a face at and said, "Go away." Her mum laughed, looked meaningfully at her, took a deep breath and disappeared into the house.

Once at playschool Alfie made for the sandpit and seemed all right so she returned home highly expectant at what she would find.

Her mother was sitting sobbing in the kitchen as she returned with one of the police officers crouched down in front of her trying to offer comfort. She threw her arms around her mother saying "Mum, what is it? What's the matter? Have they found him? Is Daddy all right?"

Her mother sobbed, "He's dead, your daddy is dead. What am I going to do? How can I tell Alfie that his daddy is dead?"

She just stood there hugging her mother, genuinely unable to say something. Goodness, she thought, I'm in shock, I'm actually grieving for that bastard. Tears ran down her face as she lay her head down on top of her mum's, inhaling the lavender conditioner her mum loved in the process.

The police officers were looking awkward and she moved away from her mother and moved out into the hallway and listened to what they had earlier told her mother, then thanked them for being so kind and let them out.

As soon as they had gone she leant back against the front door and laughed, then turned the sound into a cough in case her mum thought she was being heartless. She was ecstatic that she was actually feeling what it was like to grieve. It was painful, she had to admit, but thought that the experience could only enhance her acting career. She went into the kitchen and put the kettle on to make a cup of tea then answered the phone and handed it over to her mum, telling her it was her dad's work place on the line. She watched her mum's face to get any clues about what the caller was saying but in the end had to wait until her mum put the phone down. "They've had a collection," she said, "they've had a collection for Tommy, isn't that kind?" as a fresh flood of tears invaded her face. "I didn't tell them that he's dead, I couldn't, I can hardly accept it myself."

She found the next few days very difficult as she not only dealt with her emotions but watched her mum and little brother cope with their grief. She hadn't realised it could be so debilitating, that it could sap the life out of you and now she realised why people whose funerals she had attended looked the way they did.

Matthew was devastated for her loss and asked if there was anything at all that he could do but she found it easier to say nothing and simply cry. He would hold her and rock her and murmur in her ear and promise to be by her side if and when she needed him, all she had to do was ask.

Her mother floated between knowing that something awful had happened but could not remember what, to remembering what had happened and wishing she couldn't. In the end she took her mum to the doctor to see if he could help. The doctor gave her a certificate for a blood test, noted her mum's weight and height then asked her to leave the room whilst he talked to her mum. When she was called back in the doctor said he wanted to wait for the results of the blood test before prescribing any medication but suggested that counselling might help in the near future.

She couldn't believe the cost of funerals. She had gone from one funeral parlour to another but had found all their prices exorbitant to her way of thinking. She didn't want to spend a lot of money. After all what was the point? Her dad was dead, they should save on the cost and go on holiday or something instead. She suggested to her mum that, for the sake of the environment, they should have a cardboard coffin and received a sharp slap across her face for the suggestion.

Chapter 30
It Worked Before!

The days until the funeral seemed to drag but perhaps that was a good thing as there was so much to organise., although for every step she took forward she seemed to then take two steps backwards as her mother thwarted her arrangements at every turn. She wondered if her mum was doing it deliberately to frustrate her. She wouldn't put it past her after all was said and done.

There was something going on with her mum, something that was not quite right. She was sure that she had heard her mother humming happily in the kitchen the other morning though as soon as her mum sensed her presence she stopped humming and made out she was turning off the radio before pretending to notice her daughter and smile a sad smile at her. Unbelievable. She had spent years at acting college and yet her mum, without any sort of training, was putting on a performance of the bereaved wife that was amazing. If she hadn't gone to acting college she wouldn't have noticed the little signs that told her that her mum was playing a role for her benefit as well as for the benefit of his work colleagues and neighbours.

She decided to play along with it but this time carefully watched her mum who had decided that she would give her husband the best send-off ever even if she could not afford it. The wording of the announcement in the paper was changed, the date of the funeral was changed as her mother did not like even numbers, only yellow flowers were allowed and she chose the same old boring hymns that most people seemed to choose to say goodbye to their loved ones. She was visibly shocked when her daughter suggested live music.

Alfie was the only one in the family it seemed who missed his daddy and continually cried for him. His mum took him to the doctors as he was refusing to eat and throwing tantrums almost one after the other. He refused to be cuddled and pushed his mum and sister away when they tried to comfort him. "Go way," he cried.

Matthew had insisted on going to the funeral with her although she had repeatedly tried to put him off. They stood next to her mother in the church surprised at how full the church was as almost all the pews were taken, then realised that members of the firm where her dad worked were in attendance. There were even some members of the company she was going to work for. She was surprised, didn't they know what a real-life bastard he was? When her turn came to speak she should tell them a few home truths. She smiled as she imagined the shock appearing on their faces but knew she wouldn't say it, she would keep it dead and buried, or should she say dead and cremated. She couldn't help herself, she burst out laughing then quickly turned it into a coughing fit and dabbed at her eyes as she whispered loud enough for a few rows back to hear, "I love you, Daddy, I miss you." As the saying goes there wasn't a dry eye in the house. Matthew, his face a picture of sadness, put an arm around her and briefly hugged her and placed a gentle kiss on her nearest cheek.

A pigeon had somehow got into the church and was fluttering above them and the attention to the service wavered as some of the congregation watched it fearing that its droppings might adorn their clothes.

She watched it, fascinated whilst thinking of course, there should be white doves set free in the service where her funeral takes place, wouldn't that be something?

The curtains finally closed around the ornate coffin as the last dreary hymn was sung then she took her mum's arm and walked slowly down the aisle to wait outside and say thank you to the mourners as they exited the church. She looked out for her distant cousin, easily recognised in a wheelchair and was surprised that she hadn't attended.

An hour later she was standing outside the hotel greeting mourners who were attending the wake. Her legs ached and she wished she had put on her boots instead of the dainty high heels. They might not look too good but they would have been so much more comfortable.

At last they returned home having collected Alfie on the way. Matthew wanted to come in with them but she said she was tired after such a long sad day and he immediately apologised and left. As the big black car he drove smoothly moved off she watched him turn the corner then took a deep breath and went indoors. Her mother busied herself putting Alfie to bed then called her daughter into the kitchen and poured each of them a glass of chilled white wine. She took the glass from her mother and they clinked the glasses together then her mother said, "OK, the pretence stops here," and then downed the glass in one go, then refilled her glass. "Come on, you're falling behind," she said as she waved the bottle in her daughter's direction.

She was startled. What did her mother mean? What did she know? She downed her glass and held it out for a refill as her mum spoke. "It may or may not shock you what I am about to say but I don't care, I am going to say it anyway." She refilled her glass and said, "I am glad your dad's dead, glad he's out of my life. You don't know what I have had to put up with over the years. Come on, drink up, let's celebrate."

Of all the things she was expecting her mother to say this wasn't one of them. She was shocked, she had no idea that her mum felt this way. She said nothing but held out her glass for a refill and her mum got up and fetched two bottles of wine from the fridge and opened them saying, "Sod filling up the glasses, let's be rebels and drink from the bottle," so they did.

They spent a long time chatting, often incoherently as the wine took hold but she learnt a lot about her mum. That she had held down a well-paid position in a prestigious firm of city solicitors when she had first met her future husband and how she had given everything up for him. At their wedding day reception she had found him sexually active in one of the side rooms of the restaurant. She had forgiven him, she loved him but he continued to cheat on her and even consorted with street girls.

When her mum told her this she was startled, remembering the time she had gone to the red-light district. Bloody hell, she could have picked up her father! All these years and she never had the faintest idea of what was going on. What a little prick he was. She was so glad he was dead, so glad she had killed him. Part of her wanted to spill the beans, tell her mother that she had killed her husband and she almost did. "Mum, it was me who…" when suddenly she felt nauseous and quickly moved over to the butler sink and threw up in it, gagging even after her stomach was empty. She wiped her face with cold water and turned around to see her mother slumped in her chair fast asleep.

She had no idea how she managed to get her mother and herself up to bed. At one stage she seemed to remember they were crawling up the stairs giggling as the went but she woke up in her own bed the following morning so had managed it somehow.

She awoke late to find Alfie drawing on her wall with her make-up pencils. She watched him for a little while, then simply turned over and went back to sleep. Alfie continued his drawing until he heard his mother calling him and left the room and his sister in peace.

Later that morning he was sitting in his pushchair in a queue in the local supermarket chatting away to a child in the pushchair next to him whilst his mother chatted to her mother until it was time to move on and pay for the purchases they had made. Apparently there had been a spate of burglaries in the area and the local neighbourhood watch was holding a meeting that evening to discuss people's concerns. Leaving with a promise to attend the meeting, Mrs Bailey returned home to find her daughter sitting bleary-eyed in the kitchen. They exchanged greetings then she unpacked the shopping whilst her daughter went upstairs to wash and brush up.

Time passed and she worried as it seemed to fly by and kept checking the mirror for signs of aging. Her mum had started a course to refresh and update her skills with a view to approaching her former boss when she had requalified. She thought about her mum and her enthusiasm for learning new skills and couldn't believe how much she had changed since the funeral. She became philosophical for a moment and thought of her mum as a butterfly emerging from a cocoon, then turned her thoughts to her own life which, compared to her mum's seemed to be at a standstill.

She thought about her relationship with Matthew and whether she loved him or not. She liked him and she definitely liked the attention that she got when she was out with him but wondered if that was enough. He wasn't sexually exciting and she was beginning to get fed up with pretending to have orgasms. What she wanted, no, no, what she needed, was a rough diamond, someone who didn't show her respect, didn't shower her with gifts.

She sighed and went to the window and stared outside and saw a tiny moth struggling in a spider's web. She used a cotton bud to try to free it but managed to kill it in the process. She was mortified and thought of herself as the little moth trying to break free and being crushed by society.

Wow. Where did that come from. She brushed her hair and went downstairs just as her mobile rang. Her mum glanced at her then continued to prepare the dinner. The kitchen was such a mess, not at all like the gleaming kitchen she was used to when her dad was alive but she decided she liked it, it looked lived in, homely.

She checked who was ringing then answered her mobile, "Yes."

"It's Matthew, darling."

"Yes."

"Are you all right, sweetheart."

She raised her eyes to the ceiling. "Yes."

"I'll pick you up around eight thirty all right?"

"Yes," she replied, and switched off her mobile and made growling noises in the back of her throat. Alfie came into the kitchen at that moment and immediately copied her and for the next five minutes or so the three of them made similar growling noises and giggled. Her mood lightened considerably and she picked up her baby brother and sat him on her lap but he immediately wriggled down and left the kitchen.

"Who was that then?" asked her mum knowing perfectly well who it was.

"Matthew."

"Oh," she uttered in a disinterested way then, "you going out later?"

"Mum, you know I am, you overheard me. I know you did."

"How is he?"

"Same old, same old."

"What does that mean?"

"I dunno, when I am with him I love him but when I'm not I don't."

Her mother sat down at the table with her and took hold of one of her daughter's hands "If he doesn't make you happy, darling, you should tell him."

"It's not that simple, Mum. Oh, I dunno, I think I'm going through the menopause or something. I keep getting loads of mood swings and stuff."

"Stuff?"

"Yes, stuff."

"Make an appointment with the doctor, dear," her mum said as she kissed her daughter's forehead, "be careful or you might lose him."

After dinner she helped wash up then went upstairs to get herself ready.

She and Matthew attended an opening night of one of his father's new productions and had a box near the stage. She became mesmerised by the leading lady and followed her every move. She didn't know what it was about the woman that attracted her attention but knew she had star quality and at the reception afterwards she sought her out to see her more closely. She was disappointed momentarily, the woman wasn't ugly as such but she wasn't pretty either, but as soon as she switched herself on, became the actress, those around her were captivated.

She was quiet in the car on the way home thinking over the evening. She knew the actress was streets ahead of her but she wanted to be on stage with her so that she could watch and learn from her. She had thought she was good but now she realised she had so much more to learn. She thought about what the woman, Cyran, had said to her as they left. "Never stop learning, never think you are better than anyone else, darling."

Matthew got out and opened the door of his car to let her out and she thanked him absent-mindedly and gave him a peck on the cheek before going indoors. Matthew stood and watched her and wondered what he was doing wrong. He worshipped the ground she walked on yet she felt distant a lot of the time. As her front door closed behind her he sighed then got back in his car and drove away.

Alfie started Infant school the term after Christmas and as she looked at her excited little brother all squeaky clean and shiny in his new school uniform she remembered back to when she had started school all those years ago. She had felt excited and nervous at the same time and expected that that was how Alfie was feeling now, although to be honest, he didn't look at all nervous. She waved her mum and Alfie goodbye then closed the front door and leaned against it briefly pushing herself off it when her phone rang. Drat it, she could hear the phone but where the heck was it. The phone rang off as she found it and found a missed call listed, stupid bloody thing, she thought, I know I missed it. She threw the phone down just as it rang again. "Hello!"

"Darling, when are you coming to see me?"

"Cyran, it's lovely to hear from you, I was hoping you'd call me sometime."

There was silence for a little while then Cyran's husky voice said, "Me too, darling, come round, I'll send the car," then she put the phone down.

She was in a tiz, what should she wear? Cyran had phoned her, she had actually phoned her, oh my gosh I'm dreaming, she thought, as she sorted through her wardrobe discarding everything she pulled out. In the end she chose her white trouser suit and just managed to scribble a note to her mother before the doorbell rang announcing the arrival of the chauffeur driven car.

She spent the rest of the day and most of the night in bed with Cyran as they explored each other and found new ways to bring delight. She was infatuated with everything Cyran did and decided that she wanted to be like her. She left early the following morning on cloud nine expecting to hear from Cyran again but, as the days passed, she became more and more anxious. Should she call? Yes, no, she didn't know what to think or do. Had she upset her? Should she send her flowers? She couldn't make her mind up. She didn't know what to do, but a small niggle at the back of her mind telling her that she had been used, wouldn't go away.

She went out for a long run then found herself in a pub and downed a pint of lager in one go. OK, it was not ladylike but she didn't do it to impress anyone. She did though and found herself drinking and chatting with a fresh-faced cockney boy. She was fascinated with his accent and copied it much to his amusement.

She awoke next morning in a strange room beside the young man she had been chatting with. He stirred then leant up on one elbow and grinned down at her. "Morning, darling, want more of the same."

She was confused for a moment, then realisation dawned and she pushed herself away from him saying, "Who the hell are you? Get away from me. Go."

"You didn't say that last night, sweetheart, couldn't wait to open your legs for me. I bounced on you all night and thank you very much indeed for asking I had a great time and guess what, I've even got some nice little photos to remember you by. Though come to think of it none are of your face." He held the phone out to her so that she could see the photos as well as hear the gasps, grunts and groans on a video.

She flew at him. "You bastard," she cried, and tried to grab the phone but he neatly sidestepped her and held the phone up out of her reach as he laughed at her futile attempts. She did manage to gouge his face with her nails before he caught her forearms and thrust her roughly back on the bed then dressed, blew her a kiss and was gone.

Date rape. Date rape she repeated with horror not being able to remember a single thing about the previous night. She jumped up from the bed and had a hot shower thoroughly rinsing herself out in an attempt to deal with what had happened. She should go to the police but she knew she wouldn't. After all, what had happened would do her reputation no good at all. Life was unbelievable, she thought, one moment she was ecstatic with Cyran and the next she was mortified with finding out she had been used and hung out to dry with a handsome stranger. She crept, shame-faced, out of the boarding house keeping her head down so that nobody would recognise her but her way was blocked and money for the rent of the room for the night was demanded in a loud accusing voice that drew everybody's attention.

She was surprised how the feeling of shame overwhelmed her and of herself ending up such an easy target. She had thought she was street wise but if the past recent events were anything to go by she must be walking around with an 'I'm easy' notice pinned to her back.

The house was empty when she got home for which she was grateful and once in her room she stripped naked and examined herself horrified at finding love bites all over intimate parts of her body, but try as she might she couldn't remember a thing. She was furious with herself and knew she had to be punished and immediately took a thin belt from her drawer and beat herself till she could stand no more.

Why, oh why, was she such a fool? Why was she such an easy target? She stood in front of the mirror and looked at the lash weals on her body and told herself she deserved worse, that she had got away lightly although she knew she couldn't have taken any more pain but the trouble was she didn't feel punished and couldn't understand why. What on earth was wrong with her? Surely normal people didn't beat themselves almost senseless. She lay on top of her bed and masturbated, treating herself roughly. She cried with the pain but eventually reached a draining climax.

As she lay on top of her bed she heard her mum come in with someone whose voice she didn't recognise whom she had invited in for a cup of tea. She quickly hid the evidence of her activities and climbed under the duvet holding her breath as long as she could so that her cheeks looked flushed but she needn't have bothered as her mum did not come upstairs or even call up to see she was in.

As she lay in her bed she remembered what had happened the last time she had beat herself; she had ended up in Ward 3. She needed to make sure that her mum never found out, didn't see evidence of self-harm because, plain and simple, that was what it was. She wondered if she would feel suitably punished if someone else beat her. Would that then be the end of it? It was a possibility and the mere thought of it excited her so that she masturbated again but this time much more gently.

She should be feeling on top of the world she thought, she was young, pretty, talented, had a roof over her head, people who loved her maybe, a handsome well-connected boyfriend, a flourishing career, she should just pull herself together. Her mum on the other hand, who was old, prettyish, tied down with a young child was, for some reason she had yet to work out, happy. She got up singing or humming and spent the day smiling so much it should have made her face ache.

Whilst sitting at the breakfast table with Alfie one morning she noticed her mum's mobile left on the table. Her mum was upstairs hoovering so she pulled the mobile over to her and quickly scrolled through the messages whilst keeping an ear out for the hoovering to stop. Unbelievable, there were at least ten messages from someone who signed out D. followed by two hearts and two crosses. Was this D. her boyfriend? Were these messages the reason her mum was so happy? What on earth did the D stand for? Dennis, yuk she hoped not, Douglas, Derek, Daren, Donald? The hoovering stopped and she quickly turned the mobile off and pushed it back to where it had been. Alfie said,

"Phone" and pointed to his sister as his mum, entered the kitchen but her mum simply said, "Thank you, darling," and kissed him as she picked it up. Alfie grimaced and pulled away and his mum laughed and patted him lightly on the top of his head.

It took her a long time to track the one night stand down and the irony was that she came across him by accident. On a whim she had called into the local sports centre to find out about jujitsu classes for Alfie and there he was on the court playing basketball. He was good she had to admit and she spent a little longer than she wanted to watching him. His name, she heard from his fellow players was Tommy. How strange that he should have the same name as her dad though perhaps not, after all they were both bastards. She signed Alfie up for a judo class as he was too young for jujitsu and considered she had done a good day's work. Judo was the perfect excuse for her to be at the centre and would, perhaps, help to expend some of Alfie's energy.

Matthew took her to Aintree and out of the blue, in front of hundreds of people got down on one knee and proposed to her. She flushed with embarrassment as people stopped to stare at her. The ring, sapphires and diamonds, dripped money and sparkled in the sunlight and she said, "Yes," to a loud round of applause and flashing cameras. Matthew kissed her deeply feeling relieved, he knew that she would have rather him ask her in a quiet little out of the way restaurant but he didn't want to give her the chance to refuse him which is why he had made his proposal public. After all she was a budding actress and would bound to be playing to her audience. At the end of the day he had got what he wanted even if he had to tip the scales a fraction and it never even crossed his mind that she could or would refuse him. After all, he loved her with all his heart.

She went back to his luxury flat and allowed him to make love to her, making sure the lights were out so that he could not see the fading marks where she had beaten herself. He was gentle, loving and thoughtful which was none of the things she needed. She had wanted him to strip her and beat her then take her by force, telling her all the time it was what she deserved. She faked an orgasm to please him but was left feeling empty, cold.

Back home she showed her mum her engagement ring and was swamped with kisses and cuddles from her. Her mum started talking wedding plans and she backed out of the kitchen with a smile and went up to her room and thought things through. Even though she had flushed herself out thoroughly in the shower after her night with Tommy she knew that there was a small chance that she could be pregnant. She had planned to sleep with Matthew at the first opportunity to cover herself and couldn't believe her luck when everything fell into place. True he was a lousy lover but if she became pregnant now he would carry the can and after all, he could change. Perhaps she could teach him a few tricks! She could wind him up, get him really angry to see what he would do and just hoped he wasn't one of those men who dissolved into tears.

She suddenly sat down with a thump, slapping an open palm onto her forehead a few times. Here she was congratulating herself on blaming a pregnancy on her fiancé when she needn't have bothered. She couldn't get pregnant even if she wanted to; the rape all those years ago had put paid to that. The older she was getting, the more mistakes she was making. It just wasn't good enough.

Whilst Alfie was in his judo class she took the opportunity of checking out the men's washroom just to check out the lay of the land but she needn't have bothered as except for the urinals the layout was the same as the ladies. Just as she was stepping out of 'The Lad's Changing Room' (the legend on the door) another idea came to her and she turned and went back in. She'd have to be quick as she had no idea when anybody would come in and the only hiding place was under some of the coats and jackets hung on the pegs. She was surprised that although lockers were used none of them were locked and some didn't use lockers at all. She went through these first placing money, and phones in a pile but didn't come across anything belonging to Tommy. She pushed the stash collected so far under one of the benches then turned to the lockers and struck lucky with the fourth locker down. All she took was the mobile from it replacing it with the stash she had taken from her earlier search, carefully tucking it inside one of his trainers. She knew she should get out of there but her curiosity made her sit down and check through the phone from Tommy's locker. Luckily the phone wasn't locked and scrolling through, hidden in a 'Legs 11' file, she found the photos she was looking for plus many more, too many of them to look through where she was. The door hinges protested as the door opened and she melted behind some coats and listened to someone using the urinal then going straight back out. She gave whoever it was a few seconds then followed them out pleased to see the corridor was empty. There were multiple cameras around the building but she knew from casual chatting and fluttering her eyes at the caretaker that they weren't active, a money saving project using dummy equipment. Nice.

Once home and settled for the night she took out the mobile she had taken from Tommy's locker and scrolled through it. She couldn't believe the number of pornographic images that were on the phone and could not identify the photos she was in, after all one crotch being penetrated, was much like another, apart from the colour and style of the pubic hair. Tommy had obviously been a busy lad. Her first impulse was to delete the images and she almost did, her disgust compelling her to do so, but then she had second thoughts. All the evidence she needed to put him away for a very long time was right here in her hands, right here to do with as she pleased. She dropped the mobile on her bed frightened that she would accidentally delete the images she had found. She had heard rumours of what happened to sex offenders in prison and hoped they were true. She wouldn't do anything with the mobile just yet, she would choose a time when he thought he had got away with it. The little Tommy bird was about to get his wings well and truly clipped and didn't know it, oh what joy.

Alfie was booked in for two judo lessons per week and was loving practising rolling break-falls and generally being able to throw himself around. He had no sense of danger at all and if he was hurt he simply shrugged it off and carried on. It was in the sports centre canteen nearly a month later before she saw Tommy again not that she was in a hurry, his cards were marked and he would get more of the same when the time was right. He was on crutches with one lower leg encased in plaster sitting watching the basketball game through the glass windows. She left the canteen and watched the remainder of Alfie's lesson knowing that she had to be very very careful in case he recognised her.

The local paper printed a positive article about her at the same time that one of the glossy magazines ran an article on her as 'the one to watch' and she began to be asked to give autographs, one or two at first but this increased as her fame grew. She was very gracious to everyone that approached her and before long she had a flourishing fan club which she supported wholeheartedly and gave the people who ran it some of her trinkets to offer as prizes. She wondered if she should go on line and get people following her but decided against it for it took a commitment to keep it updated that she wasn't prepared to give.

Her career was suddenly flourishing though why it had suddenly taken off she didn't understand as she still hadn't played the lead role in any production yet so she put it down to her engagement with Matthew or the newspaper and magazine articles, perhaps. She decided, it was a bit of both. She regularly visited her father-in-law, much to his discomfort, and wouldn't have been at all surprised to hear about the angry scenes he had with his son as he tried to dissuade him from marrying her. Matthew had always given in to the pressure exerted on him so when he wouldn't back down Mr Bainridge couldn't accept it. He called his son's fiancée a whore, a tart, a money grabber and made out that she had virtually dragged him in a side room to get a piece of him but all to no avail and in the end he called a truce though he didn't like to, his own son had got the better of him!

Her mum announced to her that she was going to work part-time at the solicitors where she had worked when she had first met her father. She was obviously delighted and they had a take-away to celebrate. She was pleased for her mum but couldn't understand why she was going to work when she didn't need to. The insurance she had taken out for her husband when she had first met him had paid for the house but she wasn't a stay-at-home type she realised, she had spent far too many years chained to the kitchen sink and now it was time for her to fly and fly she would!

She idly fiddled with the mobile she had stolen from Tommy whilst staring at nothing, her mind working overtime. She had been tempted to report the rape to the police, at the same time handing in the mobile as evidence, but realised that it could be detrimental if she came under their scrutiny. It went against the grain for her to do nothing, to not retaliate. She imagined Tommy being sent to prison for a long time and his fellow prisoners dealing out the justice they saved for sex offenders, then shook her head to clear her thoughts. It wasn't going to happen. Tommy had got the best of her, the only person to do so, but she couldn't waste her time dwelling on the fact, for she soon would be going on tour. Soon she would be a star. She dropped the mobile onto the floor and stamped on it but gained no satisfaction from doing so.

The company she was in were going on a six-month tour in a fortnight's time or maybe even longer if it was successful and she was offered the part of the leading lady as the actress who was currently holding down that role had no intention of going on tour. She was ecstatic, leading lady at last. Matthew promised to come up and visit her regularly and gave her a diamond pendant for luck.

Her mum was so pleased for her that she began to suspect ulterior motives. She would be away for at least six months. Was her mum glad to be rid of her one and only daughter, glad to have a break, or was there something else going on?

She watched her mother whilst trying to appear not to and realised that she had been so wrapped up in what she had been doing lately that she hadn't picked up on the signs her mum was giving out. That her mum had a boyfriend she was certain, after all she had seen the messages signed D on her mobile. What she couldn't understand was why it upset her. After all her mum had a life, had a right to go out with whom she wanted, didn't she?

She had seen her mum coming home with flushed cheeks, leaving the kitchen to answer her mobile, noticed she was staying out longer than usual, asking her to be sure to collect Alfie from school as something had come up. She wanted to ask her mum straight out and was in two minds about going on the tour. Nobody was going to usurp her. It was her home as much as anybody's. In six months' time, if she was right, the man, whoever he was, would have his feet well and truly under the table.

She decided that today she was going to confront her mother and marched in to the house and down the hall into the kitchen. Her mum was talking to someone she didn't know and glanced up as she entered, the ready smile on her face dropping as she saw the set of her daughter's face. "Darling, what is it, what's wrong?"

She had expected her mum to be on her own and coming face to face with a stranger put her on the back foot and she found that, for a moment, she was speechless.

Her mum came over to her and put an arm around her shoulder and squeezed her, then said, "Dorothy, let me introduce you to my daughter."

Dorothy smiled pleasantly enough and simply said, "Hello."

Her mum seemed satisfied and went over and stood beside Dorothy, cleared her throat and said, "Dorothy is my lover, she will be moving in with us," and left the statement hanging in the air.

Dorothy, Dorothy, she must be the D that she had seen on her mum's mobile, the D with the two hearts and the two xxs. She smiled suddenly, totally relieved and said, "Oh Mum, Dorothy, I'm so happy for you," and threw her arms around both of them, and they stood for a few precious moments in a group hug. The surprising thing was that she genuinely was delighted for her mum. There wasn't going to be another man moving into the house, there was going to be another woman. Hurrah, she could now go on the six months tour feeling happy.

Chapter 31
Getting the Needle!

Two months into the tour and she had had enough. She understood why the original leading lady had refused to go. She had no time to herself; she couldn't think. Each minute of her day was mapped out, rehearsals, costumes, make-up and all the other little bits that go to make a successful tour, even her understudy was getting on her nerves, silly little bitch, pretending she was in awe of her. She had been there and bought the T-shirt so to speak. She knew what went through the mind of most understudies.

She had called her understudy a bitch but she knew she was turning into one herself. Her plan to be pleasant and kind to everyone had gone out the window as her energy drained and her frustration mounted.

Matthew was her only distraction and she made the most of her time with him, usually under or on top of her duvet. She was gradually introducing him to some techniques and sexual toys and there were signs that he was coming out of his shell at long last. She only hoped that she could hang in there long enough so that he would be the ardent lover she needed.

In the meantime she had formed a liaison with one of the stage hands. He had caught her as she tripped and faked a swoon which had got her a night off the production and she made full use of it. She whispered the name and number of her room in her hotel to him before she was supported to the car to take her there. Once there, she insisted she was all right to be left. She wanted to sleep and so was left on her own.

When he first came into the room she was disappointed and thought she had misjudged him as he was almost doffing his cap. She told him to go and shower and come out naked and she would be on the bed ready for him. He simply nodded his head and disappeared into the shower room which was still steamy from when she had used it. She heard the shower running and quickly went through his pockets and took out and tucked his mobile phone in the waste bin after she had turned it off. She had been caught once too often before and did not intend to make the same mistake again. She was tempted to go in there and grab hold of his penis, she loved wet men and wanted to see what he would do. She spent a good ten minutes fantasizing before she realised the shower had stopped. She positioned herself near the door and waited then, as he came out of the shower room she slapped him twice as hard as she could across his face and was going for a third when he caught her arm and said, "So that's how you want to play it is it," and before she knew it she found herself bent over his lap as he gave her a sound spanking then turned her over and made violent love to her. She was in heaven, at last, someone who understood her, at last someone who met her needs though at the same time she realised what a thoughtless selfish beast he was; he had made no attempt whatsoever to wear a condom and no attempt whatsoever to pull out before he climaxed. She wondered if she had bitten off more than she could chew but, in the calm after sex she pushed the thought aside. After all she had dealt with better men than he and would do so again when the time came, she was sure of it.

She woke the following morning feeling better than she had in a long time. Matthew had sent her an enormous bunch of yellow roses and had phoned her full of concern for her welfare but she told him the rest had done her a power of good and she was ready to carry on. She thanked him for the roses but took the edge of his pleasure when she reminded him that she didn't like cut flowers.

She continued her affair with the stagehand sometimes even having a quickie backstage with him. She didn't love him and wasn't even sure if she liked him but boy could he fuck and she wasn't prepared to give that up until she was ready.

She had phoned her mum regularly during her absence and most times she got Dorothy on the phone. She found she was able to chat to Dorothy about Matthew, her performance and anything that came to mind. Dorothy had told her that her mum was back at work full-time and that Alfie was doing well at school and in his judo classes which she had taken over the responsibility of taking him to.

The six-month tour was nearly at an end and the cast heard that there were no plans to extend it even though it had been extraordinarily successful with packed houses every night and raving reviews in the papers and glossy magazines. Fans called her name as she swept in and more and more thrust autograph books under her nose and she made sure that she played the part, smiled sweetly and blew kisses and said, "Darling," in a husky voice.

After a particularly robust romp with the stagehand she showered and started to dress then said, "Darling heart, I think we should stop seeing each other, I can't keep up with you," but was in no way prepared for his swift response. She found herself violently pushed back onto the bed, his face, a picture of menace a few inches above her. She screamed at the suddenness of it all but her scream was cut off as he clamped both of his hands across her mouth. There was a sudden knock on the door. "I say, are you all right in there?"

He nodded his head towards the door and narrowed his eyes then hissed in her ear, "Answer them."

She cleared her throat then called, "It's all right, I found a spider on my bed."

"Well, if you're sure!"

"Yes I am, thank you for checking."

"No problem."

They lay there for a few moments their warm breath making them sweaty. He pulled away and continued to dress. "No one finishes with me, you understand. It is I who does the finishing when I am good and ready and not before." He stood over her, menacing and she fell into role play after all she had played out this scene so many times before.

"I'm sorry, my sweet, it's just that I feel I'm not good enough for you," she whispered as she allowed a few tears to overspill her eyes and run down her cheeks.

He laughed, pleased that she admired his sexual prowess. He thrust out his chest with pride and strode manfully out of the room turning at the door to give his parting shot. "Remember, my sweet, I've got too much on you," as he blew her a kiss and left the room.

She was so furious she did not know what to do with herself. She clenched her teeth and tried hard not to give vent to her emotions just in case he was still outside the door listening then, unable to hold back any longer she grabbed hold of a pillow and screamed into it. Blackmail, the bastard was going to blackmail her, oh shit, that's all she needed, especially when all her dreams were coming true and she was going to be famous. She would have to do something about it of course, she couldn't possibly have any skeletons in the cupboard, could she?

After the final performance all the cast dressed up in various costumes and had a wild party to celebrate. She people watched making sure that she kept her glass topped up with water as she needed a clear head. Matthew had bought her a simply stunning necklace of sapphires, diamonds and rubies and she had insisted putting it on immediately, then thanking him with a passionate kiss then a hug. As she hugged him she looked over his shoulder and saw the stagehand watching her, a wry smile on his face, then turn away and start talking to her understudy. She couldn't believe it, she felt jealous. She had everything she could possibly wish for, well nearly everything, and she was jealous that the stagehand was flirting in front of her with her understudy of all people! She was sure he was doing it on purpose to wind her up although since that first glance he hadn't looked at her again.

Matthew sensed something was wrong and pulled away from the hug to look into her face. "What's wrong?"

"Nothing, darling, nothing at all. I was just thinking how much I want to be alone with you."

He laughed. "You're a little minx and I wouldn't want you any other way," and kissed her lightly on the cheek then, "will you be all right on your own for a moment or two? I need a word with Dad," and moved away as she nodded.

She moved out into the cool dark hallway pleased to be away from the fray and sipped her glass of water then decided she needed the ladies so quietly glided down the passage mentally waving her hands left and right to adoring fans as she went. She could hear sounds of other people in the toilets as she silently entered but was not in the least prepared for the scene that confronted her, for in one of the cubicles she could see the back of someone obviously, going by the grunts and groans, giving someone a good servicing. She took out her mobile and put it on video and let it run for a good twenty seconds or so before stopping it and entering the cubicle next to it. She sat on the toilet seat listening to the sounds coming from the next cubicle as she ran through the video again to check she had captured the action, thrilled to be so close to it and excited that the people involved were unaware they had been discovered. She then sent it to the mobiles of most of the people in the main room then deleted it from her phone then waited a few moments, noisily flicked the catch on the door as if it was stuck then opened it hearing the door of the cubicle next to her being shut. She laughed and wondered if they were still at it, excited by the fact that they might be caught but desperate to finish what they had started, albeit without the sound accompaniment. Imagine trying to fuck quietly when you were reaching for an orgasm! Impossible. She thought about standing on the toilet seat and peering over into the next cubicle and shouting, "Boo," but she managed to contain this childish response. When she noisily left the cubicle, she washed and dried her hands, deliberately taking her time then knocked on the closed door just before she left unable to resist the urge to do so. "You all right in there?" There was a faint reply to the affirmative and she left quickly whilst putting a hand over her mouth to smother a giggle.

Back in the main room there was a different atmosphere as people accessed their mobile phones. She went over to a group and asked what they were watching and she watched the twenty second clip faking a gasp of horror. "Oh no, that's dreadful, who is it?"

"At a guess it looks like one of the stagehands, you know, Steve, the good looking one that is always watching you."

"Is he, how awful. What do you mean always watching me?"

"He just is that's all. Can't see who the other one is though. oh, talk of the devil here he is."

Steve she thought, all this time I've been bonking him and I never knew his name.

Steve looked around the room puzzled by the surreptitious glances he was getting and went over to some of his mates who showed him the clip and patted him on the back obviously impressed by his temerity.

She had had enough and decided that she wanted to leave and went over to Matthew who was still talking earnestly to his father, both of them obviously having missed all the mobile entertainment, and hung on his arm to get his attention then told him she was tired and needed to lay down. Matthew went immediately to get her coat and Mr Bainridge gave her a tight smile then excused himself to be replaced by Steve hissing in her ear, "I know it was you, it won't make a difference you know. You think you're something, think you're extraordinary but I'm here to tell you that you're not, your just an ordinary little bitch." Matthew returned with her coat and she swept out of the hall with her arm around Matthew's waist. She could feel Steve's eyes boring into her but, resisting the temptation to turn around, she allowed her hand to drop down to caress and squeeze Matthew's buttock.

Back in the hotel room she lay back on the bed saying, "The last night here, thank goodness, what shall we do to celebrate?"

Matthew looked at her and smiled, then said, "Let's get an early night, I'm done for."

She sat up. "What! You're kidding me right!"

"I've had a pounding headache all evening, not helped I may add by speaking with my father, and now I need peace and quiet please," he replied, as he sat on the edge of the bed and removed his shoes then wriggled his tie off.

She had no sympathy for him whatsoever, she was feeling randy and wanted him there and then so she flung her arms around his neck and started kissing him and whispering in his ear but was shocked into silence when he gently removed her arms from around his neck, turned and kissed her then lay down and closed his eyes and within a few moments was snoring gently.

She was furious, she had never ever been rejected by anybody, it was unheard off. She looked at his sleeping form and fought off the desire to pound him with her fists. Bastard had gone to sleep on her. She shoved herself off the bed and changed her clothing then picked up her handbag and checked she had enough money for a drink or two. She had deliberately drunk water all night and now she just wanted to get rat-arsed. Reject her! She'd show him.

The contents of her handbag amazed her, she couldn't remember putting half of it in there, pencil sharpeners, safety pins, sewing needles, one small knitting needle, a packet of condoms, a crochet hook. She couldn't think what she was looking for, for a moment, then saw her purse, picked it up and checked the contents then shovelled the rest of the stuff back in her handbag thinking she must really sort it out sometime, then marched out of the room without a backward glance towards the sleeping figure on the bed.

She bought two bottles of malt in an off-licence and hadn't gone more than a few paces before she started swigging it from the bottle. She hadn't eaten too much and before long she felt the impact of the alcohol. Feeling decidedly dizzy she slumped down and heard a concerned voice. "You all right, love?"

A sharp woman's voice said, "Leave her, she's a prossy," and she made out their blurry figures moving away from her.

"Fuck you too," she shouted at the top of her voice and giggled then slid sideways and fell asleep to awake the following morning stone cold sober in a police cell. She was mortified and had no recollection of the events of the previous evening. It was late morning before Matthew came in to collect and vouch for her. She held her head down in shame as she was severely reprimanded then released. Matthew did not say a word to her on the way back to the hotel, though she tried desperately to engage him in conversation, and kept telling him she was sorry and that she would never do it again.

Once back in the hotel room she thought to get around him and pacify him but the look on his face shocked her. She had never seen him so angry and it frightened her. "Go and shower, you look disgusting," he said in a harsh voice and she meekly obeyed. The shower refreshed her and she came out of it feeling much better. She wrapped a towel around her hair and sauntered saucily out of the shower room but Matthew did not take any notice of her as he was busy packing her suitcase. He spoke to her without turning around. "I've had to pay for another night's stay, we were meant to be out by ten."

Feeling sure of herself she moved up close behind him and rubbed her groin against him whilst whispering his name. He turned to face her with a strange smile on his face and took hold of her and dragged her over to the bed. She was not in the least bit reluctant to go with him, he was her He-man and she was his woman, she felt she was on safe ground.

Matthew sat down on the bed and jerked her to fall across his knees, pushed her flimsy dressing gown aside although it would not offer her much protection and proceed to give her the hiding of her life which went on for several minutes as he emphasized each bouncing slap with verbal accompaniment. "I'm going to teach you a lesson you will never forget, my little lady, by the time I've finished you won't be able to sit down for a fortnight." She tried to put a hand back to protect her buttocks but Matthew simply laughed as he held it out of the way and seemed to slap her even harder. When he had finished, he pushed her from his lap so that she fell to the floor and left the room without saying another word.

She had needed him to make love to her after the beating, needed the reassurance of sexual contact but she didn't get it. He had walked out on her, this time she had gone too far. She didn't know she could cry so much, gently at first as she hoped that Matthew might return and see her upset and love her, then loud gasping sobs as she realised that he wasn't coming back, she had pushed him too far.

It was a very subdued young lady who travelled home alone the following day. Matthew had been right, she couldn't sit down so had to stand all the way home. She should be riding high on the crest of a wave with the success of the play but she did not feel successful, she felt sad and lonely, she needed to be home amongst people who loved her.

Alfie squealed with delight when he saw her and jumped up into her arms and she hugged him like never before. "We saw you on telly, we saw you on telly," he shrieked as she put him down to cuddle Dorothy. She stood in the kitchen feeling so good to be home and Dorothy put the kettle on and brought her up to date with all the news and how well Alfie was doing in judo having graded the previous week.

One minute she was chatting away and then she burst into tears. She hurriedly wiped them away with the back of her wrists and turned to go but Dorothy took hold of her upper arm and said, "Wait a minute," and took Alfie out to the sandpit to make her a castle. Once back indoors she made two steaming cups of coffee, passed one over, then said, "Talk to me."

She shook her head and looked down at the floor to avoid the searching brown eyes but Dorothy cupped her hands under her chin and raised her head up. "Talk to me," and, though she had no intention of telling her anything she told her everything (well nearly everything). She told about the productions last night party and how she had left arm in arm with Matthew, then about Matthew going to sleep when she needed him to cuddle her and of her going out and getting drunk and waking up in a police cell. She told about Matthew arriving at the police station and bailing her out and that he had been really angry and that she hadn't seen or heard from him since. As she finished telling her story huge teardrops spilled down her face again. Dorothy simply threw her arms around her and fiercely cuddled her whilst stroking and patting her head and saying, "There there."

She stood still comforted by the cuddle for quite a long time it seemed then Dorothy looked into her face and wiped her wet cheeks with her sleeve whilst saying, "He'd be a fool to let you go and you know it, just give him time to calm down and see reason, all right?"

She snivelled and sniffed a few times then nodded her head and whispered, "Thank you, Aunty Dorothy," then gave her a final hug before going up to her room, outside of which was a big poster to welcome her back. She gave a big sigh then lay down on her bed and promptly fell asleep.

The days went by without a word from Matthew and she went from being sorry to being angry with him several times a day which she found very exhausting but seemed unable to stop. Her mother looked amazing, she was obviously very happy and content and, although she was happy for her she couldn't help feeling a little jealous. She took off her engagement ring and threw it across the room, then spent the next half hour panicking as she searched for it. When she finally found it she noticed that one of the rubies was missing and although she used a magnifying glass to go over the area she had thrown it she couldn't find it. It was a bad omen she just knew it was.

She started swimming again, getting up very early to avoid the crowds and, although she practised hard she never returned to the speed and grace she had when younger. She determined to swim a hundred lengths without stopping but found herself struggling when she had only swum half that amount but pushed herself and finally managed seventy lengths before she had to give in. She realised she was letting herself go, no wonder Matthew didn't want her any more, she was unfit, she had let herself go, after all those years of training hard she had suddenly stopped and now she was getting fat and ugly, or so she thought.

Why had she stopped swimming? She used to love it, used to challenge herself to get better and now, apart from the occasional run, she did nothing. Run, she thought that's it, running, swimming one day and running the next that would get her fit and would also keep her mind occupied, stop her thinking about Matthew.

The weeks went by and her fitness improved but she still had heard nothing from Matthew. Well sod it, she thought, if he thinks that I am going to go crawling back to him he's got another think coming, I should have had him up for assault. He's lucky I didn't. She nodded her head as if agreeing with her thoughts then decided she needed to get out more. She grabbed hold of her handbag spilling the contents in the process then proceeded to shovel them back into the bag except for one or two items and left the house.

As she walked the darkening streets, she knew she was kidding herself. She wanted Matthew and nobody else, she would do whatever it took to get him back, crawl on her belly, grovel, promise anything, anything at all. Her mind pre-occupied she wasn't ready for the hand that went across her mouth and nose. She had a whiff of something strange and heard a familiar voice then nothing until she came to a few minutes later to find herself being raped. She kept her eyes closed, not sure if her attacker could see her face in the dark alley and reached into her pocket but her outstretched fingers couldn't find what she was seeking, drat it, it must be in the other pocket. The other pocket was not so easy to reach as it was caught beneath her and she had to lift her hip slightly so that she could reach into it. Her attacker felt her movements and laughed. "Hold on, darling, way to go yet." She knew the voice but took a little while to pin it down, then the name "Steven" burst from her lips before she could stop it.

He almost stopped mid thrust as he laughed down at her then said, "You're losing your touch, babe, been following you for days."

She had had the feeling of being followed over the last few days but had chosen to ignore it. Shit, she was losing her touch, she should have trusted her instincts. She began to groan as if with pleasure saying, "Oh yes, yes, don't stop, please don't stop."

"You're a strange one, I should have known you'd like it hard and fast."

"Oh Stevie, Stevie, I've missed you really missed you."

"Course you have, I believe every word out of your lying mouth."

She groaned again and arched her hips up to meet him as she desperately felt around for her other pocket. "There's no one like you Stevie, nobody has a tackle like yours." Although she couldn't see him she sensed him grinning down at her. She finally found her pocket and reached what she was looking for and slowly withdrew her hand. "Kiss me, kiss me."

He didn't kiss her but dropped down onto his elbows and clasped his hands over the top of her head pulling it down as he thrust upwards.

She panted and groaned then said. "You should be called Don not Stevie."

Without breaking rhythm, he said," Don?"

"Don, as in Wimbledon, two balls and a racket."

He started laughing. "You're a strange one and no mistake."

Silence reigned and the pace quickened as he neared his climax. She put her hands up and gently caressed his face whilst feeling for his ear, whispering her admiration at his endurance. She circled his ear to make sure she had the target to rights then, as he climaxed, she thrust the knitting needle deep into his ear and brain. She was not prepared for his reaction as almost immediately his dead weight collapsed on top of her, his penis still spurting semen inside her. She struggled desperately to free herself and began to panic as she didn't seem to be getting anywhere but suddenly she was free of him, she could breathe. She lay on her back panting noisily then struggled up to her feet and looked for her knickers but was unable to locate them in the blackness of the ally and guessed he had shoved them in one of his pockets or simply chucked them but it was far too dark to see and she didn't fancy going through his pockets. She listened for a moment, sensing for danger then felt about the body and, moving up to his head, removed the knitting needle although she had to think for a moment which ear it was in as his head was now 'looking' up from the ground instead of being the other way round. The knitting needle was not as easy to pull out as it had been to thrust in but eventually it came free and she melted into the night stopping only to thrust the knitting needle down in some waste ground. She was desperate to get home as the semen that Stevie had pumped into her was seeping out of her vagina and making the top of her legs sticky. She grimaced in disgust and on reaching home went straight into the bathroom and showered away all traces of him.

She felt good, proving that she could take care of herself when taken by surprise had given her a boost. She decided that although it seemed quick (she only had one person to go on by that method) she definitely did not want to die that way, it was almost too quick. Shame really that it was so dark as he could not have her image in his eyes when he died, the alleyway was too dark to see anything. Never mind, she consoled herself, at least she would have the pleasure of reading about his discovery in the papers and maybe, if he was a local man, she would be able to go to his funeral.

The man's body was discovered the following day and was in the six o'clock news but no other information was forthcoming. The local newspaper said that the body of a man aged twenty-five or thereabouts had been discovered by a paper boy doing his rounds and that police were investigating and appealing for witnesses.

Dorothy was horrified at the close proximity of where the body had been found and had extra locks fitted on the front and back doors. The workman who fitted the locks was easy on the eye and when Dorothy left to fetch Alfie from school they had an enjoyable time fitting other things together.

Back at rehearsals for the new play she couldn't seem to do anything right and the stage manager kept sniping at her: she was in the wrong position, she'd fluffed her lines, her voice was too loud/too quiet. On the break she sat in her room and thought through the morning rehearsals and knew she was being set up to fail. She knew that her understudy and the stage manager were an item and that he would continually find fault with her till she cracked but she wasn't going to crack, she wasn't going to give them that satisfaction. She would take everything meekly on the chin but would not give in. She breathed slowly and deeply and went out for round two.

"Darling," the stage manager called out in a peevish voice, "you are supposed to be an actress so for goodness sake act." She smiled at him and they went over the same scene again and again and it started with the same old whinging the following day. She would not be beaten but she was beginning to feel the strain as the days passed and the relentless barrage continued. "Get her understudy on stage now, we have less than two weeks to polish this and we are way behind schedule."

She had noticed Matthew walk around the orchestra pit whilst the stage manager was in the middle of another tirade and, despite her resolve she was distracted. She excused herself for a loo break and hurried to her dressing room when out of the corner of her eye she saw movement further down the corridor. She flattened herself against her door and watched her understudy standing up on tip-toes to kiss somebody then turned her head to see the store manager turn into the corridor and wondered if he had just seen what she had just seen and judging by the look on his face he had. The understudy went into her room a few doors down as Mr Bainridge came out into the passageway from the side room, adjust his tie, cough a couple of times as if to clear his throat then stride up the passage passing the stage manager on his way and giving him a brief nod. The stage manager turned and watched Mr Bainridge walk away, a calculating look on his face, he was no fool and knew that something was not right. As he passed he barely glanced at her standing as if stuck to her door and went straight to the understudy's room and entered without knocking.

Strange how times changes things she thought as she waited with the rest of the cast to continue the rehearsals, not looking forward to the continual negativity aimed at her but determined to ride it out. Time passed and still there was no sign of the manager and the cast began to shuffle their feet and whisper to each other.

When he finally appeared the stage manager was not the calm authoritative figure he had seemed to be previously. He strode onto the stage and, without looking at anyone in particular said, "That's it for today folks," and strode off again. The cast didn't need telling twice and vanished from the stage as if by magic.

She was the last one to leave the stage. She stood looking out into the seated area for a moment as if looking for her audience, then turned and went to her dressing room to change and collect her coat. She had entered the room and had closed the door behind her, so occupied by her thoughts, before she saw Matthew. She stopped, startled then bowed her head to look at the floor and stood stock still. She did not know how long the silence reigned but suddenly it was broken. "Look at me."

She kept looking at the floor and again the voice said gently, "Look at me" as his hand cupped her chin and raised her head. She looked at him but said nothing, her eyes wide and glistening.

"I'm sorry," he said as his thumbs gently stroked her cheeks. She was startled. What did he have to be sorry about? It was her who was in the wrong.

"Don't say that," she whispered as a single teardrop ran down her face. "I'm the one who should apologise."

"I shouldn't have reacted like that, I should have just walked away," he said earnestly.

"No, no, I deserved it. I acted like a spoilt brat and I will never ever be like that again," she said as she crossed her fingers behind her back.

Matthew groaned and held her tightly saying, "I thought you would hate me, I thought you would never want to see me again."

"Oh, my darling, I'm so sorry to have put you in that position. It was all my fault, really and truly it was."

They kissed each other gently then stood holding each other tightly until they laughed and let each other go, smiling into each other's faces.

"I love you too much to lose you," Matthew said in a gruff voice as he reached for her hand and held it up to his lips then "Where's the ring I gave you?"

"One of the rubies came out when I threw it across my room and I can't find it," she answered truthfully.

Matthew laughed. "No matter, I shall get you another," as he picked her up in his arms and swung her around.

"Stop, stop, you are making me dizzy. I don't want another ring. The missing ruby will forever remind me that I nearly lost you, my darling." She was amazed where the words were coming from and hoped that she would remember them for they were too good to forget.

Matthew drove her to his luxurious flat and once inside she became demur again lowering her head to look at the floor but Matthew simply picked her up and carried her into the bedroom and laid her gently down onto the bed, then began kissing her all over. They made gentle passionate love and she was fulfilled like never before, she was amazed. She loved him, she really loved him.

It was three days before she returned to rehearsal expecting a vitriolic comment from the stage manager but, to her surprise, as soon as she appeared the understudy was waved off the stage and the rehearsals continued. As the understudy left the stage she kept her head down but not before a painful looking black eye and fat lip had been noticed.

The rehearsals continued with only minor blips and by the end of the day even the stage manager was looking like a cat with cream.

Matthew collected her at the stage door and took her out for a fancy vegan meal, then took her back to her home as he had to go abroad for a few days. She desperately wanted to go with him but accepted that she couldn't.

Alfie and Dorothy were playing card games on the kitchen table and the house was full of laughter. The news was on in the background and when she saw a picture of Stevie's face she went over and turned the volume up to hear that the body found in an alleyway earlier that week was that of Steven Wallon, a twenty-five-year-old local man. She put her hand to her face as if in shock saying, "Oh no, I know him, he's one of our stagehands, oh no, how dreadful."

Dorothy made her sit down and have a cup of coffee and breathe deeply to calm then continued playing cards with Alfie. She watched them for a while then went up to her room which was as untidy as she had left it. Up yours Stevie Wallon she thought.

Alfie was doing really well in his judo classes and had taken another grade which Dorothy had been allowed to watch. She promised Alfie that she would watch him take his next grade and he went on to describe his lessons to her. He was full of pride of his achievements and she wished she had taken up a martial art when she was younger.

In no time at all she was back at Matthew's flat comfortably ensconced on his enormous water bed. He sat up suddenly and said, "OK then, when are we getting married?"

"I don't know."

"Wrong answer."

She laughed and sat up with him. "Next year then."

"January 1st!"

"Too cold."

"February then!"

"Still too cold."

"March" then, "I know, still too cold."

"Well it is."

"All right then, April."

"May," she said, "let's get married in May."

"May it is then," he replied, as they both lay down to cement their agreement of the month of their wedding.

Her mother was over the moon and started thinking about what outfits they would wear and pretended to be stern when her daughter laughed at her saying it was far too early for that and that the wedding wasn't as far away as she thought it was and that if she wasn't careful she would run out of time.

Although she laughed at her mother she found her words to be true. She thought it strange that she had spent most of her life planning how she wanted her funeral to be and here she was up to her eyes in trying to plan her wedding and having to be guided by her mother.

At Christmas the family moved into Matthew's flat for three weeks and had a glorious time. His ground floor flat was twice as big as their house and had a garden to match and Alfie had a glorious time, as not a penny had been spared on putting up decorations including snowfall in the garden. Her family were given free range of the flat and Alfie had been spoilt rotten with Father Christmas and his elves actually coming to see him. All in all it was the best Christmas ever and she looked forward to arriving home from her performances to snacking by the fire with her family. It was the best Christmas and she never wanted it to end but one morning she found herself fiercely hugging then waving goodbye to her family as they were driven home. It was too quiet, far too quiet and she didn't like it one bit. She was living at the flat full-time now as they both decided in one hilarious moment that they wanted to live in each other's pockets. She kept waiting for the bubble to burst but rain or shine she was contented more than she ever thought possible.

Her dress fittings were not going to plan though as her weight seemed to keep fluctuating and at one point she convinced herself she was pregnant even though she knew she couldn't be, Matthew was far too careful for that since she had moved in full-time even though she told him she wanted to have his child, a little girl named Matilda. They had spent hours in bed discussing what their child would look like and what names they would choose. Matthew didn't like the name Matilda but agreed to it when she said it was the closest girl name that she could think of to his.

Matthew had no idea that she couldn't have children as she had never got around to telling him. She didn't feel in the least bit guilty, though, as she was sure he wouldn't mind. If he did mind, she was sure she could put on a performance to reduce him to tears; after all, she was a star.

She gave her last performance at the Easter break and was overwhelmed with the accolades she received. She took curtain call after curtain call and gave a sigh of relief when at last the curtain stayed down.

Keeping her promise to Alfie she went along to watch his next grading and was amazed at his prowess. She was recognised in the audience and was inundated with pleas to give signatures. She played the rising star role to perfection and left having more fans than when she arrived. Alfie loved the attention given, telling everyone in a loud voice that she was his sister.

Finally, the day of the wedding arrived. It was cold and raining hard whilst April had been glorious. Nothing though was going to spoil their day, not even the thunder and lightning which started mid-way through the ceremony. They both thought it highly amusing and smiled and laughed their way through the rest of the tiring day.

She was Mrs Bainridge and she loved it. They had decided to have the weekend at home then drive up to Scotland for a honeymoon in a luxury cottage by a loch. They spent most of their time being horizontal whilst gently loving and exploring each other.

Mid-morning on Monday they drove off without a backward glance, their future beckoning. Their journey went well and they were only a few miles off the Scottish border when a tyre burst and Matthew fought to keep control of the car which ploughed into an oncoming lorry. It all happened so quickly but at the time seemed to happen so slowly. She remembered screaming as the lorry approached then nothing until she woke up in an intensive care unit covered in bandages and drips. She kept falling in and out of consciousness all the time calling for Matthew and eventually she was told that he had died at the scene of the accident.

She was put on suicide watch for a brief time as she couldn't stop screaming and pulling out the drips in her arms. She wanted to die too, she wanted to be with Matthew, let me die, please please let me die but she didn't, despite everything she started to recover. After six months she was transferred down to the city and started receiving visitors for brief periods. She didn't want visitors, all she wanted was to look into their faces and see that everything was all right but all she saw was sadness and tears and she didn't want that especially from his parents who simply stood staring at her, honour bound to visit, but unable to say anything.

At last she was home, two days after what would have been their first wedding anniversary. She pushed her frame around the flat feeling Matthew everywhere. There was a pile of post to sort out and she sat on the sofa tossing them unopened into the waste bin until she came across one with Matthew's writing on it and, for a brief happy moment she thought he was alive. She tore open the envelope and took out an anniversary card enclosed with a long letter. Matthew, as thoughtful as ever, had arranged for it to be sent to her along with a cuddly fluffy yellow teddy bear on every anniversary for the rest of her life wanting to make sure he never missed one.

She worked hard to regain her mobility. She wanted to go on stage again and she was sure that she had never yet seen anyone perform on stage with a walking frame. She decided that when she got back on stage she would address that.

Another year came and went and she was now only using a walking stick to aid her. She was so frustrated with what she saw as slow progress although her physio kept telling her she was remarkable. She didn't feel remarkable, every time she looked in a mirror she saw a sad lonely person looking back at her. She thought that if Matthew was here and saw her looking like this he would leave her.

Mr and Mrs Bainridge had long since given her the urn which held Matthew's ashes and she had hugged them to her as fiercely as she used to hug him. They visited her regularly and took her to the pretty little church where they had held his funeral. She stood outside the church and stared around her at the beautiful countryside that stretched as far as the eye could see, wild flower meadows alive with buzzing insects, she didn't know that there were still such places in England.

Once home she decided that moping around would not get her anywhere. If she chose not to work she was secure for the future, Matthew had made sure of that but the stage called her and she wanted to return to it. One of the glossy magazines arranged to visit her to do a feature. She briefly flicked through some previous copies they had brought with them to show her what they were after and she noted an article on Cyran and decided that perhaps she would look at it later. She did not like her but that was no reason not to have an interest in her and what she was doing.

The interview went well, she had put her acting hat on so that she could talk about Matthew without dissolving into tears and showed off the flat and garden. Once they had left she sat down and read about Cyran and had to admit that she scrubbed up well. She wondered if it was time to call on her but in the end decided that she would wait till Cyran called her and she wouldn't hold her breath.

One day she decided she would sell the flat and move back in with her mum. Matthew was everywhere in the flat and she thought that she needed to move on whilst at the same time she didn't want to sell it because he was everywhere in it. She hated being indecisive but, in the end decided she would never leave the flat. She would go and see a solicitor and leave it in her will to her mum and anyway it was about time she updated her will and made it official.

Her chauffer drove her to the college where she had started her acting career and she called in to see Mrs Hibbitt seemingly unaware of the gasps and stares she was receiving. Mrs Hibbitt hugged her like an old friend and she spent an enjoyable time with her which boosted her no end. She went with the teacher to one of her classes and gladly gave a talk and answered questions, then signed autographs. She was exhausted by the time she reached home but considered the day a positive one.

As she lay in bed she thought over the day. The students she had seen at her former college thought she was a star, thought she had made it but she knew different, knew she had a long way to go yet but still, it was nice to have fans.

The following day she rang Mr Bainridge and began to pester him for her next role. He said he didn't think she was quite ready yet to return to the stage and she insisted she was. Stalemate. Eventually she wore him down and he told her about a new production that he thought would be successful. Once he started talking about it he couldn't stop and she was caught up in his enthusiasm. The rehearsals were due to start in two weeks' time in a theatre she had never been to before.

Whilst waiting impatiently for the script to arrive. She decided on some minor improvements to the flat and had a horizontal gap made at the base of each and every window to ensure that moths or little insects weren't trapped. She couldn't bear to find their dead bodies millimetres away from freedom and now they had a chance of freedom, a chance to escape.

As soon as the script was delivered by courier she made herself comfortable and sat down to read through it. It was called 'Innuend-0' and she loved it more and more as she read through the lengthy script. This was her, or rather this was going to be the making of her. The last act was missing, she checked and checked again irritated that the script wasn't complete, then found the letter which had been included but must have dropped out unseen as she took out the script.

She threw the letter down in exasperation after she had quickly read through it then picked it up again. Ridiculous, this was ridiculous. The play was in three parts and the last act, the third part, would not be given to the performers until the finish of the second act. Ridiculous, how on earth were the actors supposed to learn their lines for the final act in a fifteen-minute break.

She phoned Mr Bainridge to complain and stated her case saying that after the first night everyone would know who the murderer was and even though the audience may be asked to keep a secret not all of them would and the plot would be blown. Mr Bainridge told her that the murderer would not always be the same, the person murdered would not always be the same and the method used to murder would be different each time. She could not think of a reply when told this and it wasn't until she put the phone down that she queried how he could make it work. It seemed impossible to her and she thought that maybe he was losing his marbles and that she should get out whilst she still had a good reputation.

The rehearsals started, still with much controversy and the national and local newspapers got hold of the story, and the way the tabloids printed it put it in perspective. The play was a murder mystery saga and the audience were the detectives. At the end of the second curtain fall they had fifteen minutes to select from one of six buttons to choose who the killer was. In the brochure there would be five named people from the play labelled from one to five and the sixth button was a 'none of the above' button. "Whodunnit" screamed the tabloids and the booking demands exploded though not all of the tabloids were complimentary and some were scathing about the use of gimmicks to sell tickets calling it a cheap trick and telling people not to be tricked.

Mr Bainridge was not in the least put out by the negative press reviews, after all, even bad publicity was still good publicity in his books.

As the rehearsals continued the cast stopped worrying about not being able to learn their lines for the last part and focused on what they did have to learn.

She did not like her new understudy (not that she liked the previous one) as she saw a lot of herself when she was younger in her. She made the life of the girl as difficult as possible for her without seeming to and was always there to pick up the pieces when the girl dissolved into tears. She couldn't stand grizzling of any sort. She remembered her young brother Alfie grizzling when teething and it had always set her teeth on edge.

She had to have frequent rests during rehearsals but didn't complain of the constant pain she was in; she was alive and you had to be alive to feel pain or anything else come to that.

Since his son had died Mr Bainridge had changed for the better, he became a much nicer caring person. She had often talked to Matthew about him wondering if his mother knew about his dark side and Matthew had said that he was sure she suspected something but until she had solid proof she would stand by him. She had upset Matthew by saying his mother was only staying with his father for the money and Matthew had defended his mother saying she deserved every penny she got.

She lay in bed full of painkillers and thought about how her life could be if Matthew was here with her and the floodgates opened and, after many hours, she eventually cried herself to sleep.

She was not fit enough to attend rehearsals for the next two days and the studio sent her huge bunches of get-well flowers. She was furious and would have thrown them out as she couldn't stand cut flowers, but on second thoughts sent them by courier to her fan club along with a dozen complementary tickets for the show and some trinkets.

When she returned to rehearsals her understudy tried to express how pleased she was to see her back and hoped that she hadn't returned too soon. She looked kindly at the young woman and thanked her profusely whilst mentally calling her a conniving little toad. If she thinks she is going to climb over me to get to where I am, she's got another think coming, she thought, as she went to her dressing room.

There was a ten-minute slot in the play where she was not required to be on stage and she used the time watching from the back of the stage and looking through the props. She found a realistically looking dagger in which the blade pushed back into the handle as it touched anything and wondered where it would be used in the play. She was intrigued. Was it to be the murder weapon? And if so who was to be murdered with it?

Her mum and Dorothy were going on holiday in Dorset for a fortnight taking Alfie with them. Since Matthew had died she had drawn away from them a little though she didn't know why. Perhaps she envied them their obvious contentment and happiness.

Alfie had progressed well in judo and had now started his Jujitsu classes. He loved martial arts and applied himself fully to the rigorous training. She went along to watch him when she could, fully aware (though seemingly unaware) of pulling in crowds. She remembered when she had been fanatical about swimming, often pushing herself to the limits and of how she had gained a place in the county swimming team. So long ago, she thought. Where had it all gone?

It seemed the minute her family went on holiday she wanted to be with them and she wondered if she was just being perverse. The thought of going on holiday had not even entered her mind but now she longed to go and promised herself that when the play had run its course she would go to Scotland as she and Matthew had planned all that time ago.

Despite their reservations the cast began to have positive feelings about the play. The dress rehearsals had gone smoothly and even the negative members of the cast gave grudging approval. The cast held bets amongst themselves as to who would be the murderer or the murdered and the kitty became quite large and well worth winning especially amongst the lower paid workers. There were only two days left until the opening night and the cast were yelling 'bring it on'.

She had set an early alarm but managed to wake up before it went off which it did whilst she was in the shower. By the time she came back into the bedroom the alarm had nearly run itself out and was giving half gasp squeaks and grunts. She clicked it off and turned on the radio for some morning music which she then hummed along to as she got dressed and went into the kitchen for her morning revival cup of coffee. She drank far too much coffee she knew, and people were always telling her it was not good for her but she told them as nicely as possible that if they didn't like coffee then they did not have to drink it, she did and she would.

Her mobile rang and she quickly checked who it was before answering. The name Edward Bainridge was displayed on her phone and she nearly declined the call.

"Hello."

"It's me, Matthew's dad."

"Yes."

"It's about the theatre, the one where we are doing the play."

She looked at the ceiling wishing she hadn't answered the mobile. "What about it?"

"Look, have you got the news on?"

"No, why?"

"It's on the news, now. The theatre has been burnt to the ground."

This got her attention. "What?"

"Look put the news on, I'll ring you later," and with that he switched off.

She sat there for a moment staring at the mobile then galvanised into action and turned on the widescreen television and there it was for all to see, the blackened remains of the theatre. The newscaster was saying that apparently the fire started in the early hours of the morning and that firefighters had been battling all night to save it and stop it spreading. The cause of the fire was yet unknown and an investigation would be ongoing. He also said that the new play Innuend-0 that was due to open the following day obviously now would have to be kept on hold until further notice.

She didn't know what to think, whether she should be happy or sad. Happy that she didn't now have to attend any more rehearsals or sad for the same reason. She knew that the theatre had a lot of dodgy wiring, she had found that out when she had found exposed live wiring in the kitchen. She had mentioned it casually to the maintenance crew then forgot about it. She wondered if the faulty wiring was the cause of the fire but knew she would have to wait until the investigation was completed.

The newspapers were having a field day and there was a picture of Mr Bainridge standing outside the ruins of the theatre giving his thanks to the efforts of the firefighters to save the theatre and saying that the show would go on as soon as an alternative venue could be found. She looked at the picture and almost felt sorry for him though not for the reason of losing the theatre but for the reason that he looked so old and haggard.

There were crowds of people and reporters hovering outside her front door and where she usually loved them being there, she now felt intensely irritated by them, why couldn't they leave her alone, give her space to breath.

After two days of lazing around she was bored. She phoned Mr Bainridge to see if the holiday cottage in Scotland was vacant and, for a few moments was met by silence.

"Hello, are you still there?"

"Oh yes, yes, my dear, I'm still here. It's just that you took me by surprise, erm. Do you think it's a good idea, you know, is it a good idea to go there of all places?"

"Yes, yes I do. I need to lay some ghosts there."

"When do you plan on going?"

"Tomorrow."

"Oh, that doesn't give much time but I'll phone through and tell Mr and Mrs Keay (the live-in caretakers) to get ready for you."

She suddenly remembered her manners. "How's the business going with the fire? I meant to ask you sooner."

"Not going anywhere I'm afraid, sorry business."

"Give my love to Mrs Bainridge."

"Will do, take care."

"You too." She put the phone down with a thoughtful look on her face then started packing for the following day. It was surprising in the end how much she was taking seeing as she was going to be in the wilds of nowhere. In one of her cases were the little fluffy golden teddy bears that she received each anniversary, they were her treasure and she would not dream of going away and leaving them alone even for a few days.

The chauffer arrived early and packed the car with her cases and, after leaving final instructions to her housekeepers she settled back for the ride. She was determined to stay awake and watch the scenery but the smoothness of the ride lulled her to sleep and they were well into Scotland before she awoke. She had dreaded passing the spot where Matthew had been killed but luckily sleep had protected her from seeing it, although it was doubtful whether she would remember the exact spot.

On arrival at the cottage (twice the size of her city flat) the chauffer unpacked the bags, alerted the housekeepers then drove to his lodgings in the nearest town seven miles away. The housekeepers had prepared a hot meal for her which she forced down even though she didn't fancy it, thanked them for their trouble then went to bed.

The next few days she slept, woke for meals and slept again. On the third day she awoke early feeling wonderfully refreshed. She looked out across the heather and decided to explore and, full of excitement she set off with instructions to the housekeepers to come and find her if she didn't return in a few hours. She was warned to keep, where possible, to the pathways as the heather covered uneven ground and holding a hand up in brief acknowledgement she strode off, leaning heavily on her walking stick. She turned to look back every now and then, a trick Matthew had taught her to sight landmarks for when they returned from somewhere new but the trouble was that once the cottage was out of sight the only landmark was a distant mountain. She desperately didn't want to get lost on her first venture out and be gossiped about as 'that silly English woman who got lost outside her own back door'.

To her surprise she found her way back to the cottage thoroughly amazed that she had and thanking Matthew profusely. She spoke to Mr and Mrs Keay and asked if they would be so kind as to show her the loch the following day and perhaps, if the weather permitted take her out on it.

The loch was as calm as could be and all she could hear was the splashing as the oars dipped in and out of the water. She had thought to take the boat out by herself but now was pleased she hadn't, she doubted she had the strength. She felt that heaven must be like the place she was: wild, peaceful, beautiful with the song of the wind ruffling around her. The wind was getting up and Mr Keay rowed the boat back to the small jetty. By the time they reached the cottage the sky had darkened and it was blowing a gale with the rain lashing down on them. Her housekeepers were worried for her to get inside out of the rain but she stood still with her arms out to the sides and her smiling face turned up to the heavens then suddenly twirled around in the glory of the moment. She noticed that her housekeepers were still outside waiting for her to go in and suddenly felt silly. She guessed that they would not go in until they had seen her go in so she hurried inside and closed the door behind her, laughing at what she thought they would be saying to each other.

She got up early the following day and, once dressed opened the front door and stepped outside. From the inside the clear blue sky was deceiving but once outside the wind threatened to drag her away from the cottage. Perfect, she thought. She went into her bedroom and picked up Matthew's urn and hugged it oh so tightly, then left the cottage and with the wind at her back she allowed herself to be blown along. She stopped suddenly knowing that the place where she was, was to be the place where she released Matthew, her darling darling Matthew. She kissed the urn and hugged it with all her might and offered a heartfelt prayer, then unscrewed the lid and watched the contents swirl up into the atmosphere and disappear. She called out his name. "Matthew, you are free," and for a moment felt glorious then panicked. What had she done, now she had let go of his ashes and she was alone? She fell to her knees sobbing and calling out his name asking him why he had left her, telling him she couldn't go on without him. She finally curled into a foetal position and slept only to awaken hours later by hearing her name called over and over again. The look of relief on Mr Keay's face when he saw her at last made her realise how foolish she had been to wander out alone in a strange place. She was treating it like the city she had grown up in, wandering about without a care in the world and that was foolish. There were dangers out here, different dangers perhaps to the city but nevertheless dangers.

The rest of her stay she kept near the cottage and went to a market town with Mrs Keay and then enjoyed a few hours baking with her. She also walked around with Mr Keay mending holes in perimeter fences and repairing the chicken coops and all too soon it was time for her to leave.

She had grown very fond of the housekeepers and strained around to catch the last sight of them as she began her journey home. She was going to miss them.

Back in the city she soon fell into the rhythm of city life. There was no mention at all of the theatre in the news and she realised that yesterday's news was no news unless a new angle could be found.

She called in to see her mum and found the family fit and well and arguing over who was going to have the last chocolate éclair. She decided for them by scooping it up and putting it in her mouth in one smooth action and was rewarded by three open mouths of surprise. "Hmm, lovely, thank you very much." They fell about laughing and each brought the other up to date with their holiday adventures.

She couldn't believe how much Alfie had grown; it hadn't been that long since she had seen him last but he seemed to have shot up. They spent a little while discussing the burnt down theatre then Alfie said, "Can I have your room?"

"No," she said without thinking, "it's my room."

Her mum looked at her, then said, "Alfie needs a bigger room and you don't need it now, you're never here and anyway you live somewhere else."

She couldn't believe what she was hearing, her throat seemed to swell up and tears threatened to spill down her cheeks. She felt like she was being thrown out like garbage, they didn't want her any more. "But it's my room," she said, "it's always been my room."

Her mum could see how upset she was and said, "Let's talk about it another time when you've been given space to think about it."

She nodded her head then said she had to leave and gave them all a brief hug before hurrying out.

Within two days she was bored. She couldn't go out without being recognised and she didn't fancy staying in and there was only so much chilled white wine to drink before that too got boring. Perhaps she should get a dog for company. After all she had read that there were thousands of animals in rescue centres waiting for homes but then decided it was not such a good idea as she couldn't take it out. Well, she could but not without being pestered by photographers and fans.

If she lived in Scotland she could have a dog, she could have two or three, now wouldn't that be fine. All that open space for them to run about and enjoy themselves and in the evening they could all curl up together in front of the hearth. The picture was so vivid in her mind that she was disappointed to come back to reality when her mobile rang. She saw it was her father-in-law, although he now kept insisting that she should call him Dad. Fat chance.

Twenty minutes later she put the phone down not knowing what frame of mind to be in. The College of Acting that she had attended all those years ago had suggested that they stage the play Innuend-0 for one night only so that some of the people who had bought first-night tickets would have an opportunity to see it through for maybe the one and only time it was performed. Of course the facilities in the college were not as opulent as the theatre had been with its plush velvet seats, options of binoculars, seats rising in tiers so that nearly everyone had a good view, but it was better than nothing.

Mr Bainridge stopped by on the way to the college to collect her and neatly dodged the questions from the crowd outside whilst wondering how on earth they got their information. "Is it true you are going to put on a performance of Innuend-0 for one night only?" Cameras flashed and microphones were shoved in the direction of their mouths but they both smiled and gave nothing away although she did manage to get her good side captured on film as she blew kisses at them.

The college was buzzing as they arrived, it seemed that the grapevine was working well. The facilities were examined and everyone dredged up a negative point of view except her. She had listened to the, "We can't do this," and "We can't do that," with growing irritation then suddenly stood up and told them to shut up. She asked them what other options were available. She reminded them that some companies didn't have the luxury of working indoors, they had outdoor theatres and come rain or shine they performed. So what if they didn't have this or that, so what if they had to work with the basics. They had been given a golden opportunity from the college and they should grasp it with both hands.

The stage manager and Mr Bainridge were taken aback by the speech realising the truth in the words spoken. They had to climb down from their high horses and accept the reality of the present rather than dwell on the reality of the past. The outcome was that they graciously accepted the proposal generously offered by the college and plans to progress were drawn up.

The cast were delighted to be together again, even if it was to be only for one night and the rehearsals got under way. The newspapers were full of the story, some positive and some scathing at what they felt was a feeble attempt to promote the company, but none of it mattered, progress was being made. The college hall would only play host to an audience of five hundred people so it was advertised that the first five hundred applications would be given free tickets and that everybody who had bought a ticket for the previous first night show would be given a full refund.

She wondered if Mr Bainridge was using a publicity stunt when he made the announcement on national television, after all it would cost him thousands, then decided that no one was that nice and that there must be a failsafe plan, perhaps he was insured against such things happening. She had never really bothered before about the funding being happy to receive a regular wage but now she realised that she should have a say in it after all, when Matthew's parents died she would be the sole heir. She started to study the stock market and realised that the company was supported by many investors who were not putting their money into the company because they liked the name, or liked Mr Bainridge, they were putting their money into the company to make money out of it. It was a revelation to her and she could not understand why it hadn't dawned on her sooner.

From what seemed total mess and chaos to start with soon became a palatable piece of work as stagehands, lighting engineers, sound engineers, costume makers and everyone else involved learned to adapt to the different surroundings and all too soon it was the opening night.

The hall was packed and throbbed with expectation. Mr Bainridge stood on the stage and introduced the show then moved to the side as the curtains rose. The audience was captivated within the first few minutes and gasped, held their breaths or groaned as the play unfolded. The play was a masterpiece as it wove its spell, entrapping them like a spider's web as they hung on to every word, every act, sometimes scared witless by the dark thoughts meandering through murky minds.

At the end of the second act the curtains went down and the lights went on and many people regained their composure. When most people had settled back into their seats the stage manager came on stage and asked for a show of hands if they thought number one was the murderer all the way up to number five. Number six was 'none of the above' and perhaps there were only a dozen hands raised followed by laughter. It was agreed that the majority thought that number four was the murderer and they settled themselves down for the final act.

Meanwhile back stage they had for the first time, read through the final script. There were no words to say, it was acting pure and simple, positioning and lighting was crucial.

The curtains rose and the third part of the play unfolded before them in total silence except for the occasional cough from the audience and when the curtain fell the whole audience stood clapping and cheering and there were five curtain calls before the she came on stage using a walking stick to support her and waited for the noise to die down. She smiled her sweetest smile and spoke in a husky sensual voice that drew everyone in as she thanked them from the bottom of her heart for attending and blew kisses to them, then thanked all the backroom boys, the people without whom the production couldn't go ahead and all her fellow actors. She was a star and she shone, holding their attention seemingly without effort. Cameras flashed and then the whole cast joined her once more as she put a single finger to her lips and told them all to keep the secret.

It was a sensation and was all over the tabloids and she found the number of people waiting outside her flat had at least doubled. She was in demand and offers were pouring in but she found that all of a sudden she wasn't interested. Since returning from Scotland she had longed to return there, a wild free land where she felt she belonged. Matthew was there and she wanted to be there too.

Chapter 32
What Goes Around Comes Around

Mr Bainridge tried hard to persuade her to change her mind but, in the end signed over the Scottish property to her saying that he had no further use for it as his wife now needed a warmer climate for health reasons. She put her flat on the market and waited impatiently for all the legal proceedings to take place and for the contracts to be signed. She had thought the flat would be easy to sell but the estate agent simply told her to be patient. He told her that at the moment it was a buyer's market and she said that if that was the case where were they!

Be patient, huh, if he wasn't careful he would be a patient, she could ring his neck the way he simpered around her.

She decided to start going through her belongings to see what she wanted to keep and managed to sort out a few trinkets for her fan club but, after a few days of sorting out she had had enough. Sod it, she thought, let the removal firm do it and soon was sitting in the back of her car as her chauffer drove her to the little church in the country where Matthew's funeral had been held. Although it was a completely different season to the one when she had last visited she was still blown away by the beauty of the place and spent a peaceful two hours or so drinking everything in, so that, when in Scotland, she could revisit it in her mind's eye.

It was Wednesday morning and she felt better than she had in a long time. She decided that she would go and visit her mum completely forgetting that her mum would still be at work. She had decided to use public transport for old time's sake but was beginning to rue that decision as the injuries from the accident began to kick in with a vengeance. She would not give in though and at last she was in the house leaning heavily against the front door and panting to regain her breath. After a few moments she felt better and limped into the kitchen deciding that she would take a taxi home when it was time to leave. It was stupid to travel on public transport when she could have just been driven here. She didn't need to challenge herself any more she decided, it was time to be kind to herself.

Looking out through the kitchen window she saw Dorothy in the garden planting some roses and stood and watched her for a few moments. She heard a noise from upstairs and went out into the hallway calling, "Mum, Mum," but there was no reply. She decided to go upstairs anyway as she wanted to see her room one more time but halfway up she had to stop and rest, she had forgotten how draining stairs could be. She called, "Mum," again as she was nearing the top of the stairs and was surprised to see Alfie emerge from her room and cross the landing towards her. "Hello, Alfie," were the last words she said as a violent push propelled her backwards down the staircase causing a violent lurch of her stomach. Time seemed to stand still as she watched Alfie's face get further and further away her arms propelling madly as if she had wings and could fly away out of trouble. She didn't and she couldn't.

She lay still at the bottom of the stairs, her body twisted at an awkward angle, alive but unable to move. She lay staring up at the ceiling and could see every aspect of it quite clearly which surprised her. Alfie's face suddenly appeared a few inches away from her blocking her view of the ceiling. She could see every detail of his face as clearly as he could see hers as he stared intently at her. He was not looking so much at her face as into her eyes for what seemed a long time but really was no more than a minute or so then suddenly he was gone. She heard him moving about and begin to whistle a tuneless song as he did so then heard the front door open and close and all was quiet, she was on her own. She was amazed at how acute her hearing was and wondered if her uncle, all those years ago, had been alive when she had stared into his face as he had lain at the base of the stairs. She would have been a picture in his eyes as Alfie was now a picture in hers.

She felt herself begin to panic and fought to remember the calming techniques she had been shown when she had been a patient in Ward 3 and gradually she began to calm and take what control she could. The thought arose that she wasn't going to Scotland, she was going to die here in the hallway of the house she had lived in all her life. As the negative thoughts sought to overwhelm her she knew she had a battle on her hands, a battle against herself she must win. She could either lay here and let the panic overwhelm her and die in torment or she could defeat it once and for all.

She told herself sternly that she was an actress and if she couldn't use the skills she had learnt over the years then everything had been a waste of time. She began to visualize herself as being somewhere else.

She lay on the side of a gentle hillock with the warm early morning sun shining down upon her and a gentle breeze ruffling her fine hair. She looked as if she was sleeping and indeed, to all intents and purposes, she was but not a sleep as we know it. Her head was turned to one side and her eyes, wide open as they were, seemed to be looking at the dew-frocked grass as it shimmered in the breeze looking like a casket of jewels to anyone who had time to watch. She had plenty of time to watch but unfortunately she was dead, the last shallow breath she had taken now seeping out through her nostrils.